HAUNTED CORNWALL

Haunted Cornwall

Edited by
DENYS VAL BAKER

Published by Heritage Publications
Merchants House, Barley Market Street,
Tavistock, Devon
(associate member of Cumbria Tourist Board)

in association with

NEW ENGLISH LIBRARY
TIMES MIRROR

First published in Great Britain in 1973 by William Kimber & Co. Ltd.

*

THIS EDITION 1980

*

ISBN 0-903975-92-0

Made and printed in Great Britain by Hunt Barnard Printing Ltd, Aylesbury, Bucks.

Contents

Acknowledgements

An Act of Charity by Ronald Duncan was first published in *The Perfect Mistress* (Rupert Hart Davis, 1969): *The Old Man* by Daphne du Maurier was first published in *The Apple Tree* (Victor Gollancz, Ltd, (1952): *The Ghost at the Old Ford* by C. C. Vyvyan was first published in *The Helford River*, (Peter Owen, Ltd., 1951): *Christmas Honeymoon* by Howard Spring was first published in *Eleven Stories and a Beginning* (William Collins and Co, 1973); *The Sacrifice* by Denys Val Baker was first published in *The Strange and the Damned* (Pyramid Books, 1964): *Shepherd, Show Me* by Rosalind Wade was first published in *Unlikely Ghosts* (Cassell and Co, 1967): the remaining stories – *The Chocolate Box* by Frank Baker, *Window in the Attic* by J. C. Trewin, *The Wheel* by James Turner, *Night on Roughtor* by Donald Rawe, *Snow* by Kenneth Moss, *Inheritance* by David Eames, *The Lost Ones* by Mary Williams, *The Castle* by M. E. Simpson and *Episode* by Nigel Tangye – have not previously appeared in book form.

Introduction

This is a hideous and wicked country
Sloping to hateful sunsets and the end of time,
Hollow with mine shafts, naked with granite, fanatic
With sorrow. Abortions of the past
Hop through these bogs: black-faced the villagers
Remember burnings by the hewn stones.

That was how a well known poet, John Heath-Stubbs, reacted to Cornwall when he lived in a cottage on the cliffs near Zennor. It was an emotional reaction rather like that of Walter de la Mare, on the occasion of his first visit to the county: he wrote afterwards that he did not feel safe again until he had crossed the River Tamar back into Devonshire.

Many other famous writers – among them D. H. Lawrence, Compton Mackenzie, John Betjeman, Hammond Innes, Winston Graham, Daphne du Maurier, Howard Spring – have been equally stirred and provoked by this unforgettable corner of England, this brooding land of mystery that sometimes seems to be drenched with dramatic mythology. Ruth Manning-Sanders, a novelist who lived for many years at Sennen Cove, near Land's End, put the matter very well when she wrote of a walk out on to the cliffs in the twilight of a wintry afternoon when nothing was to be seen but the dim shapes of the silently withdrawing cliffs and the red rhythmically winking eye of the Longships Lighthouse:

> It is then that the drowned sailors of the past can be heard hailing their names above the moaning of the waters. It is then that the sense of the primordial, the strange and the savage, the unknown, the very long ago, fills the dusk with something that is akin to dread. It is then that the place becomes haunted: a giant heaves grey limbs from his granite bed; a witch sits in that stone chair on the cliff...

The very long ago! How much it has been impressed and impregnated into the granite body of Cornwall, how much it remains alive, a part of the daily life. Once when climbing to the top of a hill above St Ives a man said to a little boy, 'This was where the Druids worshipped their idol gods.' When the boy asked, 'How long ago?' the man replied vaguely, 'About a hundred years ago, I s'pose.' Past and present, moments and centuries, all are entangled and interwoven in Cornwall. Eternity is contained in a hundred years. It was George Meredith who observed that to the Celts the past is at their elbow continuously:

> The past of their lives has lost neither face nor voice behind the shroud, nor are the passions of the flesh, nor is the animate soul, wanting to it. Other races forfeit infancy, forfeit youth and manhood, with their progression to the wisdom age may bestow. These have each stage always alive, quick at a word, a scent, a sound, to conjure up scenes, in spirit and in flame.

In such a land, among such a people, it is hardly surprising that the world of the supernatural has remained very much a real world. Cornwall is after all a land of echoes – a haunted place where the wind whistles more eerily in the old mine stacks, where the lonely sea breakers boom forever in subterranean caves, where on bleak moorland hilltops strange granite circles point to heaven like fingers – a place indeed full of ghosties and ghoulies and things that go bump in the night. In such an atmosphere the imagination has full play and even the most mundane and down to earth visitor can quite quickly come to believe in strange happenings, in fairies and pixies and gnomes, in brooding giants of Trencrom and St Michael's Mount, in satanic figures like old Tregeagle, doomed forever to labour on the impossible task of emptying a bottomless pool on Bodmin Moor – in whole mysterious worlds, like the Land of Lyonesse, buried beneath the seas that now stretch between Mount's Bay and the Isles of Scilly.

After a quarter of a century living in various parts of Cornwall, but mostly in that most mysterious corner of all, Penwith, I remain as baffled and fearful of its secrets as any visitor. This, of course, is part of the fascination of Cornwall, there is a kind of magnetism which draws one irresistibly. I can quite understand why the infamous Aleister Crowley, meddler in the realms of black magic, came to Cornwall on many occasions and so the legend goes, conducted black masses. It would be difficult to think of anywhere else in Britain, perhaps in the world, which would make a more natural setting for such occult ceremonies. Occultism is very much a part of Cornwall. I defy anyone to stand on some lonely hilltop, such as Trencrom or Brown Willy – especially on a moonlit night! – without a sense of awesome contact with the past. If those granite boulders could only speak – what strange tales would they tell? There is in fact an answer to that question. Granite boulders do speak, if you will only listen. Put your hands on a stone and apply your mind to what you are doing, think backwards into the past from which that stone came, and you may be surprised. This aspect was put very vividly, perhaps not surprisingly, by a sculptor, Sven Berlin:

> The open coliseum of each little cove of sand or rock may be the theatre for any natural, supernatural or unnatural event. The unending presence of the sea breathing ceaselessly over the shoulder of each hill, the rock charged with a thousand sunsets or carved by a hundred years of rain, the little trees loaded with berries growing away from the prevailing wind, offering crimson to green, the mind's incessant vertigo at the cliff edge, and the slow constructional flight of the seagull – these things in some way act as the charming of magicians and open up the deeper rooms of experiences in man, making him aware of his being part of the natural universe, at the head of a great unseen procession of gods and devils, spectres and dragons; of being a channel for unknown and undefined forces, of facing the mystery of life, awakening powers of perception which search beyond the frontiers of normal events.

The stories in this anthology are all attempts, in one way or another, to search beyond the natural frontiers, to peer into the shadowiness. In the past there have, of course, been many well known writers about the supernatural in Cornwall – R. S. Hawker, Sabine Baring Gould, Charles Lee, 'Q', C. C. Rogers, the Hocking Brothers, J. C. Tregarthen – even some distinguished visitors, like Thomas Hardy and Wilkie Collins and Alfred Lord Tennyson. Some of today's contributors are equally famous, others less known outside Cornwall – all are united by a common link. Whether they are Cornish born or 'furriners' who have come to settle in Cornwall, or even occasional visitors, they have all been visibly affected by the brooding mystery of Cornwall. It may not be there on the surface, but it is there somewhere – an unacknowledged sense of unease provoked in an almost physical way by the weird granite clad confinements of Cornwall's world.

So read on and enjoy these tales of hauntings and happenings, of strange atmospheres and weird occurrences, of steps back into time – and prods into the future. They are meant for your entertainment, of course – but some of them may remain with you hauntingly, as reminders that perhaps not everything is quite as it seems.

As we who live in Cornwall are reminded every day . . .

THE EDITOR

I

The Chocolate Box

Frank Baker

Intense repugnance. That is one definition of horror to be found in the dictionary. Or, *power of exciting such feeling.*

I think it is more. It is also what is totally unexpected: the long sunlit lane that has only a brick wall at the end, the worm in the rose, the sudden ravaged image of one's own tormented face in a window pane. That which has sudden power to corrupt and defile. A stench where sweetness should be; darkness where light should be; a grin where a smile should be; a scream searing into a night where silence should be. An old withered hand where a young hand should be . . .

And no escape from whatever it may be that has suddenly come upon the visitant. No escape.

*

I write those words by way of preface to the story of something that happened to me fifty years ago. And immediately I ask myself whether I want to tell the story, or *why* I have to tell it. I must. That is all. If only because – but let the reason come later.

It does not seem possible that it was fifty years ago, and I – a young man living alone in a mine-pitted valley near Land's End where on nights of no moon the darkness had a surging, living quality in which I could hear not only the waves of the sea but the waves of the music I knew I would write; a young man with great ambitions that have only been sparely fulfilled. With my music – scores of composers then considered avant-garde, such as Stravinsky, Schoenberg, Hindemith – and a few books and a stack of virgin scorepaper, I had rented a cottage in this remote valley, barely furnished, but containing all I needed except one thing – a piano. And the arrival of this, my old black Bord, I awaited from London. Against the advice of parents and friends I had come as far west as I could go, there to come to terms with the music I knew I must compose. Nothing else mattered.

But this is not a story about music. I must keep it out, otherwise it will flood the pages and consume me. I am writing of a particular night in spring, a night of pitch darkness when I was walking down the valley to my retreat, after an evening in the King's Arms.

Let me get it as clearly and simply as I can. Without comment, and no 'ornaments' to use a musical term I like. Bleak, as it was. Very bare.

Half way down the valley, along a path treacherous with jagged stones and lichenous boulders, I drew up sharply. I could not see, but I knew someone was coming up the same path towards me. I stopped. The other person stopped too. A moment of silence, then I could hear his breathing – for I knew somehow it was a man. He came closer, and I drew aside.

'Good night, Mister.'

I heard the words, husky and defensive. And almost before I could return his greeting he had passed me, and I could hear his footsteps, getting dimmer, crunching over little stones. I had no idea who he was, nor did it much trouble me, after the first shock. I had had too good an evening at the King's Arms, I was too full of imagined music – a theme in B minor played in my head, with a recurring B, reminiscent of the 'raindrop' Prelude of Chopin – and its supporting harmony, possible weaving of counterpoint, was beginning to form in my mind. So I went on, and in a few moments the stranger had left my mind.

Perhaps thirty steps on I stopped again. My foot had touched an object in the path, and it was not a stone. Something soft, something I felt should not be there. You must understand that there was nothing in the least frightening about this. I was far too full of music to be frightened of anything. But I stopped none the less, struck a match, and bent down, shielding the flame from the slight breeze blowing from the sea – a western breeze that smelt of rain. Already I could smell the sweetbriar from the steep hillside garden of my cottage. And the B minor theme drifted into the major. (Keep music out – oh, keep music out. It has nothing to do with what I am trying to relate. . . .)

In the light of the match I saw what seemed and was incongruous in that setting. A chocolate box, a familiar box of those times, one with a picture of King George the Fifth on it, and crossed by a red ribbon. A white cardboard box. A pound box. I laughed. It seemed absurd, lying there. It was familiar to me, because these were the chocolates my mother liked best. We had always had them at home, they belonged to my childhood. What was it doing here?

I could swear for certain it had not been there earlier in the evening, when I had walked up the valley.

Obviously, I told myself, it would be empty. And yet I had to pick it up, to be sure, even though I was not in a chocolate-eating frame of mind that night, having drunk many pints of beer (fourpence a pint in those days). So I did pick it up, and realised at once that it was not empty. The match went out, and it was the last in the box. So on I went in the enfolding darkness, holding the box, vaguely wondering if it contained chocolates, and remembering a melody by Dvorak, 'Songs my Mother taught me'.

Inside the cottage I found another box of matches, lit the lamp, then the small Beatrice oil-stove, and put a kettle on for tea. The room became warm and welcoming in the glow of the lamp which lit up score paper littered over the table. I longed for the piano. It was a night when I wanted to improvise, to hear those sounds which played in my mind. Yet I was content to wait. The piano would come in the course of the next few days. Putting the chocolate box down on the table, I cut a hunk of bread and found some cheese. The silence of the night was broken only by the trickling stream deep in the valley. And in this sound my B major theme evolved into a new episode.

I remember that I did not hurry anything. There is a kind of happiness, almost an ecstasy, which can flow into the soul when it is least expected. And this is what filled me then, coupled with the assurance that very soon with my piano I would begin to hear the music I was hearing now only in my mind.

I made the tea, ate some bread and cheese, lit a cigarette, and then looked again at the chocolate box which still lay on the table. It was damp from the night air, slightly browned. But it was, it seemed to me, friendly – like a message from home which said, 'Don't worry, you are on the right path.' I was reluctant to open it, and even wondered whether I would do so that night.

But at last – and by now it was well past midnight – I did open it. At once, I drew back a little. I saw something wrapped in tissue paper, something stained a sullen rusty red. And like a flash of lightning the whole scene changed, the whole peaceful contented mood was shattered. Whatever was wrapped in that tissue paper I knew that I did not want to take it out and examine it. Yet I had to do so.

As I looked down at the object wrapped in the tissue paper a new sound came insistently into my ears. I tried to ignore this sound. I tried to gather back into my mind the music which, only a few minutes earlier, had been moving there, making its own form and order. But it would not return. I only knew the key: B minor. And could only hear this new sound – a humming, a buzzing, which rose to a crescendo, then sank to a diminuendo until it died away completely leaving only the sound of the stream outside.

And still I was staring down at the open box.

I put my hand down to touch the tissue paper, then drew back. The sound had come again, and this time nearer, then broken by a strange blundering little thud, which should have finished it, yet did not. For now the sound was close to my ear. Something brushed my face and I put my hand up involuntarily, slapping my cheek.

It was a bluebottle. I saw it veer drunkenly above the lamplight, then swoop down in an arc towards the box, then away again.

I tried to laugh. Bluebottles are loathsome, I have always hated them. But to be almost panic-stricken by one was clearly absurd. And as to what was wrapped in the tissue paper . . .

I took it out, and drew back a little of the paper. I saw what looked like the nail of a finger – a blackened nail, horny and scored with yellow cracks.

The bluebottle swooped down. Suddenly I shouted at it, and at the same moment drew away the folds of paper from the object in my hand.

In my hand . . . there it was. A hand in a hand. A dead hand cradled in a living hand. A left hand, severed at the wrist, hacked away and still bleeding.

I laid it down, then drew back with a hiss. I felt sick. From a fold in the window curtain, drawn towards the hand like steel to a magnet, the bluebottle loomed across the room. It settled where it wanted to settle. On the dead hand.

My mouth was open, as though to release something foul inside me. I could do nothing for several seconds but stare down at the hand and the bluebottle stalking across the palm with its broken-up lines and branches. Then I looked away to the bright circle of red light from the little oil cooker – always a comforting glow. It was late April, and the air was clammy and heavy after a day of heavy showers. There was no sound now from the bluebottle. The silence seemed to solidify, I felt as though the bracken-breasted hills each side of the valley were meeting and closing in upon me. There was a faint satisfied humming again, as the insect delved deeper into the palm of the severed hand. I forced myself to look at it.

It was not a large hand. Wrinkled, with long fingers and black grimy nails, unfreckled, hairless. I put down my own hand as though to touch it, but could not. Still, in a half bemused manner, I could not quite believe it was there – the thing that should not be there.

I blew on it, which disturbed the bluebottle and sent him crashing crazily round the room, angry, defiant.

It wasn't true, I told myself. It could not be true. If I had had a piano here I could have beaten back the rising sickness in me. As it was, I retched, went quickly out to the door, and was sick.

I stayed, wiping my mouth, looking into the solid darkness. Then I remembered the man who had passed me, muttering 'Good night, Mister', and so quickly disappeared. Who was he?

Getting control of myself, I returned to the cottage, half hoping yet knowing it could not be, that the hand would not be there.

It was there. Calmly now, I put the lid back on the box, telling myself I must take it to the police station next morning.

I went up to bed. Whether it was the amount of beer I had drunk, I do not know. But, mercifully, I slept – for several hours. I awoke suddenly, before dawn – not with any memory of the hand, not out of some nightmare, but struggling to recall music which had drifted back into my sleeping mind. I sat up. If I could get downstairs now, I told myself, and touch the keyboard of a piano, the music would return.

But there was no piano downstairs. And suddenly I remembered what was there. Then, until the sun rose over the shoulder of the valley, I lay awake, remembering it was a spring morning when I should have been happy.

*

It is difficult to keep music out of this story I have to tell, and yet I must try. Try to relate the incongruous events quite simply, as though they had not happened to me, but to someone else; as though it were an account of something I might have read in a newspaper.

And when I write 'it is difficult to keep music out', I mean simply that music – or the lack of it – played so large a part in the events of the following days, days in which I tried so desperately to recall the themes which had been in my mind before I opened that box. Themes which would not return, and now, perhaps, never will.

What happened, as I came downstairs the next morning remembering what had been on the table, lying on top of the score paper, the night before? Nothing happened. I remembered the chocolate box as one remembers a dream, and still held on half love it. I had intended walking up to the village in the evening, taking what I had found to the police station, then to the King's Arms, to drink and try to forget the whole matter –

Try to forget it! As though that were possible. And it was not the kind of evening in which to take the long trek to the village; for now the rain was driving in slanting sheets, filling the gushing stream in the valley. It was one of those evenings in late spring when winter makes a sudden dramatic reappearance and you long for darkness to come But darkness is delayed, and the heart grows cold as you look at the empty grate, choked up with old cigarette packets – Player's, at sixpence for ten. Light a fire, I said. Go out to the shed and bring in some driftwood. But when I opened the door, the force of the wind almost knocked me back. I shut it fiercely, drew the curtain across the doorway to the small living-room, sat down and clenched my fists, looking at them. There were blisters at the base of the fingers of my right hand. Were there blisters on –

The Hand possessed me. I tried to read – Rimsky-Korsakov on orchestration. But the words made no sense, and a torrent of chaotic music in my mind made me want to scream. The piano – why wasn't there a piano? That could have saved me.

Save me? From what? For I am still alive to tell the tale. But I mean, a piano could have saved me from the inner darkness and rising void which like its sister darkness in the valley outside the cottage walls rose up as though to suffocate me. I did not read or even know the name of Gerard Manley Hopkins in those days; he had hardly emerged upon the literary scene. But now I can quote from him, in illustration of my condition then.

O the mind, mind has mountains; cliffs of fall
Frightful, sheer, no-man-fathomed.

(And this from the poet who died unknown, with none of his verses published, and on his lips the last words, 'I am so happy.')

Yes, the piano would have saved me, or any sound of music. But in particular I would then have played from the Well-Tempered Clavichord, for in Bach I could have found the strength, the consolation, the perfect *order* without which art and life have no meaning.

But there was no piano. And as the window panes misted with heat from the oil stove and the driving rain hissed and bubbled down the gutters I could think only of one thing: the box in the window seat. What had stopped me from going straight up to the village and handing it over to the police? Merely the drenching rain? No, it was more than that, or so my sick conscience seemed to tell me. I was afraid to become involved. There would be questions I would not be able to answer. Would my story even be believed – that I had merely stumbled upon the box in the dark? But worse than that, my conscience drove at me the awareness that in some dreadful way I could not explain to myself, *I did not want to part with it*. As that long black evening drew on to night, and midnight, and past midnight, and still I did not go up to bed, and had by now smoked the last cigarette, I knew that this was the real reason why I had rejected the long walk to the village.

It had fallen in my path. It was mine. I wanted to keep it.

I can remember now a moment of wild humour that rose in me, when I spoke aloud, trying to reassure myself. 'Bloody fool. What is it? Nothing but a Hand in a chocolate box. People are constantly leaving hands in chocolate boxes and dropping them on remote paths in west Cornwall.' And it was with a laugh of sheer bravado that at last I went to the box, and once again lifted its lid.

A thought came to me as I looked down. The box was packed with power. I bent down to take a closer look at it. And as I did so, I heard the sound I had subconsciously expected, yet had, at this moment, forgotten about.

It came from a corner of the room I could not place. Or did it come from the floor, from the tattered oil-stained rush matting before the slab, the rusty slab which had not been lit for so long? Or did it come from inside myself?

At first, I would not let this sound worry me. I felt calm, as though I were no more than a pawn in a game of chess, and must move as I was moved. So I merely looked and looked down at the Hand. Again, it seemed to have changed. Was it true that nails grow after death? I did not know, but I believe now that they do. And here, certainly, on these dead cold sticks of half curled fingers, the nails were longer, crustier, than they had been the last time I had looked.

Gnarled, tobacco-stained . . . and now the colour had a purplish-greeny glow. In the centre of the palm I could see a thick black moving spot.

It was when I saw the spot that the sound stopped. It was the bluebottle. It had settled precisely where it had wanted to settle.

Not until that moment did I lose control. The next second I was looking through misted eyes at the shattered bits of a cup I had thrown across the room. It had crashed into a mirror on the wall by the door, a small oval mirror framed in an absurd fretsaw design of little crosses. The glass was splintered, and the bits of china scattered over the table. Tea had spilled across a sheet of score paper on which I had written the beginning of a subject – a dribble of quavers.

That was the moment when I cried out the name of Christ, and snatching up the score papers, tore them in two, and then tore again, and again, and set a match to them and watched them burn. That was the moment when I threw away the work I had meant to do, the work I was meant to do, and the moment when I consented to evil.

And then I was calm again. Putting the lid back on the box, I went upstairs to bed. I slept. And that night I was not disturbed by any dreams of music.

*

'The moment when I consented to evil . . .'

It is too great a condemnation; I know that. And yet, from that moment I can now see my life as a composer was ended. What threads I have taken up have not been the right ones. And if I compose now, or play now, the sounds are not in good order.

I must finish this account of something that happened to me so long ago, which I would never have written had it not been for a letter I received recently from an old friend who lives still in that part of Cornwall – a letter I will quote from presently.

The stormy weather continued well into the following day. But by some intuition I knew it would end before evening, I knew the sun would break through the mass of cloud as the day wore on. I cannot remember now what I did with the earlier part of that day – whether I once opened the box or not. I only remember that at about six o'clock a glow of watery sun suddenly came across the opposite hillside, and again I heard the cuckoo, this time far away, yet not soothing, not on notes of ecstasy. It was to be a clear night. A night when one sees the slip of a new moon. I now had to do what should have been done twenty-four hours earlier, or even before that. I had to go to the village and give up to the police what I had found two nights before. I would tell them, I decided, that I had only just found it. For what kind of questions would I be asked if I admitted that I had kept it for nearly two days?

I am trying to remember each move I made that evening. I think it was like this. I would have to return a milk jug and a cream bowl to the farm at the top, and these I put in a haversack. Bread had to be collected from the farm on the way back, where it was left for me twice a week. Probably it was a Saturday night, when, in those days, shops stayed open late. I intended to buy stores for the next few days, and that must have been why I took the haversack.

The last thing I did was to take the box from the window seat, outside, and there I rested it on a stone hedge, while I put the milk jug and cream bowl into the haversack. I remember that moment well. For the thought came to me (and why did I not follow it up?) that I should bury the Hand; bury it and forget it. Even give it a little funeral service as they did in the superb tale of Maupassant, the tale of the fisherman's hand that had become gangrenous. Yes. I should have done that. It would have been kinder.

Instead . . . and it was not until I got to the farm that I realised what I had done. Taking the haversack from my shoulders in order to leave the jug and cream bowl with Mrs Harry I stared at her in a way that must have frightened her.

'It's nothing,' I said, in answer to her question. 'Something I meant to take to the village. That's all.'

'Tesn't the end of the world,' she said.

No. I agreed. It was the end of the world. And I went up to the village, did my shopping, and spent the rest of the evening in the King's Arms. I had left the chocolate box on the stone hedge outside the cottage.

*

Why did I not go back for it? And what would have happened had I done so? Would it still have been there, on the stone hedge, in its box where I had left it? Or would only the box have been there, as it was when I returned late that night to the cottage?

I kept asking these questions, as I have asked them many times in the last fifty years – intermittently, it is true, trying to bury the inexplicable, even to pretend that I had imagined it all, from the beginning, that I had never even found the box in my path. But it cannot be buried, any more than I can now bury the Hand; and now, because of this letter I have had, and because of something else, it has had to be written – written out of me, I hope; written right out of my system.

I have not made it clear. Would only the box have been there, I have written above, had I gone back for it? By that I mean, when I did return late at night, only the box *was* there.

There was nothing inside it.

At first, as I stared down at the empty box in the light of my torch, and saw only dark brown stains, there was a sense of lightness in me, almost of relief. It had gone. Perhaps it had never been there. The whole business the product of a disordered mind. But then I knew this was not so. The hand had been taken away. But who had taken it?

At what time, I asked myself, had I again met the man I had passed in the dark two nights earlier? At what time had I passed him that evening? And hardly noticed him?

Yes, it had been a few moments after I left the farm, continuing my walk into the village. An old man, wearing a long shabby grey overcoat that had once been good, an old man with a shuffling walk and a furtive expression, an old man who did not show his hands, for they (if two there were) were in his coat pockets. He had passed me with a quick upward glance at me, and he had muttered something I hadn't heard. I had hurried past, not wanting to admit his presence even into my mind. But he had been walking down in the direction of the valley. And I have never seen him again, I never found out who he was.

I had spent an almost convivial evening in the King's Arms. I remember making jokes about hands to the landlord, old Bill Jago he was called. 'Hands,' I had said, 'funny things when you look at them. Think what they can do.' And he had looked at me a little oddly, wondering what I was talking about, and why I was so closely examining my own two hands laid palm upwards on the bar counter.

'Never thought much about them meself,' he said.

'Well, do,' I advised him. 'Because they're precious things. If you lost one, then you'd think about it.'

A crude, macabre joke, which I had enjoyed, perversely relishing the knowledge of what I thought still reposed in the box on the stone hedge. No need to report this matter to the police, I told myself. It had been taken out of my hands . . .

At first, as I have said, I had this sense of lightness and relief, when I found the empty-box, and took it in, and looked again and again at it. Tonight, the cottage was dead silent. The wind had dropped. In the window seat I saw a dead bluebottle. Scattered all over the floor the charred bits of score paper. Then, and not till then, did I begin to feel a dreadful sense of loss. Even if it had been the hand of a killer, *I wanted it back*.

As I grow older, and my left hand hardens and becomes more useless so that I begin to drop things from cramped and bloodless fingers even on fine summer mornings, I feel how much easier it could be if I had the Hand safely back in the chocolate box. What would be left of it now? A writhing mess of maggots? But no. That happened a long time ago. Or did it? For here is a part of the letter

lately; I'm speaking of several years back – but even now you can see what he must have been once. Such power and drive behind him, and that fine head, which he carried like a king. There's an idea in that, too. No. I'm not joking. Who knows what royal blood he carries inside him, harking back to some remote forebear that gets the better of him and drives him fighting mad. I didn't think about that at the time. I just looked at him, and ducked behind the gorse when I saw him turn, and I wondered to myself what went on in his mind, whether he knew I was there, watching him.

If he should decide to come up the lake after me I should look pretty foolish. He must have thought better of it, though, or perhaps he did not care. He went on staring out to sea, watching the gulls and the incoming tide, and presently he ambled off his side of the lake, heading for the missus and home and maybe supper.

I didn't catch a glimpse of her that first day. She just wasn't around. Living as they do, close in by the left bank of the lake, with no proper track to the place. I hardly had the nerve to venture close and come upon her face to face. When I did see her, though, I was disappointed. She wasn't much to look at after all. What I mean is, she hadn't got anything like his character. A placid, mild-tempered creature, I judged her.

They had both come back from fishing when I saw them, and were making their way up from the beach to the lake. He was in front, of course, she tagged along behind. Neither of them took the slightest notice of me, and I was glad, because the old man might have paused, and waited, and told her to get on back home, and then come down towards the rocks where I was sitting. You ask what I would have said, had he done so? I'm damned if I know. Maybe I would have got up, whistling and seeming unconcerned, and then, with a nod and a smile – useless, really, but instinctive, if you know what I mean – said good day and pottered off. I don't think he would have done anything. He'd just have started after me, with those strange narrow eyes of his, and let me go.

After that, winter and summer, I was always down on the beach or the rocks, and they went on living their curious, remote existence, sometimes, fishing in the lake, sometimes at sea. Occasionally I'd come across them in the harbour on the estuary, taking a look at the yachts anchored there, and the shipping. I used to wonder which of them made the suggestion. Perhaps suddenly he would be lured by the thought of the bustle and life of the harbour, and all the things he had either wantonly given up or never known, and he would say to her, 'Today we are going into town.' And she, happy to do whatever pleased him best, followed along.

You see, one thing that stood out – and you couldn't help noticing it – was that the pair of them were devoted to one another. I've seen her greet him when he came back from a day's fishing and had left her back home, and towards evening she'd come down the lake and on to the beach and down to the sea to wait for him. She'd see him coming from a long way off, and I would see him too, rounding the corner of the bay. He'd come straight in to the beach, and she would go to meet him, and they would embrace each other, not caring a damn who saw them. It was touching, if you know what I mean. You felt there was something lovable about the old man, if that's how things were between them. He might be a devil to outsiders, but he was all the world to her. It gave me a warm feeling for him, when I saw them together like that.

You asked if they had any family? I was coming to that. It's about the family I really wanted to tell you. Because there was a tragedy, you see. And nobody knows anything about it except me. I suppose I could have told someone, but if I had, I don't know . . . They might have taken the old man away, and she'd have broken her heart without him, and anyway, when all's said and done, it wasn't my business. I know the evidence against the old man was strong, but I hadn't positive proof, it might have been some sort of accident, and anyway, nobody made any enquiries at the time the boy disappeared, so who was I to turn busybody and informer?

I'll try and explain what happened. But you must understand that all this took place over quite a time, and sometimes I was away from home or busy, and didn't go near the lake. Nobody seemed to take any interest in the couple living there but myself, so that it was only what I observed with my own eyes that makes this story, nothing that I heard from anybody else, no scraps of gossip, or tales told about them behind their backs.

Yes they weren't always alone, as they are now. They had four kids. Three girls and a boy. They brought up the four of them in that ramshackle old place by the lake, and it was always a wonder to me how they did it. God, I've known days when the rain lashed the lake into little waves that burst and broke on the muddy shore near by their place, and turned the marsh into a swamp, and the wind driving straight in. You'd have thought anyone with a grain of sense would have taken his missus and his kids out of it and gone off somewhere where they could get some creature comforts at least. Not the old man. If he could stick it, I guess he decided she could too, and the kids as well. Maybe he wanted to bring them up the hard way.

Mark you, they were attractive youngsters. Especially the youngest girl. I never knew her name, but I called her Tiny, she had so much go to her. Chip off the old block, in spite of her size. I can see her now, as a little thing, the first to venture paddling in the lake, on a fine morning, way ahead of her sisters and the brother.

The brother I nicknamed Boy. He was the eldest, and between you and me a bit of a fool. He hadn't the looks of his sisters and was a clumsy sort of fellow. The girls would play around on their own, and go fishing, and he'd hang about in the background, not knowing what to do with himself. If he possibly could he'd stay around home, near his mother. Proper mother's boy. That's why I gave him the name. Not that she seemed to fuss over him any more than she did the others. She treated the four alike, as far as I could tell. Her thoughts were always for the old man rather than for them. But Boy was just a great baby, and I have an idea he was simple.

Like the parents, the youngsters kept themselves to themselves. Been dinned into them, I dare say, by the old man. They never came down to the beach on their own and played: and it must have been a temptation, I thought, in full summer, when people came walking over the cliffs down to the beach to bathe and picnic. I suppose, for those strange reasons best known to himself, the old man had warned them to have no truck with strangers.

They were used to me pottering, day in, day out, fetching driftwood and that. And often I would pause and watch the kids playing by the lake. I didn't talk to them, though. They might have gone back and told the old man. They used to look up when I passed by, then glance away again, sort of shy. All but Tiny. Tiny would toss her head and do a somersault, just to show off.

I sometimes watched them go off, the six of them – the old man, the missus, Boy, and the three girls, for a day's fishing out to sea. The old man, of course, in charge; Tiny eager to help, close to her dad; the missus looking about her to see if the weather was going to keep fine; the two other girls alongside; and Boy, poor simple Boy, always the last to leave home. I never knew what sport they had. They used to stay out late, and I'd have left the beach by the time they came back again. But I guess they did well. They must have lived almost entirely on what they caught. Well, fish is said to be full of vitamins, isn't it? Perhaps the old man was a food faddist in his way.

Time passed, and the youngsters began to grow up. Tiny lost something of her individuality then, it seemed to me. She grew more like her sisters. They were a nice-looking trio, all the same. Quiet, you know, well-behaved.

As for Boy, he was enormous. Almost as big as the old man, but with what a difference! He had none of his father's looks, or strength, or personality; he was nothing but a great clumsy lout. And the trouble was, I believe the old man was ashamed of him. He didn't pull his weight in the home, I'm certain of that. And out fishing he was perfectly useless. The girls would work away like beetles, with Boy, always in the background, making a mess of things. If his mother was there he just stayed by her side.

I could see it rattled the old man to have such an oaf of a son. Irritated him, too, because Boy was so big. It probably didn't make sense to his intolerant mind. Strength and stupidity didn't go together. In any normal family, of course, Boy would have left home by now and gone out to work. I used to wonder if they argued about it back in the evenings, the missus and the old man, or if it was something never admitted between them but tacitly understood – Boy was no good.

Well, they did leave home at last. At least, the girls did.

I'll tell you how it happened.

It was a day in late autumn, and I happened to be over doing some shopping in the little town overlooking the harbour, three miles from this place, and suddenly I saw the old man, the missus, the three girls and Boy all making their way up to Pont – that's at the head of a creek going eastward from the harbour. There are a few cottages at Pont, and a farm and a church up behind. The family looked washed and spruced up, and so did the old man and the missus, and I wondered if they were going visiting. If they were, it was an unusual thing for them to do. But it's possible they had friends or acquaintances up there, of whom I knew nothing. Anyway, that was the last I saw of them, on the fine Saturday afternoon, making for Pont.

It blew hard over the weekend, a proper easterly gale. I kept indoors and didn't go out at all. I knew the seas would be breaking good and hard on the beach. I wondered if the old man and the family had been able to get back. They would have been wise to stay with their friends in Pont, if they had friends there.

It was Tuesday before the wind dropped and I went down to

the beach again. Seaweed, driftwood, tar and oil all over the place. It's always the same after an easterly blow. I looked up the lake, towards the old man's shack, and I saw him there, with the missus, just by the edge of the lake. But there was no sign of the youngsters.

I thought it a bit funny, and waited around in case they should appear. They never did. I walked right round the lake, and from the opposite bank I had a good view of their place, and even took out my old spy-glass to have a closer look. They just weren't there. The old man was pottering about as he often did when he wasn't fishing, and the missus had settled herself down to bask in the sun. There was only one explanation. They had left the family with friends in Pont. They had sent the family for a holiday.

I can't help admitting I was relieved, because for one frightful moment I thought maybe they had started off back home on the Saturday night and got struck by the gale; and, well – that the old man and his missus had got back safely, but not the kids. It couldn't be that, though. I should have heard. Someone would have said something. The old man wouldn't be pottering there in his usual unconcerned fashion and the missus basking in the sun. No, that must have been it. They had left the family with friends. Or maybe the girls and Boy had gone up country, gone to find themselves jobs at last.

Somehow it left a gap. I felt sad. So long now I had been used to seeing them all around, Tiny and the others. I had a strange sort of feeling that they had gone for good. Silly, wasn't it? To mind, I mean. There was the old man, and his missus, and the four youngsters, and I'd more or less watched them grow up, and now for no reason they had gone.

I wished then I knew even a word or two of his language, so that I could have called out to him, neighbour-like, and said, 'I see you and the missus are on your own. Nothing wrong, I hope?'

But there, it wasn't any use. He'd have looked at me with his strange eyes and told me to go to hell.

I never saw the girls again. No, never. They just didn't come back. Once I thought I saw Tiny, somewhere up the estuary, with a group of friends, but I couldn't be sure. If it was, she'd grown, she looked different. I tell you what I think. I think the old man and the missus took them with a definite end in view, that last weekend, and either settled them with friends they knew or told them to shift for themselves.

I know it sounds hard, not what you'd do for your own son

and daughters, but you have to remember the old man was a tough customer, a law unto himself. No doubt he thought it would be for the best, and so it probably was, and if only I could know for certain what happened to the girls, especially Tiny, I wouldn't worry.

But I do worry sometimes, because of what happened to Boy.

You see, Boy was fool enough to come back. He came back about three weeks after that final weekend. I had walked down through the woods – not my usual way, but down to the lake by the stream that feeds it from a higher level. I rounded the lake by the marshes to the north, some distance from the old man's place, and the first thing I saw was Boy.

He wasn't doing anything. He was just standing by the marsh. He looked dazed. He was too far off for me to hail him; besides, I didn't have the nerve. But I watched him as he stood there in his clumsy loutish way, and I saw him staring at the far end of the lake. He was staring in the direction of the old man.

The old man, and the missus with him, took not the slightest notice of Boy. They were close to the beach, by the plank bridge, and were either just going out to fish or coming back. And here was Boy, with his dazed stupid face, but not only stupid – frightened.

I wanted to say, 'Is anything the matter?' but I didn't know how to say it. I stood there, like Boy, staring at the old man.

Then what we both must have feared would happen, happened.

The old man lifted his head, and saw Boy.

He must have said a word to his missus, because she didn't move, she stayed where she was, by the bridge, but the old man turned like a flash of lightning and came down the other side of the lake towards the marshes, towards Boy. He looked terrible. I shall never forget his appearance. That magnificent head I had always admired now angry, evil; and he was cursing Boy as he came. I tell you, I heard him.

Boy, bewildered, scared, looked hopelessly about him for cover. There was none. Only the thin reeds that grew beside the marsh, but the poor fellow was so dumb he went in there, and crouched, and believed himself safe – it was a horrible sight.

I was just getting my own courage up to interfere when the old man stopped suddenly in his tracks, pulled up short as it were, and then, still cursing, muttering, turned back again and returned to the bridge. Boy watched him, from his cover of reeds, then, poor clot that he was, came out on to the marsh again, with some idea, I suppose, of striking for home.

I looked about me. There was no one to call. No one to give any help. And if I went and tried to get someone from the farm they would tell me not to interfere, that the old man was best left alone when he got in one of his rages, and anyway that Boy was old enough to take care of himself. He was as big as the old man. He could give as good as he got. I knew different. Boy was no fighter. He didn't know how.

I waited quite a time beside the lake, but nothing happened. It began to grow dark. It was no use my waiting there. The old man and the missus left the bridge and went on home. Boy was still standing there on the marsh, by the lake's edge.

I called to him, softly. 'It's no use. He won't let you in. Go back to Pont, or wherever it is you've been. Go to some place, anywhere, but get out of here.'

He looked up, that same queer dazed expression on his face, and I could tell he hadn't understood a word I said.

I felt powerless to do any more. I went home myself. But I thought about Boy all evening, and in the morning I went down to the lake again, and I took a great stick with me to give me courage. Not that it would have been much good. Not against the old man.

Well . . . I suppose they had come to some sort of agreement during the night. There was Boy, by his mother's side, and the old man was pottering on his own.

I must say, it was a great relief. Because, after all, what could I have said or done? If the old man didn't want Boy home, it was really his affair. And if Boy was too stupid to go, that was Boy's affair.

But I blamed the mother a good deal. After all, it was up to her to tell Boy he was in the way, and the old man was in one of his moods, and Boy had best get out while the going was good. But I never did think she had great intelligence. She did not seem to show much spirit at any time.

However, what arrangement they had come to worked for a time. Boy stuck close to his mother – I suppose he helped her at home, I don't know – and the old man left them alone and was more and more by himself.

He took to sitting down by the bridge, humped, staring out to sea, with a queer brooding look on him. He seemed strange, and lonely. I didn't like it. I don't know what his thoughts were, but I'm sure they were evil. It suddenly seemed a very long time since he and the missus and the whole family had gone fishing, a happy contented party. Now everything had changed for him. He was

III

An Act of Charity

Ronald Duncan

The morning started badly, it ended worse. That is, if it ended.

I had been more than usually annoyed when I had received a phone call the previous night calling me up to a rehearsal in London the next afternoon. It was not that I was particularly busy or writing anything important, but it was November. The weather was unusually cold. I felt most disinclined to move from my fire.

To begin with, my alarm call had been ten minutes late: the operator apologised, but starting late put me in a panic. I had to dress, have breakfast, and then drive forty miles. British Railways had closed the station at Bideford and my nearest is now Barnstaple. Hurrying to dress, I could not find my links; making the coffee, I spilled the coffee, and halfway to the garage I remembered that I had left my car keys in my other suit. . . .

There had been a hard frost. It took me five minutes to start the car. When I had backed it out of the garage I had to get out, breathe on the windscreen and scrape it with the back of my glove before I could see through it. A skid at Welcombe Cross told me I had better drive more slowly. There were patches of black ice on the road which I couldn't see. I went slowly down the hill towards the West Country Inn, only to run into a herd of cows being brought in for the morning milking. The cowman stamping his feet on the road, his breath vaporising in the raw air. I was surprised to see a herd of Guernseys still out at night.

Treading my way through them, I drove on across Bursdon Moor. I had just reached the Forestry Commission plantation there when I saw a gaunt, tall figure walking along the road fifty yards ahead. I could tell by his slow ambling gait that he was a 'runner'. That is the Devon word for tramp, though sometimes we call them 'mile-stone inspectors'. He had a long overcoat with the hem half undone, flapping round his ankles, a piece of binder twine tied around his middle. The coat pockets were torn. He carried a paper bundle under one arm. As I drove up he turned his head, but like any professional tramp, he made no gesture for a lift. It was a cruel morning. I stopped beside him, opened the door and indicated that he was to get in. I glanced at my watch: if I was not careful I would miss the train. Having acquired my passenger, I now felt embarrassed by him. I do not make a habit of being a good Samaritan; and casual passengers in cars irritate me when you have to make conversation with them. The tramp sensed this; and, for a mile or two, did not say a word until I offered him a cigarette.

'No, thanks, I roll my own.'

He took out a packet of cigarette papers from his inside pocket, shook some tobacco into one, and dexterously rolled a weedy cigarette with one hand. I passed him my lighter. He immediately began coughing. It was a dreadful cough. He brought up some phlegm. It would not have surprised me if he had coughed up his feet.

'That's a terrible cough you have got,' I said, needlessly.

'It should have killed me years ago,' he replied.

We drove on a few more miles in silence, while I formed unspoken questions about my passenger.

He continued to smoke his filthy cigarette.

'Are you a Catholic?' he asked suddenly.

'No,' I was surprised at his question. 'Though I suppose you are, being Irish. Whatever makes you think I am one?'

He nodded towards the dashboard of the car. I saw that my daughter had left her Missal there.

'It's not mine,' I said, almost aggressively, 'somebody has left it in the car.'

'Do you mind if I look at it, sir?' he asked, reaching for the book. 'I have not had one of these in my hands since I left Ireland thirty years ago.' He opened the Missal and picked out one of my small daughter's Holy pictures and stared at it. I glanced up at the driving mirror, and studied his reflection as he looked at the card in his hand. His dark, unshaven face expressed nothing of his feelings, whatever they were, but his eyes were moist. Seeing this I began to despise him for being a sentimental Irishman. But his next remark disillusioned me. As he put the Missal back under the dashboard, wiped his eyes with the back of his hand.

'That's the worst of whiskey,' he said, 'it always walks out of a man's eyes, if he can get enough of it.'

I found myself wondering against my will how this wretched creature had been on the road so early in the morning. I assumed he had slept in a hayrick, I glanced at his coat and saw there was no sign of that. My curiosity got the better of me.

'How far have you come this morning?'

'Bude,' he replied. 'Had a good night's kip there. Found a railway carriage in a siding. Porters often let us sleep in a compartment until they have to couple up.'

'Where are you heading for now?'

'Anywhere. I have nowhere to go. Odd, this is the second lift I've had this morning.'

I drove on for another five miles, cursing the ice on the road. It was likely to make me miss my train. I watched him roll another cigarette, then start another fit of coughing. He was in a terrible condition. Obviously consumptive; two stone underweight, with nothing but his old overcoat round him. His trousers had been corduroys, but were now entirely smooth with wear. I decided to take him as far as Bideford, and began to wonder whether to give him ten shillings or a pound to put him on his way, wherever that was. My concern for him began to irritate me, especially as he appeared to have none for himself.

'Have you been on the road long?' I found myself asking.

'Twenty years or so. Never thought it would happen to me, but it did.'

'How?'

'It is quite simple, really,' he replied, 'and all my own fault.' There was not a note of self-pity in his voice. 'Soon after my wife and I married, we came over from Ireland, and I got a job masoning in London. We were very happy. Then my wife died, so I went to live with my married daughter. That didn't work out well. I was already drinking a fair sop and didn't get on with either of them. So I moved out into digs. The loneliness of that room in Brixton made me take to the bottle more. If I got a job, I fell down on it. So eventually I took to the road. That's my story; it's not a very good one, is it?'

I now began to hate the fellow beside me; having made a good Samaritan out of me he was now turning even me into an earnest social worker.

'There must be something you can do,' I said. 'Have you tried Public Assistance?' He smiled tolerantly.

'Funny,' he said, 'a lot of people who give me a lift ask that question. But of course people in my condition cannot get any Public Assistance, for the simple reason that if you apply for it, you have to give a permanent address. So that counts us out for a start. Nobody who keeps lodgings is going to take a scarecrow like me in anyhow.' This was a bit of a set-back to my attempt to be constructive, but I was not to be defeated.

'But if somebody gave you a couple of quid so that you could pay your rent in advance, and you then applied for Public Assistance, you would be all right?' I said.

'Don't waste your money. If you gave me a quid, I would do what I always do: wait till the nearest pub opened, get as tight as a lord and sleep till I could wander off again.'

'Can't you leave the booze alone?'

'Never tried it. Being drunk is the only thing I have got to live for. And that is becoming difficult enough.'

'Have you ever heard of Alcoholics Anonymous?' I heard myself saying. This was appalling. I should soon find myself handing out tracts.

'No,' he said, 'what's them?' I skipped that one. I could not imagine a member of that Society being able to ring him up in the middle of the night.

'What you don't realise,' I said, 'is drinking is a kind of disease. It is easily cured nowadays if you go into a hospital and get treatment. Why don't you do that? If you like, I will drive you to Barnstaple Infirmary and get you a bed.' He shook his head.

'I tell you, drink is all I have to live for. Don't try to take that from me. With this cough, there can't be much more round the road for me. If it weren't for my wretched strong heart I would have pegged out years ago. I have often fallen down in a ditch and woke up sober and soaked, having been through a night that would have snuffed any normal man. But I hope this damn ticker is getting weaker now, for I'm tired of carrying my thoughts along the road. That's the worst of being sober – they are so heavy then, and so monotonous too. Most of a man's thoughts are regrets.'

At Bucks Cross I had to slow down to let another herd of cows pass, and for the next few miles we did not speak.

'Isn't there anything I can do for you?' I said at last. He shook his head.

'Just put me down in Bideford, and forget all about me.' he replied. I glanced at him occasionally as I drove along. It seemed that his eyes were closed and it was not until we were about four miles outside Bideford that he spoke again.

'You asked me some way back' he said, turning to look at me kindly, 'if there was anything you could do for me.'

'Yes,' I said, already feeling for my wallet. He smiled at my gesture and shook his head.

'No, I want something more than that. Stop the car and I'll show you what it is.' I pulled up and saw him open the door and get out. He walked quickly ahead of me, then stopped about twenty paces in front of the car, and turned round.

'Put an end to me, guv'ner,' he shouted.

I did nothing. 'You think you are charitable,' he yelled sneeringly, 'come on, prove it. Prove it!'

I put the car into gear and drove straight at the fellow. A look of gratitude was on his face as my bonnet approached him. It hit him hard in the chest, sending him straight on his back. There was a sickening crack as his head struck the frosty road. I pulled up and ran back. Blood trickled from his lips: there was blood matted in his hair. I felt unusually charitable. Then the wretched creature's eyes opened.

'Damn and blast my bloody heart,' he whispered. 'You'll have to have another go.' I raced back to the car, reversed, and drove over his body again, only succeeding, because it was along the road and not across it, in merely going over one of his legs. I pulled up again. This was ridiculous. Should I put the body across the road, reverse again and steer for his head? Fear of oncoming traffic made me take another course. I ran back to my car, found the jack-lever and went back to him.

'Bless you, guv'ner,' he said, seeing what I held in my hand. I brought it down on his skull with all my force. The blow broke the skin. But still he was conscious. I was reminded of when I had been driven to kill a cat in a sack with a hammer having failed to drown it in a tub. I brought the handle down on his temple as hard as I could. With his right hand he scrawled the sign of the cross on the frosty road. His eyes closed.

My first impulse was to fling the iron bar marked with blood into the hedge, then I realised it would be found so I wiped it with grass and put it in the boot and drove on. I felt strangely elated. It was the one good deed that I could recall I had ever done. I decided that I would drive straight to Bideford Police Station and report that I had found a body lying on the road and then catch a later train. The sergeant was making a cup of tea. He offered me one.

'Now, let's get these details down,' he said, without much concern. 'What time would it have been when you found the body?'

'7.30.'

'And from the marks on the head it had obviously been hit by a car?'

'What else?' I said. 'You had better come and see for yourself.' The wretched man seemed so casual. He insisted on another cup of tea.

'It was there,' I said, pointing to the gate some twenty yards ahead of us. But there was nobody on the road.

'Somebody must have picked it up and taken it into the hospital,' I said.

'Are you sure it was here, sir?' he asked.

'I'm certain,' I replied. 'If you look there are all the marks of my car where I stopped.' But the frost had melted, and there was not a trace of them.

'Maybe he was only stunned,' the bobby suggested.

'No,' I insisted, 'he'd been hit twice. . . .'

'Twice?'

'Twice as hard as to just stun him,' I said. 'He was dead already . . . I made sure of that.'

'Then he'll be at Bideford Hospital,' the sergeant said conversationally. 'Let's go in there and see. If he's not there, you must have had what they call an hallucination, sir.'

We drove to the hospital. He made an enquiry at the gate, then walked back to the car.

'What they call an hallucination, sir,' he said. 'They would not have taken him anywhere else but here.'

I dropped him back at the police station, apologised for troubling him and drove on to Barnstaple, wondering and worrying how much of this I had imagined. Then I saw in the ashtray on the dashboard the proof of my charity: a weedy, hand-made cigarette stub. I picked it up and put it in my wallet. It is good to have proof of one's Christian virtue.

IV

Inheritance

David Eames

The girl Elly was twenty one years old when her grand-mother's will came into effect and she became the rightful owner of the big, bleak granite house out on Bodmin Moor. It was a moment she had been secretly preparing for ever since she had first heard of the bequest from her puzzled, already estranged parents. They could not understand, or forgive the temerity of an eccentric old lady in by-passing a whole generation in the bestowing of such a formidable favour.

'That's what comes of buttering up the old girl, I suppose,' said Elly's mother sourly. 'By rights it should go to your father.'

But Elly knew that her father, a weak and self-centred man, had cared little about his aged mother and had done nothing to deserve such an inheritance . . . and as for her own relationship with the old lady it had been born of no unworthy or ulterior motive but rather out of a spontaneous bond of sympathy. She had never forgotten the occasion of her first visit, when her parents had responded to an invitation by making excuses ('Bleak forlorn place, no thank you,' her mother had muttered) and sending her down as if in compensation.

While the ancient lumbering taxi from Bodmin Road Station had made that first haunting journey through winding narrow lanes, often across wide desolate areas of moorland where the only signs of life would be a lonely cluster of black bullocks. Elly had found herself growing increasingly nervous. Looking back she could see that anyone might well have been apprehensive about such an apparent journey into nowhere, especially one culminating in the arrival at such an enormous, lonely, even sad looking house. And yet the moment she stepped out and took in the unfamiliar, almost eerie sight, she felt immediately a sense of peace, even contentment. When the huge oak doors opened and she recognised the frail white-haired figure of her grandmother she felt that they were joined together at once by some kind of elemental link.

After that she had never minded the long journey from London, had grown to treasure the strange, rather secretive periods with her grandmother, just the two of them wandering in the afternoons across the wild moors, or sitting in the evenings by the big log fire in the long sitting room from whose bay window, on a clear day, you could catch a distant glimpse of the grey Atlantic Ocean. It was at these times, listening entranced to the reed-like voice of the old lady recalling dim memories of the lonely life of the moors, that Elly had become aware of the significance in her life of that remote, mysterious place. She had never openly expressed this feeling to her grandmother, she felt sure – and yet somehow, when the solicitor's letter arrived one day like a proverbial missile out of the blue, the generous bequest did not seem altogether a surprise. Instead, it bore the touch of the inevitable. . . . All her rather solitary, curiously unfulfilled life, she realised with a throb of excitement, might have been merely a preparation for such an inheritance.

It was the beginnings of a Cornish spring when the business of clearing up her previous life was completed and she was able at last to make the long journey westwards. For some years she had lived on her own, inhabiting one dreary bed sitting room after another on the fringes of Earl's Court and South Kensington. Fulham and the King's Road, participating superficially in the life of her own lost generation by wearing black leather jackets, sweaters and jeans and high heeled boots, squatting for hours listening to cool jazz in smoky cellars, drinking when the occasion demanded . . . working now and then, once as a waitress in a coffee bar, another time as assistant in one of the big, anonymous departmental stores, a third time, more pleasurably, behind the colourfully lined shelves of a bookshop . . . never somehow becoming really involved with anyone else, remaining stubbornly a lone wolf, withdrawn into her secret self . . . and all the time a part of her already far away, across the miles of uniform, soul destroying roofs and chimneys, beyond the neat suburban parks, far out to where the wind blew eerily among the tiny Cornish hedges and fields, bending the few trees still obstinately clinging to their moorland roots.

When the time came to give all this up she did so gladly, without a qualm. It was as if when finally she settled down in a corner of the train at Paddington and watched the familiar environment sliding gently away, so she wiped clean the slate of the past in preparation for entering a new life, perhaps as a new person.

By the time she stepped off the train at the lonely halt station, steeply and unexpectedly surrounded by high trees, perhaps already she was someone else, or perhaps this was more likely, the real Elly . . . this waif-like, pale-faced boyish figure, moving as if always alone, shoulders hunched up, dark hair dishevelled and brushed carelessly back, eyes peering eagerly forward into the imponderable mysterious future.

She could hardly wait until the familiar taxi had driven up to the stone steps, the driver had helped her out with her two suitcases, all her worldly possessions – and suddenly she was left all alone.

Nothing that Elly had imagined could compare with her experiences and sensations during the ensuing days as she took up her new life in the big, bleak old house. She had imagined a certain oneliness, a feeling of strangeness, perhaps some domestic difficulties – she was unprepared, on the contrary, for the immediate sense of belonging. It was almost as if the house had been waiting for her to come, now enfolded her in its bleak embrace, like a lover. She never tired of walking from room to room, standing in the doorway and enjoying the exquisite pleasure of surveying this particular domain . . . admiring the gracious Georgian structure, the frescoed ceiling, the elegant line of the windows, the gleaming polished wood of the long floors . . . the richly coloured tapestries and the strong, beautifully proportioned furniture.

Altogether her response to the house contained a strong element of earthy, almost physical awareness; she loved walking down the curving staircases, caressing the smooth wood of the bannister, fondling the intricately carved headpiece at the bottom. Always she was finding new surprises, new sensations. Picking up a tiny ceramic mask, brought back once by her grandfather as a momento of mining years in Mexico, she was at once aware, vividly, indeed disturbingly, of ancient influences. Probing with her fingers around the thick curves she might almost have been probing, as if by instinct, into the mysteries of all supernatural life.

It was the same wherever she went in the house, upstairs, downstairs in my lady's chamber. Down in the basement the huge room that had once been a smoking kitchen for the large families of other generations now lay empty and unused – yet, somehow, among its subterranean shadows, the girl was aware of the element of surprise, the unknown, perhaps danger. And if again, she ascended the steep winding stairs that led up to the enormous attic, with tiny dormer windows tucked at every corner, then indeed there was a sense of unexpected awe, looking out upon the wide unending panorama of bare moorland. Sometimes in the early evening, when the orange sun was dying behind the western hills – illuminating starkly the distant slag heaps of the St Austell claypits – Elly would throw open one of the dormer windows and stare out, feeling the caress of the evening breeze on her cheeks, watching once-normal shapes of the landscape waver and tilt and become fearfully unfamiliar in the gathering dusk.

It was easy then to forget herself and her cramped position, to become sunk in some kind of dream, to be lost in that vast sea stretching everywhere in darkening brown, turning to indigo, broken perhaps forlornly by some distant wavering star, first one, then another – messengers with whom she felt at once more contact than with any of her own human kind.

For day after day, indeed week after week, the girl Elly gave herself up to the joyous task of entering into this new, private world. Perhaps because of the very intensity of her new passion there were few external problems. Every morning one of the local farmers dropped in a jug of milk, and if she wanted it, eggs and vegetables. Twice a week the baker from the nearest village, a speckle on the far horizon, called with her solitary loaf – and once a week a smart modern grocer's van came out from Launceston with a parcel of groceries. In one of the outhouses she found a stack of wood logs, enough to last a year or two, perhaps a lifetime . . . What else did she need? Everything she valued and cared about, suddenly, was here, in the lonely midst of the moors.

Once, after a couple of weeks, she walked the two miles to the main road and caught one of the infrequent buses into Launceston: but after half an hour's idle walking round the few shops she became bored, waiting impatiently to catch the return bus.

After that she did not attempt the pretence of caring about the outside world again. Soon, indeed, she grew to distrust even the occasional visits from the postman on his bicycle, though after a while anyway the letters grew fewer, dwindling to an occasional remonstration from her mother, whose suburban world already seemed part of another planet. At first Elly scanned these letters curiously, but then she gave up even that pretence, and began tearing them up unopened. Instinctively she knew she was safe there from her parents, indeed from everyone.

It went on like this all the time. What might have seemed a routine, even a dull one, was for Elly always a kind of continuous and joyful surprise. She would awake to the silent, sunlit mornings, aware with pleasure of the huge silence, and of being safe and secure behind the sheltering walls of her own secret home. When she got up and wandered from room to room she gloried in the sense of familiarity with so much that was old and wise and beyond the normal comprehension. She lived a strange, monastic life: in the mornings she did the housework, tidying the rooms, cleaning and polishing, attending to the needs of her home – in the afternoons she donned jeans and a sweater and went out into the rambling garden, digging and hoeing, forking and raking, tending with loving care to the growing plants, taking a pride in keeping alive the luxuriant patches which her predecessor had cultivated.

In the evenings – in the evenings she delighted in going up to her bedroom, spreading out her best clothes and spending perhaps half an hour in selecting from among them the one that suited her mood. There was a long mirror in one corner of her room, and it gave her a strange pleasure to stand in front of this as she dressed and undressed. To know that she was completely and utterly alone encouraged in her an unfamiliar sense of liberation. First she would flick on the subdued light at the side of the mirror, whose glow illuminated her silhouette softly. Then, with quick, almost irritable movements she cast off the day's dull garments, until she was quite naked. Standing thus in front of the mirror, her body glistening in the dimmed lighting, she was aware of the pleasing effect. She had long, almost boyish limbs that were now filling out with the promise of womanhood: the whiteness of them seemed to flare up to where her breasts hung gently, mysteriously touched by shadows. Yes, she reflected, it was her body that seemed brightest and most vivid in the revealing mirror, that was most vibrant and alive. The face above it – she examined it critically – somehow made less impact; it was detached, observing, curiously anonymous, a watchful, wary face, as if aware of the hidden flamboyancies of that secretive flesh.

Often the girl Elly would remain for endless periods, an hour or more, in front of her mirror, looking at her young, awakening, virginal body not so much admiringly as curiously, as if surmising some experiences and sensations yet to be encountered. At last, with a secretive smile, she would run her tapering fingers up and down the rippling skin, feeling each contour and curve, lifting up the youthful breasts in homage to some unknown god. . . . Then, a little sadly, she would turn away and pick up the dress she had chosen for the evening, setting about the task of preparing herself almost as if it was some very grand occasion. And indeed when finally she went to eat her lonely meal it was hardly any longer an illusion to her that she was not really alone, but that the room glittered with lights and hummed with conversation, that all manner of strange and wild spirits accompanied her on each golden evening. . . .

It never occurred to Elly that her behaviour was in any way odd, but she perceived so from the occasional curious glances of the farmer or the postman or any other solitary caller. The effect of this sense of intrusion was to cause her to retreat even more into her circle of secrecy. It was not really difficult, for all that was pleasurable and meaningful in life was already within such a confinement. Now she took to avoiding seeing any of her callers, leaving little scribbled notes and memorandums and the money needed – a method of transaction quite adequate, but calculated to spread the gossip around the scattered neighbours.

'Bit strange, isn't she, that lady up at the big house?' wagged the tongues; and a stranger and an eccentric, someone remote from them all, she became.

Such definitions did not bother Elly, if ever she was aware of them, but perhaps the mere existence of such an attitude helped to confirm her isolation. And so, freed of all external contacts, she became curiously exhilarated, able to give herself up more completely to the compelling urges which, she noticed, seemed to come quite naturally to her since she came to live in the granite house.

Yes, even the very granite, its presence everywhere, rock-like and impregnable, surrounding her – even that had a way of communication. Sometimes she delighted in walking slowly around the outside of the house, pressing her fingers along the gnarled, curling shape of the granite blocks . . . and through their stone shape she could feel mysterious vibrations, as of echoes, of past ages. This was particularly so of the huge granite lintel which stretched across the open fireplace in the big sitting room. Often in the evenings, while the fire light danced warmly in the wrought-iron basket, the girl would stand with both hands held up to touch the lintel, probing with her fingers into the ageless cracks and crevices . . . until she would become aware of the most extraordinary sensations, as if through her fingers pulsated a whole strata of ancient sounds, of pipes, of drums, of living voices, even. Sometimes the impact would be so forceful, so realistic, that she would feel momentarily frightened and unable to let go of the hard granite surface – but then somehow it was as if the sound and the movement washed over her whole being, entering into her, binding her to that past life, and she felt a warm glow of contentment, as if lifted up to another plane of life.

Gradually the large sitting room with its long bay window looking over the barren moors became for the girl Elly her haven, her real home. She had long ago discarded the harsh electric lighting, which anyway depended on some rusting machine lying broken in one of the sheds. Now, every evening, she brought in two tall brass candlesticks which she had found and polished assiduously, placing one at each end of the long refectory table. The flickering lights seemed to fill the room with magic and mystery: in unison with the dancing shadows on the oak-panelled. walls the girl would sometimes pirouette round and round . . . and often it seemed as if the room moved with her, the shadows. becoming her own, and she would gain unfamiliar confidence, until it might be as if she was caught up in some fierce secret whirlwind of movement that whistled about the room, dancing faster and faster, tossing her head and arching her body, pounding her bare feet into the soft texture of the thick carpet. At such times a tiny, still earthbound part of the girl's mind sounded a warning note: beware, beware, of what you do not know of barriers that may not be crossed . . . but it was like applying a worn brake to a chariot hurtling down an endless hill.

And then one night, somehow, everything seemed to Elly different, elevated, removed to a higher, more marvellous level. Outside there was a huge full moon hanging like a silvery wonder-world in the middle of the indigo sky. She had watched it fascinatedly from the attic window, then when dusk had fully fallen she had felt impelled to go out into the garden and wander about, smell the honeysuckle and thyme, listening to the subdued humming of sleepy insects, the occasional cry of a bird . . . How still and tranquil everything was, and yet how disturbingly aflame from the blinding moonlight. Wherever she went it seemed that light followed her, bathing all around her as if with a magic spell. And when finally she crossed the lawn and entered the big sitting room through the French windows it was almost as if the moonlight came in with her, awakening even the inanimate things of the room to an awareness of this special and rarefied occasion.

At first Elly lit the candles as usual, but tonight their harsher yellow light seemed out of place and displeasing, and after a while she snuffed them out. As she did so, catching each flame between her two fingers and obliterating it unerringly, she had a weird sensation of power, absolute and unending power . . . as if not only did the house belong to her, and all that was in it, but the flame, too. As if perhaps everything in the world was in her possession. . . .

Except that distant, but ever closening moon. She turned at last and faced it, opening her eyes wide, letting the vast silvery moonglow fall upon her, splashing her face, raining upon her shoulders, showering her, drowning her, overwhelming . . . until she could bear the exquisite sensation no longer, was restless, had to jump to her feet and move about the room, cross to the fire, warm her hands, then place them reflectively on the warm old lintel. Yes, tonight, tonight of all nights she knew, the mysteries of the granite were there at the touch of her fingers. Why, already she could feel the pulsating heart-beats of a thousand years ago!

Compulsively, without quite knowing what she was doing, she began to dance slowly around the room. But it was a slowness of restraint, not of mood. Within her she felt burning many fierce flames, was aware of them being fanned, leaping higher and higher, to new intensities. All at once she began to increase the tempo of her movements, swirling round the room faster and faster, in and out of the long avenues of silver light flooding through the doorways. As she danced faster so she became hotter, and there welled up in her an almost frantic desire not only to feel the fresh cool night air against her skin, but also to be free, utterly and completely free, even abandoned.

It was thus, still moving round and round, that she began to divest herself of her clothes, first unpinning the ivory headband so that her coiled dark hair fell in sudden profusion, then gravely unbuttoning her blouse until it seemed to slip away of its own volition – at last unfastening her loose hessian skirt and letting it fall, unheeded, to the floor. Then while, almost unthinkingly, she struck new vigour into her dance, wheeling and stamping and jerking, she quickly stripped away her remaining garments, flinging the last speck of civilised white confinement high into the air and oblivion, aware at last of the most complete and glorious moment of utter liberation.

Now, as she revealed almost defiantly her virgin flesh, Elly became aware that the moon's watchful being had loomed closer and closer, so that its silvery rays now seemed to flood every corner of the room. Caught up in the sensuous movements, caressed by the silver warmth, she danced on round the room, suddenly no longer the former uncertain spinsterish Elly, but a newly born, awakened ageless, primeval woman, writhing sensually in the flaring moonlight, her long dark tresses whirling round and round

V

The Botathen Ghost

R. S. Hawker

There was something very painful and peculiar in the position of the clergy in the west of England throughout the seventeenth century. The Church of those days was in a transitory state, and her ministers, like her formularies, embodied a strange mixture of the old belief with the new interpretation. Their wide severance also from the great metropolis of life and manners, the city of London (which in those times was civilised England, much as the Paris of our own day is France), divested the Cornish clergy in particular of all personal access to the master-minds of their age and body. Then, too, the barrier interposed by the rude rough roads of their country, and by their abode in wilds that were also inaccessible, rendered the existence of a bishop rather a doctrine suggested to their belief than a fact revealed to the actual vision of each in his generation.

Hence it came to pass that the Cornish clergyman, insulated within his own limited sphere, often without even the presence of a country squire (and unchecked by the influence of the Fourth Estate – for until the beginning of this nineteenth century, *Flindell's Weekly Miscellany*, distributed from house to house from the pannier of a mule, was the only light of the West), became developed about middle life into an original mind and man, sole and absolute within his parish boundary, eccentric when compared with his brethren in civilised regions, and yet, in German phrase, 'a whole and seldom man' in his dominion of souls. He was 'the parson', in canonical phrase – that is to say, The Person, the somebody of consequence among his own people.

These men were not, however, smoothed down into a monotonous aspect of life and manners by this remote and recluded existence. They imbibed, each in his own peculiar circle, the hue of surrounding objects, and were tinged into a distinctive colouring and character by many a contrast of scenery and people. There was the 'light of other days', the curate by the sea-shore, who professed to check the turbulence of the 'smugglers' landing' by his presence on the sands, and who 'held the lantern' for the guidance of his flock when the nights were dark, as the only proper ecclesiastical part he could take in the proceedings. He was soothed and silenced by the gift of a keg of hollands or a chest of tea.

There was the merry minister of the mines, whose cure was honey-combed by the underground men. He must needs have been artist and poet in his way, for he had to enliven his people three or four times a year, by mastering the arrangements of a 'guary', or religious mystery, which was duly performed in the topmost hollow of a green barrow or hill, of which many survive, scooped out into vast amphitheatres and surrounded by benches of turf which held two thousand spectators. Such were the historic plays, *The Creation* and *Noe's Flood*, which still exist in the original Celtic as well as the English text, and suggest what critics and antiquaries these Cornish curates, masters of such revels, must have been – for the native language of Cornwall did not lapse into silence until the end of the seventeenth century.

Then, moreover, here and there would be one parson more learned than his kind in the mysteries of a deep and thrilling lore of peculiar fascination. He was a man so highly honoured at college for natural gifts and knowledge of learned books which nobody else could read, that when he 'took his second orders' the bishop gave him a mantle of scarlet silk to wear upon his shoulders in church, and his lordship had put such power into it that, when the parson had it rightly on, he could 'govern any ghost or evil spirit', and even 'stop an earthquake'.

Such a powerful minister, in combat with supernatural visitations, was one Parson Rudall, of Launceston, whose existence and exploits we gather from the local tradition of his time, from surviving letters and other memoranda, and indeed from his own 'diurnal' which fell by chance into the hands of the present writer. Indeed, the legend of Parson Rudall and the Botathen Ghost will be recognised by many Cornish people as a local remembrance of their boyhood.

It appears, then from the diary of this learned master of the grammar school – for such was his office as well as perpetual curate of the parish – 'that a pestilential disease did break forth in our town in the beginning of the year A.D. 1665; yea, and it likewise invaded my school, insomuch that therewithal certain of the chief scholars sickened and died'.

'Among others who yielded to the malign influence was Master John Eliot, the eldest son and the worshipful heir of Edward

Eliot, Esquire, of Trebursey, a stripling of sixteen years of age, but of uncommon parts and hopeful ingenuity. At his own especial motion and earnest desire I did consent to preach his funeral sermon.'

It should be remembered here that, howsoever strange and singular it may sound to us that a mere lad should formally solicit such a performance at the hands of his master, it was in consonance with the habitual usage of those times. The old services for the dead had been abolished by law, and in the stead of sacrament and ceremony, month's mind and year's mind, the sole substitute which survived was the general desire 'to partake', as they called it, of a posthumous discourse, replete with lofty eulogy and flattering remembrance of the living and the dead. The diary proceeds:

'I fulfilled my undertaking, and preached over the coffin in the presence of a full assemblage of mourners and lachrymose friends. An ancient gentleman, who was then and there in the church, a Mr Bligh, of Botathen, was much affected with my discourse, and he was heard to repeat to himself certain parentheses therefrom, especially a phrase from Maro Virgilius, which I had applied to the deceased youth, "*Et puer ipse fuit cantari dignus*".

'The cause wherefore this old gentleman was moved by my applications was this: He had a first-born and only son – a child who, but a very few months before, had been not unworthy the character I drew of young Master Eliot, but who, by some strange accident, had of late quite fallen away from his parent's hopes, and become moody, and sullen, and distraught. When the funeral obsequies were over, I had no sooner come out of church than I was accosted by this aged parent, and he besought me incontinently, with a singular energy, that I would resort with him forthwith to his abode at Botathen that very night; nor could I have delivered myself from his importunity, had not Mr Eliot urged his claim to enjoy my company at his own house. Hereupon I got loose, but not until I had pledged a fast assurance that I would pay him, faithfully, an early visit the next day.'

The Place, as it was called, of Botathen, where old Mr Bligh resided, was a low-roofed, gabled manor-house of the fifteenth century, walled and mullioned, and with clustered chimneys of dark-grey stone from the neighbouring quarries of Ventorgan. The mansion was flanked by a pleasance or enclosure in one space, of garden and lawn, and it was surrounded by a solemn grove of stag-horned trees. It had the sombre aspect of age and of solitude, and looked the very scene of strange and supernatural events. A legend might well belong to every gloomy glade around, and there must surely be a haunted room somewhere within its walls. Hither, according to his appointment, on the morrow, Parson Rudall betook himself. Another clergyman, as it appeared, had been invited to meet him, who, very soon after his arrival, proposed a walk together in the pleasance, on the pretext of showing him, as a stranger, the walks and trees, until the dinner-bell should strike. There, with much prolixity, and with many a solemn pause, his brother minister proceeded to 'unfold the mystery'.

A singular infelicity, he declared, had befallen young Master Bligh, once the hopeful heir of his parents and of the lands of Botathen. Whereas he had been from childhood a blithe and merry boy, 'the gladness', like Isaac of old, of his father's age, he had suddenly, and of late, become morose and silent – nay, even austere and stern – dwelling apart, always solemn, often in tears. The lad had at first repulsed all questions as to the origin of this great change, but of late he had yielded to the importune researches of his parents, and had disclosed the secret cause. It appeared that he resorted every day, by a pathway across the fields, to this very clergyman's house, who had charge of his education, and grounded him in the studies suitable to his age. In the course of his daily walk he had to pass a certain heath or down where the road wound along through tall blocks of granite with open spaces of grassy sward between.

There, in a certain spot, and always in one and the same place, the lad declared that he encountered, every day, a woman with a pale and troubled face, clothed in a long loose garment of frieze, with one hand always stretched forth, and the other pressed against her side. Her name, he said, was Dorothy Dinglet, for he had known her well from his childhood, and she often used to come to his parents' house; but that which troubled him was, that she had now been dead three years, and he himself had been with the neighbours at her burial; so that, as the youth alleged, with great simplicity, since he had seen her body laid in the grave, this that he saw every day must needs be her soul or ghost.

'Questioned again and again,' said the clergyman, 'he never contradicts himself; but he relates the same and the simple tale as a thing that cannot be gainsaid. Indeed, the lad's observance is keen and calm for a boy of his age. The hair of the appearance, sayeth he, is not like anything alive, but it is so soft and light that it seemeth to melt away while you look; but her eyes are set, and never blink – no, not when the sun shineth full upon her face. She maketh no steps, but seemeth to swim along the top of the grass; and her hand, which is stretched out alway, seemeth to point at something far away, out of sight. It is her continual coming; for she never faileth to meet him, and to pass on, that hath quenched his spirits; and although he never seeth her by night, yet cannot he get his natural rest.'

'Thus far the clergyman; whereupon the dinner-clock did sound, and we went into the house. After dinner, when young Master Bligh had withdrawn with his tutor, under excuse of their books, the parents did forthwith beset me as to my thoughts about their son. Said I, warily, 'The case is strange but by no means impossible. It is one that I will study, and fear not to handle, if the lad will be free with me, and fulfil all that I desire.' The mother was overjoyed, but I perceived that old Mr Bligh turned pale, and was downcast with some thought which, however, he did not express. Then they bade that Master Bligh should be called to meet me in the pleasance forthwith. The boy came, and he rehearsed to me his tale with an open countenance, and, withal, a pretty modesty of speech. Verily he seemed *ingenui vultus puer ingenuique pudoris.* Then I signified to him my purpose. "Tomorrow," said I, "we will go together to the place; and if, as I doubt not, the woman shall appear, it will be for me to proceed according to knowledge, and by rules laid down in my books." '

The unaltered scenery of the legend still survives, and, like the field of the forty footsteps in another history, the place is still visited by those who take interest in the supernatural tales of old. The pathway leads along a moorland waste, where large masses of rock stand up here and there from the grassy turf, and clumps of heath and gorse weave their tapestry of golden and purple garniture on every side. Amidst all these, and winding along between the rocks, is a natural footway worn by the scant, rare tread of the village traveller. Just midway, a somewhat larger stretch than usual of green sod expands, which is skirted by the path, and which is still identified as the legendary haunt of the phantom, by the name of Parson Rudall's Ghost.

But we must draw the record of the first interview between the minister and Dorothy from his own words. 'We met,' thus he writes, 'in the pleasance very early, and before any others in the house were awake; and together the lad and myself proceeded towards the field. The youth was quite composed, and carried his Bible under his arm, from whence he read to me verses, which he said he had lately picked out, to have always in his mind. These were Job vii. 14, "Thou scarest me with dreams, and terrifiest me through visions"; and Deuteronomy xxviii. 67, "In the morning thou shalt say, Would to God it were morning; for the fear of thine heart wherewith thou shalt fear, and for the sight of thine eyes which thou shalt see."

'I was much pleased with the lad's ingenuity in these pious applications, but for mine own part I was somewhat anxious and out of cheer. For aught I knew this might be a *daemonium meridianum*, the most stubborn spirit to govern and guide that any man can meet, and the most perilous withal. We had hardly reached the accustomed spot, when we both saw her at once gliding towards us; punctually as the ancient writers describe the motion of their "lemures, which swoon along the ground, neither marking the sand nor bending the herbage".'

The aspect of the woman was exactly that which had been related by the lad. There was the pale and stony face, the strange and misty hair, the eyes firm and fixed, that gazed, yet not on us, but on something that they saw far, far away; one hand and arm stretched out, and the other grasping the girdle of her waist. She floated along the field like a sail upon a stream, and glided past the spot where we stood, pausingly. But so deep was the awe that overcame me, as I stood there in the light of day, face to face with a human soul separate from her bones and flesh, that my heart and purpose both failed me. I had resolved to speak to the spectre in the appointed form of words, but I did not. I stood like one amazed and speechless, until she had passed clean out of sight.

One thing remarkable came to pass. A spaniel dog, the favourite of young Master Bligh, had followed us, and lo! when the woman drew nigh, the poor creature began to yell and bark piteously, and ran backward and away, like a thing dismayed and appalled. We returned to the house and after I had said all that I could to pacify the lad, and to soothe the aged people, I took my leave for that time, with a promise that when I had fulfilled certain business elsewhere, which I then alleged, I would return and take orders to assuage these disturbances and their cause.

'*January 7, 1665.* – At my own house, I find by my books, what is expedient to be done; and then *Apage, Sathanas*!

'*January 9, 1665.* – This day I took leave of my wife and family, under pretext of engagements elsewhere, and made my secret journey to our diocesan city, wherein the good and venerable bishop then abode.

'*January 10.* – *Deo gratias,* in safe arrival in Exeter; craved and obtained immediate audience of his lordship; pleading it was for counsel and admonition on a weighty and pressing cause; called to the presence; made obeisance; then and by command stated my case – the Botathen perplexity – which I moved with strong and earnest instances and solemn asseverations of that which I had myself seen and heard. Demanded by his lordship, what was the succour that I had come to entreat at his hands. Replied, licence for my exorcism, that so I might, ministerially, allay this spiritual visitant, and thus render to the living and the dead release from this surprise. "But," said our bishop, "on what authority do you allege that I am entrusted with faculty so to do? Our Church, as is well known, hath abjured certain branches of her ancient power, on grounds of perversion and abuse." "Nay, my lord," I humbly answered, "under favour the seventy-second of the canons ratified and enjoined on us, the clergy, anno Domini 1604, doth expressly provide, that 'no minister, *unless he hath* the licence of his diocesan bishop, shall essay to exorcise a spirit, evil or good'. Therefore it was," I did here mildly allege, "that I did not presume to enter on such a work without lawful privilege under your lordship's hand and seal." Hereupon did our wise and learned bishop, sitting in his chair, condescend upon the theme at some length with many gracious interpretations from ancient writers and from Holy Scriptures, and I did humbly rejoin and reply, till the upshot was that he did call in his secretary and command him to draw the aforesaid faculty, forthwith and without further delay, assigning him a form, insomuch that the matter was incontinently done; and after I had disbursed into the secretary's hands certain moneys for signitary purposes, as the manner of such officers hath always been, the bishop did himself affix his signature under the *sigillum* of his see, and deliver the document into my hands. When I knelt down to receive his benediction, he softly said, "Let it be secret, Mr R. Weak brethren! weak brethren!" '

This interview with the bishop, and the success with which he vanquished his lordship's scruples, would seem to have confirmed Parson Rudall very strongly in his own esteem, and to have invested him with that courage which he evidently lacked at his first encounter with the ghost.

The entries proceed:

'*January 11, 1665.* – Therewithal did I hasten home and prepare my instruments, and cast my figures for the onset of the next day. Took out my ring of brass, and put it on the index-finger of my right hand, with the *scutum Davidis* traced thereon.

'*January 12, 1665.* – Rode into the gateway at Bothathen, armed at all points, but not with Saul's armour, and ready. There is danger from the demons, but so there is in the surrounding air every day. At early morning then, and alone – for so the usage ordains – I betook me towards the field. It was void, and I had thereby due time to prepare. First I placed and measured out my circle on the grass. Then I did mark my pentacle in the very midst, and at the intersection of the fire angles I did set up and fix my crutch of raun (rowan). Lastly, I took my station south, at the true line of the meridian, and stood facing due north. I waited and watched for a long time. At last there was a kind of trouble in the air, a soft and rippling sound, and all at once the shape appeared, and came on towards me gradually. I opened my parchment-scroll, and read aloud the command. She paused, and seemed to waver and doubt; stood still; then I rehearsed the sentence again, sounding out every syllable like a chant. She drew near my ring, but halted at first outside, on the brink. I sounded again, and now at the third time I gave the signal in Syriac – the speech which is used, they say, where such ones dwell and converse in thoughts that glide.

'She was at least obedient, and swam into the midst of the circle, and there stood still, suddenly. I saw, moreover, that she drew back her pointing hand. All this while I do confess that my knees shook under me, and the drops of sweat ran down my flesh like rain. But now, although face to face with the spirit, my heart grew calm, and my mind was composed. I knew that the pentacle would govern her, and the ring must bind, until I gave the word. Then I called to mind the rule laid down of old, that no angel or fiend, no spirit, good or evil, will ever speak until they have been first spoken to.

N.B. – This is the great law of prayer. God Himself will not yield reply until man hath made vocal entreaty, once and again.

'So I went on to demand, as the books advise; and the phantom made answer, willingly. Questioned wherefore not at rest. Unquiet, because of a certain sin. Asked what, and by whom. Revealed it; but it is *sub sigillo*, and therefore *nefas dictu*; more anon. Inquired, what sign she could give that she was a true spirit and not a false fiend. Stated, before next Yule-tide a fearful pestilence would lay waste the land and myriads of souls would be loosened from their flesh, until, as she piteously said, "our valleys will be full". Asked again, why she so terrified the lad. Replied: "It is the law: we must seek a youth or a maiden of clean life, and under age, to receive messages and admonitions."

'We conversed with many more words, but it is not lawful for me to set them down. Pen and ink would degrade and defile the thoughts she uttered, and which my mind received that day. I broke the ring and she passed, but to return once more next day. At evensong, a long discourse with that ancient transgressor, Mr B. Great horror and remorse; entire atonement and penance; whatsoever I enjoin; full acknowledgement before pardon.

'*January 13, 1665.* – At sunrise I was again in the field. She came in at once, and, as it seemed, with freedom. Inquired if she knew my thoughts, and what I was going to relate? Answered, "Nay, we only know what we perceive and hear; we cannot see the heart." '

Then I rehearsed the penitent words of the man she had come up to denounce, and the satisfaction he would perform. Then said she, "Peace in our midst." I went through the proper forms of dismissal, and fulfilled all as it was set down and written in my memoranda; and then, with certain fixed rites, I did dismiss that troubled ghost, until she peacefully withdrew, gliding towards the west. Neither did she ever afterward appear, but was allayed until she shall come in her second flesh to the valley of Armageddon on the last day.'

These quaint and curious details from the 'diurnal' of a simple-hearted clergyman of the seventeenth century appear to betoken his personal persuasion of the truth of what he saw and said, although the statements are strongly tinged with what some may term the superstition, and others the excessive belief, of those times. It is a singular fact, however, that the canon which authorises exorcism under episcopal licence is still a part of the ecclesiastical law of the Anglican Church, although it might have a singular effect on the nerves of certain of our bishops if their clergy were to resort to them for the faculty which Parson Rudall obtained.

The general facts stated in his diary are to this day matters of belief in that neighbourhood; and it has been always accounted a strong proof of the veracity of the Parson and the Ghost that the plague, fatal to so many thousands, did break out in London at the close of that very year. We may well excuse a triumphant entry, on a subsequent page of the 'diurnal', with the date of July 10, 1665.

*

'How sorely must the infidels and heretics of this generation be dismayed when they know that this Black Death, which is now swallowing its thousands in the streets of the great city, was foretold six months agone, under the exorcisms of a country minister, by a visible and suppliant ghost! And what pleasures and improvements do such deny themselves who scorn and avoid all opportunity of intercourse with souls separate, and the spirits, glad and sorrowful, which inhabit the unseen world!'

VI

Snow

Kenneth Moss

It began very gently. Just a few flakes which seemed first to float on the air, and then drift slowly down.

'Good God! It's snowing,' said John.

Putting his drink on the low table in front of him, Norman leaped up from the couch, clapping his hands together.

'But how marvellous!' he said.

He went over to the window and looked out, trying to see through the reflection – the easy chairs where John and Mary sat; the blue carpet; the couch; the lighted table lamps; and, in the corner, the ominous single eye of the television set – a second, ghostly room, existing on another plane.

'No John, I'm afraid you're mistaken,' he said, squinting into the darkness.

He cupped his hands around his eyes, and where they blotted out the reflection he saw a patch of garden. As he did so, a few more flakes drifted slowly down.

'Oh yes. I don't think it's going to be much, though.'

'Well, I don't know why you should be disappointed,' said Mary. 'You've a long drive in front of you.'

'But I like snow.' He turned from the window and sat down again on the couch. 'We haven't had a good snow fall for ages.'

'It makes everything so bloody cold, though,' said John.

'Yes, but it looks wonderful.' Norman picked up his drink and sipped, and as he spoke, the snowfall died again. 'I mean, don't you think it's a wonderful experience to wake up in the morning and see everything white? It's like a new world.' He leaned forward towards them. 'And it makes things look so clean. You go to sleep in one world and wake up in another.'

'Oh yes, it's marvellous,' said John with heavy irony. 'Especially when I have patients calling me out in the middle of the night, and the car won't start, and I have to dig a path to the front gate, and the snow gets in my shoes, and the pipes are frozen. That's when I really like it.'

Norman smiled.

'Ah, you've got no imagination, John,' he said, and outside a few more snowflakes began to fall. 'It reminds me of Finland. I had a marvellous time over there. But we never get snow here like they have it. And if you can survive that, you can survive anything'.

'You were over there working on this new process of yours, weren't you?' Mary asked.

'Yes. We wanted to see the effect of operating at low temperatures.'

'You didn't finish telling us what it's all about,' she reminded him.

'Ah no. Well, you see the basic idea is that it will help to make petrol engines more efficient.'

Norman, who worked as a research chemist for one of the large petrol companies, explained as simply as he could the principle of the additive he had developed. It was difficult to explain briefly and without getting involved in technicalities the others would not understand, but he did the best he could. As he finished his explanation, there was a sudden flurry of snow.

'And so you see,' he concluded, 'it will mean we can raise the compression ratios as high as we like.'

'Which means more power, I suppose,' said John.

'Precisely. More power, more miles per gallon, better acceleration, smaller and therefore lighter engines, and so on.'

'And yours is the only company to have this?' Mary asked.

'Not only is mine the only company, I'm the only chemist.' He sipped his drink. 'If I were to die tomorrow, the process would die with me. No one else knows about it yet. Mind you, once we start selling, the other companies will soon catch on, but we'll have a head start'.

'Good God! Look at it now,' said John, pointing towards the window.

The snow was falling quickly now, and Norman again went over to the window.

'That's better,' he said. 'I wonder if it's going to settle. You know, I think it is.' He felt as though his trip to Finland had given him a proprietary interest in snow.

'Well if it goes on like this,' said Mary, 'I think you'd better stay the night, Norman.'

'What, a hardened old campaigner like me?' he replied.

'Nonsense. I wouldn't dream of it. Besides, I promised my parents I'd be there tonight, and I can't disappoint them.'

'But surely you're not going to Tremesca tonight? You can't drive across Bodmin Moor in this,' she protested.

'Why ever not? I've got a good car, a full tank of petrol, an efficient heater, and on the back seat I've an overcoat and a raincoat. Now what more do I need?'

'But the roads. . . .'

'What about them? If it's snowing like this, there'll be nothing else about – I'll have the roads to myself.'

'Just the same, she's right you know,' said John. 'You'd far better stay the night and go on in the morning.'

'John, you're becoming an old woman. What difference will the morning make? I know that road like the back of my hand, and besides, it'll be worse in the morning – there'll be more traffic about. No, I can't let my parents down. They'll be terribly disappointed if I don't arrive tonight.'

John finished his drink.

'You know best,' he said. 'Now, how's your glass?'

He re-filled Norman's glass, and they talked and drank, and the snow was still falling, and the garden and the road slowly turned white.

John had become involved in a long explanation of how the human body has vast reserves of physical strength which are never used. He told them that these reserves can be tapped under hypnotism, and that in a hypnotic state people can perform amazing feats of strength. 'Of course,' he said, 'if a man's life depended upon it, maybe he could harness that strength himself. We don't know. It's an experiment that we can't carry out.'

An hour had passed. It had stopped snowing, and Norman stood up to go.

'That's a date,' he was saying. 'You'll be out to Tremesca a week from today. My parents will be awfully pleased to see you. You know how fond of you they are, and being so isolated, they rarely see people.'

As he moved towards the front door, Mary laid a hand on Norman's arm.

'I do wish you'd stay the night,' she said.

John opened the front door, and they felt a blast of cold air. The snow gleamed.

'Go on with you, Mary,' said Norman. 'Look – it's stopped now, and it's only a couple of inches deep. I'll be all right. You forget, I got used to this sort of thing in Finland, and it was a damned sight worse than this. Good night, now.' He kissed her forehead. 'See you next week, I hope. Don't forget.'

'I won't,' she smiled. 'Bye for now.'

John walked with him along the garden path to the car, and their feet sank into the snow. As they walked, a solitary snowflake drifted down, and Norman caught it on the palm of his hand.

'Amazing, isn't it?' he said. The delicate crystals began to change colour as they melted in the warmth of his hand, and finally they became a tiny drop of water. 'That's what stopped Napoleon at Moscow. Thousands of men, tons upon tons of materials, and military genius. And that's what stopped them – snowflakes! Incredible! And all it means to me is waking up in a new world, where everything's white and clean.'

'And to me it's just a damned nuisance, the blasted stuff,' John said. 'It sticks to your shoes, gets into your feet. I think I can do without it.'

Norman opened the door of his car and held out his hand.

'Good night, old chap,' he said.

'You're sure you won't stay?' John asked him.

'Certain. I don't want to disappoint the old folks. Thanks all the same.'

'Well, goodnight, then.'

Norman started the car, switched on his lights, and drove off into the snow.

Because there was only a light covering, he was able to make good progress, for which, in view of his 50-mile drive, he was thankful. There was more traffic than he expected, but it seemed to move almost silently.

Because of the whiteness of the snow, he did not use his headlights until he was clear of the town. When he switched them on, the glare that was reflected back was momentarily dazzling.

He decided that perhaps he should stop and telephone his parents, just to re-assure them that he was on his way. Maybe when he reached Redruth.

At Camborne, he came upon a line of slow-moving traffic, but in spite of his exasperation, he was unable to overtake.

Then it began to snow again.

Coming down the slope towards the Redruth by-pass, he could see that the traffic was mostly going up the opposite slope, into the town. He took the by-pass.

Now that the traffic had thinned out, he was able to drive more quickly, despite the falling snow. Suddenly he remembered the telephone call.

'Oh to hell with it,' he whispered. It was best to keep going.

With the heater on and the car gliding quietly over the snow, he felt as if he were in his own warm, private universe.

He left the by-pass, and then turned off at Scorrier along the road towards Bodmin.

There was something satisfying about seeing the cold world around him while he sat snugly in his warm, motorised cocoon. Like being back in the womb.

It began to snow faster. Around his windscreen, the area unswept by the wipers was now thickly covered, and the inside of the car was illuminated with a ghostly white light.

After a while, he noticed that the rest of the traffic had dispersed, and it was now snowing so fast that the tracks made by other cars were quickly disappearing.

Now he was travelling over virgin snow and the whole world outside seemed to have turned white. He felt totally alone. To Norman, it was exhilarating. He began to sing softly. Why, he wondered, did he feel so elated? Perhaps it was because the feeling of being so alone, but yet protected from the cold world, warm and comfortable in his car as it glided gently and quietly along, intensified the womb-like sensation.

What was that saying about English poetry depending upon the fact that in English, womb rhymes with tomb? What was the phrase, exactly? Then there was doom, of course. Womb, doom, tomb. In his exhilaration, he shouted the words. 'Womb, doom, tomb,' he called out, and the words filled his private, mechanical womb. And then he fitted a tune to them and sang them. He was enjoying himself immensely. 'Womb, doom, tomb.'

Still the snow fell. It thickened on the windscreen, impeding the movement of the wipers, which were cleaning a smaller and smaller area.

Norman adjusted the heater control, so as to divert some of the warm air directly on to the screen and melt the snow. After a while, a slab slid down off the screen, and the wipers were able to resume their full sweep. But again, the swept area slowly shrank, until another slab dropped off the glass, and the process settled into a rhythm.

As the miles passed, the car began to slide on the bends, and Norman was compelled to reduce his speed progressively until he could only travel quite slowly. Visibility, too, was a problem, not only because of the constant shrinking of the area cleaned by the windscreen wipers, but also because now, the snow was falling so quickly that it almost seemed as if it were being squirted at him from a hosepipe. For a moment he felt uneasy.

In that cold, inhospitable universe outside the car, landmarks were disappearing as everything was reduced to a flat uniform whiteness. It was difficult to see where the road was now, but he had travelled it so often that he told himself that the contour of the land was sufficient to remind him of the shape of the road.

He let the car run slowly down hill in second gear as he neared the spot where he judged he must turn off the main road on to the winding, narrow strip of tarmac that branched across the moor and led eventually to Tremesca. The farm itself was hidden in a fold in the moors some miles distant, and Norman often wondered why it was that his parents still insisted on remaining in such an isolated spot when they could easily afford to retire and move somewhere more convenient.

Faintly visible in the deep snow, Norman fancied he saw the hump made by the boulder that stood at the junction of the little lane and the main road. Slowly, he steered the car across the road and on to the snow where the lane should be.

'It's idiotic their staying here,' he told himself. 'Miles from anywhere, two old people like them – in weather like this, anything could happen to them. True, there's the phone, but if the line went dead, as it so often does in bad weather, they could be in trouble for days and no one would know.' That was how disaster came, he reflected. One moment you were comfortable and complacent, and suddenly you were exposed and vulnerable.

He should be there quite soon now, and he decided that he must speak to them again about leaving Tremesca. Perhaps persuade them to move somewhere like Carbis Bay. They'd hate it, but it would be safer for them.

The car climbed slowly to the crest of the hill, and ran down the other side. Norman sat warm and snug, as he moved across the desolate landscape.

He was now heading directly into the driving snow, and the increased volume was upsetting the rhythm of his windscreen cleaning process. Half-way down the hill, he had to stop. The warm air-current in the car was no longer melting the snow fast enough, and the screen was completely covered. He adjusted the heater control so as to turn the full blast of hot air on to the screen, and sat a few moments waiting for it to clear, but he could see that the snow was quickly thickening.

'Blast,' he said softly, and he opened the car door and stepped out into the cold. The sudden slap of the icy wind took his breath away, and the driving snow stung his face, almost blinding him.

Quickly, he cleaned the windscreen and scuttled back into the shelter of the car. The wipers were working again and he could see. But while the car had been stationary, the snow had been piling up in front of it, and instead of easing forward as he engaged the clutch, the rear wheels were spinning on the slippery surface.

He got out again into the wind and snow. Another assault from the elements. Quickly, he cleared some of the accumulated snow from the front of the car, cleared the windscreen again, jumped back into the shelter of the car, and eased it forward.

Although it was warm, Norman began to feel wet and uncomfortable. The snow that had fallen on him while he worked outside had begun to melt, and cold water trickled down his face and neck; but he knew now that it was best to keep going at all costs rather than stop while he dried his face. He was now moving very slowly, and he became aware that the snow had already got into his shoes and his feet were soaked. Thank heavens he'd be home in a moment or two.

Home in a moment or two. Home in a moment or two. Home in a moment or two. The phrase drummed in his head. Then, forming a counterpoint to it, that absurd chorus beat out behind it – womb, doom, tomb; womb, doom, tomb. . . .

The windscreen was covered again. Without a moment's hesitation, Norman stopped, leaped out, cleared part of the screen, back in, and away. This time, the car took off without difficulty.

Now he was climbing uphill, but soon the screen was covered once more. Same process. Stop. Out into the snowstorm. Quickly clean. In again. Start.

He began to watch with dread the snow gradually accumulating on the glass as the car climbed higher and higher.

Stop again. Out. Clean. In again. Start.

In his haste to get the car moving again, he engaged the clutch too quickly and the wheels spun. In a moment his foot was back on the pedal, and this time he engaged it slowly, slowly. The wheels spun, and the rear of the car slowly slithered round to the left until the lateral movement was stopped by the snow scooped up by the sliding wheels. He tried top gear. The wheels spun. Then he tried each gear in turn. Each time, the wheels spun. He sat and thought for a moment, cursing quietly. Then he got out into the blizzard and looked. The snow whirled around him in a torrent.

Where the wheels had spun they had formed a smooth patch of crushed snow and ice. As the car was facing uphill, it was obvious that the wheels would never grip sufficiently to get him started. He got inside. The only solution was to let the car run back down the hill and start again from the bottom. He released the handbrake, and the car gently rolled a few inches backwards before coming to a standstill once again. He engaged reverse gear to get it rolling, but once more the wheels spun. He tried moving forward. Wheel-spin.

'This is ridiculous!' he shouted in exasperation. Then, controlling himself, he decided he must think methodically and work slowly. He was only making his position worse through not thinking.

He reached into the back of the car and picked up his overcoat. The feeling of uneasiness came back to him. As best he could, he struggled into the coat and again got out of the car to investigate. The snow swirled around him so thickly it was difficult to see, but he discovered why the car would not run backwards. Instead of rolling back over the snow, the rear wheels had simply dug two trenches into it. The only solution was to go forward, and this was only possible if he put something under the wheels – grit, even twigs or grass would do it. Something they could grip. But there was only snow.

Perhaps he could find something in the boot. A sack maybe. The snow lay so thickly on the lid, he could not lift it. Impatiently, he swept enough snow off to enable him to get it open, but as he'd already known, there was nothing inside. His ears were stinging in the cold, and he got back into the car to think.

He told himself that having coped with winter in Finland, it was absurd to get rattled by an English snowstorm. He must think, sensibly and methodically.

As he sat in the warmth, the snow that had accumulated on him began to melt, and he now felt wet through to the skin. There were puddles of icy water in his shoes, and they squelched as he moved his feet. But it was warm and safe in the car – like a womb. He was protected from the cold and the wind and –

Suddenly he realised that time was vital. If the snow kept falling at this rate, it would not be long before it piled up around the car high enough to prevent his opening the doors. Then he'd not be able to get out and do anything. For a moment, he felt panic. Perhaps he wasn't so safe inside the car, after all.

Again, he tried to discipline himself into calm thought. If the car were on flat snow it would run back down the hill, then he could get it going again. The only way to get it on to flat snow was to lift it out of the tracks it had made. But he couldn't do that with the jack.

Then he remembered what John had been saying that evening. Enormous untapped reserves of strength. Available under hypnotism. But if a man's life depended upon it . . .

Well, of course, it wasn't that bad, but the situation was getting pretty desperate. Maybe his life didn't depend on it, but just the same, now was the time to mobilise those reserves. It was just a question of determination.

He sat for a moment or two, willing himself into a state of mind where he felt he could not fail to lift the car. Then he stepped out into the blizzard again, sank his feet into the deep snow behind the car, and standing with his back to it, he bent down and gripped the underside of the body. Then, he braced himself, and made sure of his footing. He needed to lift for only a moment, and lurch sideways under the weight. That would do it.

Slowly, he began to straighten up, and he felt the back of the car rising as he took the weight off the springs. Now he sensed that he held the full weight of the body, and just a few more inches would raise the wheels from the ground. Straighten up with a jerk and drop it sideways. He ignored the pain of the metal cutting into his hands. Concentrating every faculty into that last effort, he forgot the snow swirling around him, was unaware of the sweat which now poured from him, became oblivious of the melting snow running down his legs, and he commanded himself, 'Lift!' And with every muscle straining, he lifted. Blood spurted to his eyes, and pounded in his ears. His body seemed to be bursting. 'Lift!'

The wheels did not budge. Norman collapsed, face forward, sick with disappointment, frustration, and exhaustion. His lips sank into the snow, and he struggled up in a moment, impotent with rage, and almost too weak to stand. Then he noticed that, miraculously, it had stopped snowing.

There was a terrible stillness. Even in his present state, he turned and surveyed the countryside around him, and he was breathless at the beauty of the gently curving surface of the snow-covered landscape. The snow glinted.

Weakly, half-heartedly, he brushed the snow from himself and stumbled back into the car again. In spite of the warmth, he began to shiver.

He was on the wrong track. Think. Think. Something under the wheels. Something they could grip. Suddenly he remembered the raincoat on the back seat.

He carefully packed it under one of the rear wheels, scooping away the snow as best he could, and then tried to drive forward on to it. The car moved forward perhaps two or three inches and then stopped, with a sound of wheelspin. He got out and looked again. Yes, One wheel was on the raincoat. But, of course, the differential was causing the other wheel to spin. Sensing triumph at last, he took off his overcoat and packed this under the free wheel. Again he tried to drive forward. Two or three inches, and again, wheelspin. Another look. One wheel was firmly in the centre of the overcoat, but the other had whipped the raincoat up and it was now entangled around the axle.

No time for scruples. He took off his jacket, and working in his shirtsleeves in the bitter cold, he packed it under the wheel, leaving the raincoat where it was. The wind cut into him. Perhaps six inches or so more and he'd be on fresh snow and the nightmare would be over. Then he could pick up his coats and drive home. How his parents would smile at the story when he told them of the foolish struggles he'd had.

He put the car in gear and with infinite gentleness eased out the clutch. Slowly the car moved forward until – the whine of spinning wheels.

Once more, he got out to investigate, feeling, despite the disappointment, on the brink of success. All three coats were now inextricably entangled around the rear axle. He worked on his hands and knees in the snow trying desperately to free them, but now he was becoming so numb with cold he could not work properly.

He staggered back into the car to warm himself, and to decide what could be done. Although he now admitted to himself that the countryside had become unrecognisable, he felt certain he could not be far from Tremesca.

There were two alternatives. Either he could spend the night in the car and hope to get it moving in the morning; or he could try to walk to the top of the hill and hope to see the farm buildings – but in his shirtsleeves! The car, he knew, was immovable as things were, and it was impossible to recover his coats. He decided to wait until morning.

He had become so cold, that even in the car he could not seem to get warm. The heat only made him drowsy. He checked the petrol gauge to see if the engine would remain running until morning: without the engine there would be no heater.

Outside, it began to snow again. It must have been some time before he realised it, because the windows were now thickly encrusted, and when he did he whispered to himself in desperation, 'Good God, no! Not more!'

He sat where he was, numb with rage. Still the snow fell. Inexorably, the knowledge imposed itself – he could not stay where he was. The safe, warm car was now a death-trap. The snow would pile up until it blocked the exhaust and stopped the engine, and then the heater would not work. Then it would build up around the car until he could not open the doors. Finally, he'd either freeze to death or suffocate. He must get out! Snowflakes, so fragile, and more delicate than lace. But millions upon millions of them. And this was what had stopped Napoleon.

Wearily, he took a last look round the inside of the car, and gazed for a moment at his briefcase still clean and dry on the back seat, with his initials stamped on the front in gold: N.B. It might have belonged to another world.

He turned off the engine, braced himself for the shock, and stepped out into the flying snow in his shirt sleeves.

The sudden cold made him breathless, and it bit at his nose and ears. The snow stung his eyelids, and began to cake on his hair and his eyebrows. For a moment he hesitated, then he stumbled forward up the hill, unseeing, into the teeth of the snowstorm.

The snow beating against his shirt began to melt slowly, and run down his body in icy drops. It ran down his face in freezing rivulets. He tried to run, but the wind tore at his shirt and the freezing snow whipped his chest and pulled at his feet. On and on he went, on up the hill. He reached the top, and staggered down the other side, not even pausing to look for the farm, only conscious that he must press forward. Desperation began to take hold of him. Though at first he'd been aware of the wind whining as it tore around him and across the hills, filling his body with an unbelievable coldness, he soon became unconscious of everything but the need to battle forward against the universe of snow into which he seemed to be submerged. Earth and air were now merged into one whirling white plane, and he began to sense the impossibility of what he was attempting. Forcing himself onwards, he tried to grit his teeth, but they chattered uncontrollably. He fought the snow as if it were a living thing. And he felt unbelief at his predicament.

One foot dropped deep into a drift, and he almost fell flat on his face, but supporting himself on his hands and his free foot, he extricated himself and staggered blindly on. Breathing was difficult. and he swallowed great gulps of freezing air and snow in uncontrollable convulsions. His legs felt so weak they would barely support him, but he knew he must go on, on.

For a moment, he turned his back to the wind, and peered

back along the way he had come. There was nothing but the curving white brow of the hill, his fast-disappearing tracks, whiteness all around, and from the black sky, the snow, falling, falling, falling.

He turned into the wind again, and it stung his face and chest. Progress became more and more difficult as he grew weaker and colder, but still he staggered forward. He was now desperately tired, but he forced himself on, pushing his reluctant feet through the snow. His body felt frozen all over. His stomach felt like an ice-block inside him, and his belly heaved and shivered. The wind tore at his shirt. An icy hand gripped his back and chest. The snow that gathered on his face and caked on his hair and eyebrows was no longer melting. It no longer melted from his shirt, but thickened around his body in an icy slab.

Now he was staggering aimlessly. From the depths of his weariness, he decided he must get back to the car again, but he knew he would never find it.

Almost overcome by drowsiness and at the extremity of desperation, he struggled on through the snow. There was nothing else to do.

If only it would stop! He lifted his face to the sky. 'Stop, you bastard. Stop!' He mumbled through his frozen lips, but the snow poured down inexhaustibly.

He wandered across the featureless snowscape, all sense of direction lost. He staggered across slopes, tottered into drifts, all the time obsessed by one idea – to keep on. Through the cascades of snow that still poured from the sky, the slopes swayed before him, and his feet dragged through the snow. The snow gleamed and Norman began to lose control of his limbs. His legs moved mechanically, but he fell so frequently that at last progress was easier on all fours. A voice kept repeating in his head, 'Please, please stop snowing. Please please let me get out of this,' but he himself could no longer speak.

Still he pressed on, longing to rest, but knowing he must keep on, on.

His mind began to be overtaken by a sense of incredible loneliness as he saw himself, a tiny speck, crawling through the endless snows.

Where in God's name am I? Where in God's name am I? Where? Where? Home in a moment or two. Home in a moment or two. Who am I? Who? Womb, doom, tomb. Where am I? Where? Oh please, please.

At last the snow stops falling, but the wind whips up snow from the ground and blows it at him in huge clouds, so that it scarcely makes any difference. His drowsiness is now irresistible, and he no longer knows whether it is snowing or not.

Where? Where? He thinks of John and Mary and himself talking and drinking, warm and comfortable, how many years ago, and how many thousand miles away from this insane world of snow, snow, snow. And there is a great tiredness. But it is warm.

His arms and legs work more and more slowly, until finally, without knowing it, he has stopped. The ground moves up against his face, and he is falling into a great black lake of sleep. Too tired now to feel the cold, he rolls on to his back involuntarily, possessed by his ineffable tiredness. Sleep. Sleep is now the most blissful thing in the world. More important to sleep than to move, even.

He no longer wonders where he is or pleads with the elements. He no longer pants for breath so desperately. It is easier now. The blood slows and thickens. Sleep beckons comfortingly, and it is warm. Blissful sleep.

Still the wind whines across the great snowfield, blowing up freezing clouds of snow, but Norman sinks into the black lake, dreaming of a long-forgotten Christmas at Tremesca with the lights and warmth and the Christmas pudding burning, burning. It is warm at last.

The snow gleams.

After a while, the sky clears. Slowly, imperceptibly, the delicate nerve-endings have begun to decay, and Norman's new process for inhibiting the pre-ignition of petrol has vanished, along with his memories of childhood and Christmas, and John and Mary. The stars come out and the cold burns his body. Norman lies motionless. In the morning, a flock of birds passes, and a crow settles on Norman's chest and cranes its neck forward. Then it hops jerkily two or three times, finally landing on the frozen face before flying slowly away across the snow plain.

The clouds begin to gather and the sky turns grey above the white hills, and it snows again.

VII

Night on Roughtor

Donald R. Rawe

Three young men from one of the most venerated universities came up the steep hill road from Trebarwith Strand. They carried towels and swimtrunks and their long hair was damp and uncombed. One smoked a heavy pipe with a bowl like a small incinerator; one had a bushy ginger moustache and sideboards. The third, a dark intellectual with steel-rimmed spectacles, wore a denim shirt and cap. June bloomed benevolently round them, fresh from their finals. Thick-fingered membryanthemum hung from walls and rock-faces, and on the deep valley slope were the minute balloons of birdsfoot trefoil, yellow, and orange and shrivelling red. Viper's bugloss reared bold blue spires lower down.

'The next question is,' said Browne-Smythe in his lazy cultured tones, 'where do we go from here?'

'I suppose it'll have to be camping,' said de Vere Ellis, viewing the scene through his glasses. 'Not that I'm enthusiastic; the Cornish summer's likely to turn damp when you least want it to . . .'

'But where do we camp?' said Browne-Smythe, puffing slightly through his moustache. 'Come on, Mac; you know the place.'

'Thus speaketh the psychologist,' remarked McMahon, taking the huge pipe from his mouth. 'He must know where we're going. My dear chap, don't you ever feel like taking pot luck? Why not just load up the old jalopy and pitch tent wherever we get to at nightfall?'

'Any chance of camping here in the garden – or would your family object?' asked de Vere Ellis.

'Not a hope,' said McMahon. 'My old man's the trouble; wants it peaceful when he brings this dear old tycoon down. Sir Geoffrey Pomphrett, Bart. About ninety, as far as I can gather. Don't suppose the old boy would care, but fathers of my generation are a bit down on denims and long hair, that sort of thing.'

They turned in at the gate of the villa, spread their towels and costumes out on the privet and azalea bushes to dry, and went inside.

'What time's the family comin', Mr McMahon?' asked the woman who was sweeping out the hall and porch.

'Oh, any time after tea. About seven, perhaps,' said McMahon.

'Ah well,' she said, 'better go up an air the beds, I s'pose.' McMahon looked at his watch.

'Half past twelve,' he murmured. 'What's for lunch, Mrs Tregellas?'

'Pasties,' she said as she stooped down with the pan brushing dust into it.

'Ha!' cried de Vere Ellis in his best mock-Cornish accent, 'Carnish Pasties, eh? Ess, me dear, tull do.'

'Not for half-hour yet, though,' said the housekeeper, unamused. 'They beds d'come first.'

The three wandered into the lounge and amused themselves drinking beer and playing gramophone records. They had the latest hit, in which an ecstatic pop-star yelled:

Oh darling, oh sweetest,
My life, my all completest,
Whatll I do without you,
Whatll I do without you?

to an accompaniment of wailing electric guitars and shrieking trombones.

When they sat down to the meal and, with knives and forks, had consumed pasties. Browne-Smythe suddenly said to Mrs Tregellas as she cleared away the plates, 'Where would you suggest we go to camp for tonight?'

'She stopped and said, 'Dunno, I'm sure. Never go camping meself.'

'No,' said Browne-Smythe. 'But what about the moors?'

'Aw, no,' said Mrs Tregellas 'Not there. I wudden go there for the golden calf hisself. Not tonight, anyway.'

'Oh; how's that?'

'Well, 'tis dangerous for one thing. All they marshes and holes. An besides, 'tis Midsummer's Eve.'

'Come, Mrs Tregellas,' smiled McMahon. 'You aren't superstitious, are you?'

'No,' she said, 'not more than anybody else is round here. I dun't take no account of talk about piskies an giants an ghosts, but I wudden walk through the churchyard at midnight, not fer nobody: an I wudden go up on the moors, an specially not near

Roughtor on Midsummer night. Call me simple an mazed if you like – but I wudden do it, I tell ee; an if you go an do it, you'm very silly.'

De Vere Ellis, who was a physicist and subscribed to those theories which explain everything in material terms, was interested.

'It's merely a question of fear,' he said. 'Your reason tells you that there's nothing in these stories of the supernatural; it's only your unreasonable subconscious self that makes you afraid of these things, as our professor of psychology – indicating Browne-Smythe – will tell you.'

'Just one of the lingering hereditary animal instincts that are in process of disappearing, Mrs Tregellas,' Browne-Smythe assured her with faint amusement.

'Quite,' went on de Vere Ellis. 'We know a little too much about the subject to fear it. There's never been any ghost that couldn't be explained quite simply and reasonably. Personally, I rather enjoy disobeying superstitions; though I never walk under a ladder at any price. I once got a pot paint down my neck. . . . Is Roughtor a hill?'

'Ess,' said Mrs Tregellas. 'You can see it if you walk up on to the high ground up by Lob's Cot. But if you got any ideas about camping there tonight you better put 'em right out of yer head. Tis dangerous, I tell ee.'

'If Roughtor's only a hill, Mrs Tregellas,' said McMahon, 'it must be easy to climb. It'll be a fine night: the weather forecast is good, and there's an anticyclone just now.'

'No,' she said folding her arms, 'I dun't like it. I dun't like it wan bit.'

She stared out of the window to where between the roofs of other villas there were glimpses of leaning cliff, and Gull Rock a quarter of a mile out in the torpid sheen of Atlantic waters.

'Tis no place for you,' she said. 'What about they Jacky Lanterns?'

'Just marsh gas,' said McMahon. 'Burning methane. We shan't be fooled by them any more than by Tregeagle himself.'

'Who's Tregeagle?' Browne-Smythe asked, fingering his red moustache delicately.

'Oh, a giant ghost the Cornish say runs wild on the moors, shrieking and yelling – or something of the kind. Is that right, Mrs Tregellas?'

'So the story do go,' she said. 'But he dun't run wild as a rule – he've got tasks to do, like baling out Dozmary Pool with a limpet shell. They put un out here on the Strand once, so they say, to bind sand into sheaves. He managed it by wetting em with water on a winters night so they froze. He's ony s'posed to run wild when he do disobey the devil. Then the hell hounds come after un. But tis ony the wind an storm really, I spose.'

'Of course, of course,' said de Vere Ellis as he folded his napkin.

'Still, I dun't think tis right for you three young gentlemen to go up there. Is it Roughtor you'm thinking about? Cause if tis, well all I can say is you'm all three of you furriners when it come to the point, and where none of our crowd ud set there foot after sundown you certainly never ought to. Besides, Roughtor do mean something to we people, and some ud call it near sacriledge for you to camp there.'

McMahon got up, smiling. 'You Cornish are all the same: living in the past, born with your heads looking over your shoulders. All these legends and mysteries are all very picturesque, but they won't get you anywhere. I consider it'll be a bit of a lark to pitch camp on Roughtor on Midsummer Night. Anyway you needn't worry, Mrs Tregellas: my grandmother was Cornish, so I'm entitled to play the host and entertain friends, even on the holy of holies.'

McMahon's father was half-Cornish, half Irish. His mother was French. He called himself an Englishman.

'Huh! A fat lot you knaw about legends, Mr McMahon, being away up country all the year. As for whether theyll get us anywhere, well praps they wunt. P'raps we dunt want to get anywhere. Cornwall's good enough for me; tis good enough for half London in summer, seemin'ly. When my old grandmother was dying up to Tavistock they said to her, "Well Mrs Pengelly, you'm going to a better land". An she looked up an said, "Ess, theres no place like Cornwall".'

She smiled and then went on seriously.

'But I bain't joking about Roughtor. Sneer about the past if you like; but once you get up there you'm going to find whats past idn so dead after all. Thass where tis; now go an do what you like: I been yammering here too long. Let me get on with they dishes.'

Gathering up the pile of plates she marched out with the dignity of a duty done.

It was about half-past seven when they set off for Roughtor, the old Morris groaning up the hill with the weight of baggage and three university rugby forwards. At the wheel McMahon smoked placidly, the great pipe pushed out of the corner of his mouth so that it should not obscure his view. Browne-Smythe sat beside him and in the back seat de Vere Ellis held steady a rickety camp stove which threatened to discharge paraffin if allowed to move off its balance.

Oh darling, oh sweetest.
My life, my all completest

mooed Browne-Smythe.

'Bi-dah-bih-dah-bi-doop,' supported de Vere Ellis tattooing on the stove with a spoon. 'Bi-doom-doom-blah-ah-ah!'

They had the sliding roof back and the breeze never absent from the moors came flapping in. As they reached the level high ground – McMahon wrenching the gear lever producing a grinding cry from the engine – a few other cars passed them, their windscreens flashing red in the lowering sun. Down into grey narrow Camelford they went, and beyond through valleys and up hills until the road ended abruptly at a gate opening on to the moors. On the other side of the shallow valley was Roughtor with its crest broken, jagged like the backbone of a skeleton saurian.

They got out and unloaded. McMahon locked the car doors, lifted the bonnet and dismantled the petrol lead. He put it in his knapsack and shut the flange. They could not carry everything at once, so leaving Browne-Smythe stretched out on the turf guarding the gear – although there was nobody nearer than the farm a mile away – the others started off.

They reached the bottom of the valley and crossed the little bridge over the stream. Suddenly McMahon stopped.

'Hullo! What's that?'

'You mean that rumbling?'

'Yes. There's no railway line around here, is there?'

De Vere Ellis hauled out the Ordnance Survey map from the pocket of his large sheepskin jacket.

'No,' he said.

They stood still, the sound rushing and eddying round them. It appeared to come from farther up the valley, so they walked a hundred yards up towards it. There they found the stream plunging over a waterfall into a narrow deep pool, a small pot-hole. This must they thought be the source of the noise; there was no other explanation. Yet as they stood there twenty yards from it across the bog they could not say with conviction that it was definitely the cause; for the rumbling swirled round them enveloping the place, coming on them from all sides, hollow and uncanny.

'Hm,' grunted de Vere Ellis, and scratched his head.

'Come on,' said McMahon, almost as if he were glad to go and wanted to forget it.

They climbed stolidly up the hillside, the loud burbling receding below them. The grass of the lower slopes gave way to ankle deep bracken and ling. It took them half an hour to reach the top.

Great boulders of granite and grey basalt crowded the peak. They looked for a sheltered place, but there seemed to be none. Cold evening wind hurtled across, singing between stones. They climbed across to the eastern side where they found a rock shoulder with a small cave hollowed out on the leeward side; here it was calm like the still centre in a whirlpool. This was the place to pitch the tent. They had some difficulty in wedging the poles into the rocky soil, but with exertion they succeeded.

De Vere Ellis went back to help Browne-Smythe up with the remaining gear. Left alone McMahon secured the tent. He hammered in pegs, fixed guy ropes, laid out groundsheets inside and took in all the tins and apparatus they had brought. He tried to dig a rain trench round the tent but could not manage it. Then he took a long thick peagreen scarf from his haversack, a pair of binoculars, and wandered around the summit. It was nearly dusk and the sun was going behind another tor to the west, throwing it into bold black relief.

Below him shadows were lengthening second by second, creeping across moor and marsh and up the sides of hills like vast grey ghosts. Standing on the brow overlooking the precipitous south end, he could see vague stone pillars set in a circle immediately beneath. In daylight no doubt they would look mundane enough, but here in twilight their very vagueness seemed to promise life: at any moment they might begin to shuffle and dance. A half-forgotten tale about maidens changed into stones for dancing on the Sabbath came back to him.

Westwards there was a white hill, a china claytip which by its incongruity attracted his attention. Perhaps it was a mile off, but he could not say because at every second it seemed to be at a different distance away. It was a hill without roots or foundations; a hill that lurked and loomed, having no fixed place for its being. He found it disturbingly easy to imagine it approaching, stealing nearer and then slipping away among the other tors, all fast losing their identities in the gloom.

He looked across to his left and regarded Brown Willy, the other twin Cornish mountain. It was supposed to be higher than Roughtor, but it seemed not as tall; it sprawled loosely and carelessly against the blue night, less forceful than Roughtor and more welcome. McMahon found himself wishing they had chosen it for camping site instead.

Roughtor itself, he saw, was a place to reckon with. All around him were stones erected in illogical but natural positions by men in the lost past. He found the Logan Rock, a great flat mushroom cap of stone balanced on a much smaller rock: balanced with such precision that he could rock it unaided though it had withstood aeons of wind and storm. Like all the other rocks on this precipice it was worn smooth, rutted and grooved by centuries of west wind. Roughtor was ageless, barbaric, primitive; yet primitive in a positive sense, because it possessed the elements of a civilisation – although one alien and opposed to his own.

Now conflicting thoughts came to him unreasonably and without his summoning them. It was as though he stood now on the rock of eternity, and mere time was below him: in this sudden elevation of his historical perspective the millenia ago that the ancient men raised these stones and dolmens and barrows seemed no farther away than last week. He had an ill defined sense of having been there before. He felt he knew the place, he could almost have shouted out the day – or was it century? – ago that he had been there; but the half memory struggled in vain to free itself. Among these twilight thoughts, which welled up in his mind as his flesh chilled and goosed in the night wind, was an insistent discord saying he had no right to be there at all; there was too a very simple, perhaps childish fear of some dark retribution for breaking some fundamental natural law. Then again without his consciously thinking a voice spoke within his mind, so suddenly like a shout in his ear or a tap on his shoulder that he started. It was the voice of Mrs Tregellas saying, 'What's past idn so dead after all.'

Real voices now called out to him. Turning he saw a torch flashing and caught a glimpse of de Vere Ellis' blazing shirt and fleecy jacket. He groped his way back around to the tent and found his two friends putting down the remainder of the gear – bedrolls and blankets.

'We saw a will o' the wisp,' cried Browne-Smythe.

He spoke excitedly so that the other two, recoiled silently.

'Old Bertie here started the damned thing,' said de Vere Ellis in exaggerated laconic tones. 'Lit a match for a smoke as we started up the hill. Must have ignited a pocket of marsh gas.'

'Gave me quite a jolt, actually,' said Browne-Smythe. 'One second there was nothing there, and the next this kind of purple ghost was dancing like a monkey round us. Burnt out after a few minutes, of course.'

They busied themselves arranging the tent. McMahon lit a couple of oil lamps and tied them to the tent poles. No one spoke; they were perhaps little fearful of betraying the fact that the place was affecting them strongly. Each knew that this night on Roughtor was going to be far less of a joke than they had imagined; but none would admit it. Conversation was therefore strained, and confined to matters of immediate concern; which was mainly the cooking of supper. De Vere Ellis made a brave show of being at home by whistling the tune of 'Oh Darling, Oh Sweetest', as he fried sausages over the stove, but soon he too relapsed into moody silence.

Supper over, they prepared to turn in. It seemed to all three that they could feel the proximity of the big rock that shielded them from the wind, even within the tent. It was as though it had a personality of its own which would not permit them to forget it. Probably this annoyed Browne-Smythe; he went outside for a smoke before sleeping.

Leaving the tent he frightened several rabbits which had gathered curiously outside, attracted by the faint lamplight. They went off scuttling down across the hillside. The moon had risen, full and ominously amber. There were no clouds in the sky. Below he heard a very faint trickling sound and shining the powerful torch down into the valley between the two hills detected an answering shimmer from the stream that flowed through it. He shone the torch around to amuse himself: the beam reached well up the side of Brown Willy, and he saw a hump on the eastern end of it which appeared to be a barrow. One or two purple will o' the wisps hovered momentarily out beyond upon the marshes, and knowing what they were he smiled superciliously; then he had a great fright, for randomly turning the beam on an outcrop of rock fifty yards away he was confronted by a white face and two large horns. For a second he stood thunderstruck, the light wavering in his hand; then he heard a deep cry, half-bray and half-bleat, and a goat leaped away over the boulders.

There was no sound except for the unwavering high note of the wind. For a moment something akin to fear gripped him, and as suddenly released him. A man could go mad on these moors, he decided. The moon cast enough light to present those gaunt shapes, grey enigmas, but never enough to explain them. Browne-Smythe threw away his cigarette and went to bed.

They lay for an hour or more sleepless on the hard ground,

which their sleeping-bag did little to soften. They stared up at the indistinct canvas listening to the wind, and each sensed the others were awake. Once McMahon said, trying to sound irritated, 'Don't go much on the orchestrations up here,' – but neither of the others replied.

The wind did however gradually die away; it was a process so slow that their minds preoccupied with its sound were lowered and lulled to sleep as it waned. The other two had relapsed into an uneasy slumber when de Vere Ellis sat up in bed and whispered, 'For God's sake, what's that?'

McMahon stirred and made a grunt of interrogation, then he too sat up and listened. There was a sound of laughing; or was it singing? It was both: a crowd of voices laughing and singing very close at hand.

There was nothing at all uncanny in the sounds; they were jolly voices that made them, and it was only the unexpectedness of hearing them that made the three stare at each other for minutes before anybody spoke again.

Browne-Smythe was awake. He did not sound afraid when he said, 'Here, I'm going out to have a look.' He dragged on his jeans and a pullover; the others followed suit.

When they got outside the revelry was loud and boisterous The moon was clear and white again; they climbed across the backbone rocks of the hill and were staggered by what they saw.

There were maybe fifty dancers in a circle with arms interlinked, leaping and jigging with tremendous energy around a big boulder on which sat three figures. None of the dancers seemed to be over two feet high; they were all dressed in tight garments and little pointed caps of light green or blue. Their faces even in the half-light were shining and jovial. They sang as they danced, the little men on the boulder taking in turns to sing the verse and the whole crowd joining in the chorus with a roaring flourish. What was so stupendous, when the watchers overcame their initial surprise, was that the voices which came from the tiny beings were so loud and rich, an unhesitating unrestrained bass. What they sang none of them could understand. McMahon first thought the language was Welsh; but looking back realised it could only have been Cornish.

The three watched with a kind of astonished delight, for such merriment they had never imagined. It was naïve spontaneous pleasure that spelled them motionless like statues there on the great stones. None of the rollickers took any notice of them.

This went on for some minutes, and having become intoxicated with the mirth they saw before them they were totally unprepared for what happened next.

Clouds passed overhead obscuring the moon, and for a half a minute there was darkness. The singing and dancing ceased abruptly; McMahon thought he saw figures stealing hurriedly away. Then they heard another song, as vigorous as the first but higher pitched and somehow more disturbing; it contained a subtly menacing rhythm; as it approached a sense of vicious or evil intent assailed them. Then the moon was freed and showed them about twenty little men no bigger than the others, dressed in the same way except that they had dark caps of black or deep blue. But the main difference was not of dress form. These were ugly little creatures with spindly legs and square heads too large for their bodies. When the moonlight revealed them they were not so much dancing as fighting among themselves and tripping each other up in malevolent sport; but they soon saw the three humans watching them stupefied from the boulder, and with shouts of diabolical glee bounded toward them in a body.

Unable to control his actions, McMahon turned and fled. De Vere Ellis, afraid but still proud, hesitated. Browne-Smythe started to run with McMahon, but caught his foot in a crevice and fell. Four of the goblins were on him instantly, two twisting his foot, one pulling his ears and poking at his eyes, the other jabbing him with a sharp stick. De Vere Ellis took a stride toward them, sent one sprawling with a kick and clouted the others with his fists. Browne-Smythe got to his feet and they both ran.

They were going down over the hillside towards Brown Willy, but McMahon's voice shrieked out urgently, 'Here! To the tent, *quickly*! We're safe here!'

The tent was not more than a hundred yards away, and they sprinted frantically across, reaching it as the crowd of little people came hopping and screeching over the rocks. They stopped ten yards away from the tent and stood around it in a ring, glowering and uttering cries of chagrin. It was as though there was a circle drawn round the tent into which they could not penetrate.

The three flung themselves down inside the tent, panting feverishly.

'Safe – safe, thank God!' gasped Browne-Smythe. He felt his scratched and torn ear, and pulled up his shirt revealing little red weals and cuts bleeding on his ribs.

McMahon was looking at the map.

'Thought so,' he said relievedly, 'this spot is marked Chapel here. It – this cave thing – is a chapel to Michael the Archangel, patron saint of Cornwall; so I've heard. It explains why they can't hurt us in here.'

As though they had heard the name of Michael spoken, the crowd outside dispersed silently and loped back over the boulders into the night. Once again there was silence except for the wind, which seemed to be rising, and the hard breathing of de Vere Ellis and Browne-Smythe.

'I once went into the local folk lore,' said McMahon. 'I remember something about these things from what I heard as a boy.' He grabbed a packet of cigarettes and lit one, inhaling nervously. 'The first lot were piskies, I think; they don't do any harm. The second kind were spriggans, and their jokes are nothing to laugh at.'

Silence again. De Vere Ellis stared dully out of the open tent entrance towards Brown Willy. Then Browne-Smythe croaked with harsh unpleasant voice, 'My God – I never dreamed for a moment . . .' He did not finish his sentence; it was unnecessary. Words were indeed useless. A nightmare had taken on flesh and blood and had assaulted them; talking could not calm their confusion.

McMahon remembered a flask of whisky included in his pack, and took it out. He handed it around, and the fierce liquor made them a little more sanguine.

'I feel quite mystified by all this,' said McMahon somehow achieving reflective detachment. 'Is it possible for three people to dream the same nightmare at the same time?'

'There's no mystery,' said Browne-Smythe sourly. 'Those damned spriggans were tangible enough.'

'Oh, forget it!' snapped de Vere Ellis, savage now that for the first time in his life his logical beliefs were violently shaken. 'Forget the whole affair! Talk about it in the morning. I'm going to sleep if I can.'

'Happy dreams,' said Browne-Smythe, 'I shan't get any.'

'The blasted wind's going to stop us sleeping,' said McMahon with a yawn.

The wind was increasing in power every minute. Soon it was seething and screaming across the summit, whipping in around their corner, snatching at the tent. Through it all they became aware of a dim stony creaking rising louder and faster, the sound of boulder on boulder. It was McMahon who realised what it was.

'It's the Logan Stone,' he said, 'rocking in the wind.'

It began to rain, though not on the tent. The heavy drops went over them, protected as they were by the Chapel rock, and splashed loudly on the boulders nearby. The Logan Stone oscillated yet more wildly, a gauge of the wind's violence: clunk-clunk, clunk-clunk, like a mad thing. The tent was illuminated in a lightning flash and they saw each other half sitting up in bed with white faces. Then an enormous roll of thunder sounded immediately above them, rotating and exploding like some cosmic cannon; the rain redoubled and the windshrieks seemed to fade beside its dark drumming.

Browne-Smythe, whose bed was at the southern end of the tent nearest Brown Willy, put out his hand to secure the end flap more tightly. As he undid the knot the strings were plucked from his hand by the hurricane, and he had to half crawl outside to regain them. Then wind entered, creasing the canvas and banging the lamps against the poles. Browne-Smythe was on his hands and knees in the doorway, they saw, when the lightning blinked again, but he was making no effort to close the flap.

'What's the matter?' yelled de Vere Ellis above the wind.

Browne-Smythe turned slowly, but as he was evidently speaking in his normal voice they could not hear him. He beckoned and then pointed to something. The other two crawled over to him.

Over the south slope of Brown Willy they could just distinguish a great jet figure against the fiercely dark sky. It was of human form, but the size of a giant; it was bending and stooping and appeared to throw up its arms to the clouds and down again, as though throwing something over its shoulder. They could not be sure. They lost the figure in the darkness, thought they saw it again; then it was gone. What was it? Had they seen a real thing, or merely a trick played by the lightning and the black pregnant clouds?

'It might,' said McMahon very slowly when they had retreated into the tent, 'it might have been Tregeagle baling out Dozmary. The pool lies in that direction.'

'Giant ghosts now – Jesus!' muttered Browne-Smythe.

Insane fear and anger rushed through de Vere Ellis. Reason was playing him false tonight. He was bewildered, his brain near numb with helpless feelings. He wanted to scream but with great effort overcame that longing, only to find that when he did so there were tears in his eyes, rolling down his face, and he had no power to stop them. It was at this moment that the other two decided to light a lamp for comfort, and hearing McMahon fumble with matches he flung himself down on the nearest bed – Browne-Smythe's – and buried his face in the bedclothes.

'Hullo, old chap,' said Browne-Smythe stupidly when he saw him there. 'Anything up?'

De Vere Ellis said nothing for some moments, not trusting himself to speak without betraying emotion, and then made some explanation that Browne-Smythe in a normal time would have laughed at. But he too was confounded, and accepted the tale about hitting his head on the stony ground quite seriously. Against the voice of the wind McMahon had heard nothing of this, and having lit the lamp he began grumbling that there was very little oil left in it.

De Vere Ellis raised himself and shouted discordantly, 'You talk about the bloody lamp! What's the matter with you two; what d'you think this is, a boy scout's jaunt?'

No one replied for a minute, and then McMahon shouted back, 'You can't accept the supernatural; that's what's the matter with you I've seen it: I believe and keep sane. You've seen it and you won't believe it: if you don't look out you'll go out of your minds!'

There was no time to reply to this. They heard a long piercing wail rising above the wind; it was a loud bass tortured voice from some distance away, like a trumpet gone mad and possessing the strength of ten trumpets. It was followed by a sound that could only be described as a laugh; a maniacal fiendish laugh, a great gloating chuckle out of the clouds. But they hardly had time to experience fresh fear at this, for the wind without the slightest warning veered round and blew in from the east in giant gusts. The Chapel rock was now no protection; with the rain sheeting down on the canvas came stones flung by the gale. Then a guy rope snapped and the tent collapsed on top of them.

There was only one thing to do. Thunderstruck as they were they managed to uproot the other pegs and drag the whole gear to the cave. It was only shallow and left them half in, half out of the storm. They covered themselves up with blankets and the canvas.

Gathering stray items together McMahon found his big pipe and instinctively clutched hold of its familiar form. Like a child clutching a teddy bear, he thought, and realising this saw irony; but he could not smile. He thought of his peagreen scarf, de Vere Ellis' loud shirt, Browne-Smythe's moustache: the pop record and the cigarettes and the brandy – all futile vanities now strewn abandoned like children's playthings, or hugged but no longer comforting; and they themselves were suddenly no more than terrified children, afraid of what they did not understand.

They were now facing up the valley between Roughtor and

Brown Willy and so saw without hindrance the last satanic stormy episode. There was a glaring yellow flash of lightning lasting several seconds it seemed, which revealed that same dark figure towering against an inflamed sky and flying toward them down from the uplands. It was Tregeagle with his head in the cloud, whooping and screaming, running with thunderous footsteps. A hell-hound pack pursued with murderous baying.

Down between the two hills he came bellowing out tormentedly. His great thighs were level with them as he passed and his footsteps shook Roughtor itself so that loose stones fell down around them. His screams cut into them like knives, severing the roots of nerves and stabbing through the floors of sanity. At his heels those devil-dogs leaped, sabre fangs in cavernous jaws open for the kill. Their raucous throatings sawed the air, upward emanating like fists seizing, choking, with horror sickening them beholding. Night filled overpowering with sudden hellmighty voices, rock moor cloud abyss, two hills with terror yelling between them – were they, grovelling unbearably, the only things afraid?

Away westward they ran, echoes bellowing out among the tors even in the unabated wind, but diminishing as they went. De Vere Ellis was on his feet and ran round the Chapel rock to watch; he came back with face wet but not with rain, and gibbered for the whisky. Browne-Smythe sat moaning unintelligibly like an idiot. McMahon himself, though quivering with shock, heart racing uncontrollably, did not dare think but searched for the flask. He found it under a pile of blankets and reached out to give it to de Vere Ellis. Browne-Smythe snatched at it and they began to fight. McMahon did the only thing he could think of: he picked up a jagged stone weighing nearly half a hundredweight and snapped, 'I'll brain you both if you don't sit down and shut up!'

They calmed down a little. Browne-Smythe began his dull moaning again, looking around him piteously like a whipped cur.

'Listen,' said McMahon very firmly and calmly, 'there's only one thing to do – stay here at all costs.'

But then the gaunt baying and howling, which had never quite died away, became louder; Tregeagle and the savage yelping hell pack were returning. De Vere Ellis was on his feet in an instant, running away, scrambling frantically across the boulders. Browne-Smythe made as though to get up; McMahon leaned over and roared in his ear, 'Don't be a bloody fool! This is the only place where they can't hurt you!' He put his hand on his shoulder to prevent him rising. But now they could hear the footsteps pounding. Browne-Smythe shrieked, flung himself sideways; tripped

McMahon as he came at him and lashed out ferociously with his fist. He caught him on the jaw, and fled off across the rocks. McMahon fell, hit a boulder and lost consciousness.

When he came around it was dawn and the sun, spinning crimson up over the moors, shone full into the Chapel cave. The wind was now merely a faint placid breeze, the clouds high, white and motionless. A lark was singing up among them, his ceaseless wings whirring.

This much McMahon observed sleepily; then realising he was cold he moved to cover himself and found a sickening pain shooting through his head. He had ugly cuts and bruises on his temple.

He managed to wrap himself in blankets, and slept again for several hours. He was conscious from time to time of the gathering warmth of the sun; and though he felt vaguely impressed by some recent event he was too insensible to try and remember it, or ask himself what he was doing there so early in the morning on the hillside.

When he finally awoke his head was clear, the sun was high, and he remembered not without shuddering the adventures of the night. He got up, found a rock pool and bathed his face and wound, donned an anorak which belonged to Browne-Smythe, and went off in search of the other two.

Obviously they had gone across to the north, with the object of reaching civilisation. Crossing the rocky backbone of Roughtor he saw the car was still there by the gate at the end of the road.

He found Browne-Smythe in a gorse clump very near the rumbling waterfall. He was asleep and snoring stentorously. When awakened he gave no sign of recognition, and said nothing; the only sound he made, at long intervals, was the same low moaning he had made in the night. He could not walk; his ankle was broken.

For about a fortnight Browne-Smythe suffered a complete loss of memory concerning himself and the events leading up to the morning he was found on the moor. Gradually his awareness of his past life and who he was returned, but he never recalled the events of that night on Roughtor, nor would he believe McMahon, who told him about them. Yet though he refused to accept the story, the cuts and weals on his back healed leaving ugly red scars which no doctor could ever satisfactorily explain.

Although he now owns the property left him by his father,

McMahon does not visit Cornwall much. He lectures at a college in the Midlands, has a flat in London and is fond of travelling abroad.

De Vere Ellis was lost for two days, wandering the moors without any sense of bearing; he declared afterwards that he was convinced he was being led in circles by something, and marvelled that he had not been drowned in a bog. He has since taken up the study of parapsychology, and is in his way something of an authority on psychical research. One day, when he feels equal to the occasion, he may go back to Roughtor; but whether to spend the night there in further research, he does not say.

VIII

The Castle

M. E. Simpson

My firm were thinking of moving to the West country and had asked me to look around for a likely site, the hierarchy had unleashed the boffins of O. & M., who were having a real ball with the drawing office staff, and now they had finally given birth to a set of plans drawn meticulously down to the wrought iron gates, and a plantation. It looked more like a stately home than a business suite of offices.

I took the plans from my briefcase and became lulled into introspection. The rhythm of the wheels of the speeding train kept repeating where to start and what to find, where start where.

The train had stopped and I roused myself, feeling rather stupid and unable to focus my eyes until the train had started again and I was able to read the lettering that was leaving my vision. It was St Austell. I'd arrived in the West. I returned the scattered plans to my case and started to browse through the assorted brochures I had.

How soft and relaxing it felt, as I walked along the platform at Penzance, so different from the atmosphere I'd left in Essex. There was a fresh country smell of washed clean air. Emerging from the station I could see the sea practically lapping at the car park's wall. I stood a while looking at the small craft that darted out from somewhere. Their sails sent the light craft spinning over the waves. I supposed they came from Newlyn or Mousehole. St Michael's Mount was crowned with a light mist. It looked majestic and mysterious rising out of the sea away from the land. The view inland wasn't very prepossessing, a jumble of everything, even to a monstrous corrugated iron-covered gas works, hissing and steaming and clanking, its sheeted building rising up the hill to street level. I made arrangements for a car and driver to call the next day, and after a meal gave myself the luxury of an early night, something I had not indulged in for many a day.

Voices in the corridor! How different they sounded from those of London! A rattle of keys, and the clinking of china, then quiet. I had not ordered early tea. The car arrived on time. Truro had been mentioned by my partners, so here I started. Agents were generally sceptical. Such an area was out of the question near to the centre, and building land was in very short supply in this county of rolling hills, moorlands and granite outcrops. I got the general impression that only manufacturing firms that could shift into tailored premises would have a chance. They would help the local labour problems. We wanted to start from the grass roots and build for our own existing staff. My report that night to Essex was not encouraging. Many sites advertised as building land were out of the question because of the different levels they presented. An old mine shaft or engine house would be plumb in the middle of the boardroom. I tried farms, where it was many a long day since any farming had been done, the house and buildings were derelict. Yet directly the purpose of the purchase was mentioned, I found I was on a sticky wicket, and with some amusement had heard myself described in the local as a 'bloody foreigner looking for a holiday camp site'. So it was plain that rebuilding was going to be out of the question as well as town centres. It was all becoming very depressing.

My driver was a local man and after weeks of each other's company he began to help considerably. I learnt much about the people around and how much they would probably expect for their lands, especially if it was just one of a family left. I gathered I would be committing sacrilege to mention any land was wanted for offices.

Towards the end of three weeks he at last came up with something interesting advertised in the local paper. It was after a fruitless day spent in and around Helston, any land here being earmarked as Government projects or dormitory requirements by the Admiralty I was beginning to feel most inadequate to the task set, and was well on the way to making a return the coming weekend, when Willie pulled the paper from his pocket, rather hesitantly pointing to a heavily scored notice of an impending sale by auction of land that also had the ruins of a 16th century castle on it, not scheduled as an ancient monument or as having been occupied or farmed for some time: this seemed to be distinctly promising, so we set off to view.

The winding road from Penzance kept springing surprises today, the helicopter lifting and swinging out on its journey to the Scillies seemed to skim the car roof and salute St Michael's Mount. How different it was today. Instead of thrusting itself on rocks from the sea, it was rising from the golden sands, many people were walking along the causeway to it, kicking aside the seaweed that had been caught up and unable to float back to the seabed. Small pools glinted and sparkled in the strong sunlight, the sky was as blue as it was sometimes pictured on the postcards – a wonderful back curtain to the turrets and towers of the Priory. How drab and dull the little station of Marazion looked, its life of gay holiday traffic quenched. Willie had some trouble getting past the coaches and caravans that claimed right of way through the very narrow road that was loath to leave its way by the sea. We soon were turning into the approach road and there, standing out from the trees, were the two towers, showing red in the sun.

Leaving the car, we tramped through brambles and bracken. How still it was! I couldn't hear a bird or yet the usual stealthy rustlings one normally heard in places such as this. The first tower's entry showed that it had been used as a shelter for some knights of the road, the large gaping hole of the one-time fireplace still held charred remains and tins, a winding stone staircase faced the entrance, and daylight could be seen. There was no roof, but there was an abundance of wild plants sprouting tall and pale, reaching up for the sun that spilled through the top and lingered on each stair today. We turned away and skirted around piles of debris and came to the other tower. This had a modern door with a yale lock that was incongruous in the medieval surroundings – quite unnecessary, too, as the door was not locked. The inside was in much better shape than the other. The walls had been dressed and were carved; several incisions, though smoothed by time, could have been Latin or just designs. The arch to the great fireplace was intact, and we could stand in there and look up a perfectly straight chimney. It was a long way up too.

Willie reckoned that they made 'a proper ole smeech cooking' there. The staircase was very dark. Our torch showed the way was reasonably safe. We climbed twelve stairs and saw a platform leading to a small opening outside. I explained to Willie that unwelcome visitors were greeted by boiling oil from these openings, and thought it was a long shot getting on target even though the openings were trebled on the next platform. The third and fourth floors had circular stone rests fanning out from the central stone pillar of the stairs, each stair was of the natural granite shaped and placed into the walls of the tower and the bricks all seemed keyed into each other. There was no movement anywhere that had shaken them out of alignment in three hundred years.

That night I phoned and said I was going to make a bid for the castle, but I was well and truly caught. I hoped that the partners would be as interested as I was, for I painted in glowing terms the amount of land going with the ruins and even suggested an air strip could be accommodated. The auctioneer made a short speech giving particulars of the land and the Duchy's rights to any minerals found thereon, and that the towers must remain as they were. Bidding was slow, and in no time at all I found I was the owner, at what appeared to be a ridiculously low figure, of several acres plus the remains of a fortified castle.

On returning to the hotel there was a wire from Essex, lengthy in terms regarding my sanity. I began to delve into the history. Beyond confirming the date of the building of the castle, some books mentioned it as being the bolt hole of a murderer on the run from London, but suggested that although there were many versions none could be proved. It hadn't figured in the civil war yet it must have had a purpose in Henry VIII's schemes of fortifying the coast along with St Mawes and Pendennis. From its towers one could see from Mount's Bay to Lizard Point. Enough of conjecture: I had to convert the place, on paper at least, as suitable for a suite of offices.

On my return to Essex doubts began as to what the Partners were going to think of the transaction, and at the board meeting, when I was perhaps becoming too lyrical, the Secretary muttered that I had become pixilated by Cornwall. They heard me out and praised my layout – at least my uncle did. The rest murmured about the cost of the original plans that had been ignored. I couldn't put in the peace and calm they would all find, in that clean-washed air they would all benefit from, or the time they would gain for leisure. The portents around me were not too promising. At the worst I was the owner of a castle in the West country, but I was very disappointed at the lack of enthusiasm. Only one thing would help me – the low cost of the property – and the space there for building as they wished.

That night I tossed and turned, seeing a new building rise by the side of the towers, and with each phase of the construction a complete collapse of the new, leaving the towers as they had stood for so long. I got up and poured a drink, conscious of an exhausted feeling and great despair. I'll never know if I did really sleep, but my brain had become a computer. There it was churning out great masses of figures. Millions and millions of pounds were pouring from the castle's towers. There was masses of ticker tape rolling and snaking out of the door. I followed. They were winding around the trees, forming great loops to cross the road, an undulating sea of paper which joined the rhythm of the dark black sea and disappeared, stopping the chatter of the computer.

Phew! I was becoming obsessed. Strange, that a computer could become mixed up with a medieval castle even in my subconscious. Cheers for Sunday! I could repair my disturbed night. I thought of London. Yes, a day in London would do just that. On a Sunday it had so much to offer. I strolled along the Embankment, taking in the stillness and seeing the tall cranes high and at rest, the tied shipping not even riding a movement of the sluggish Thames. Coming to Cleopatra's Needle, I admired its clean appearance from its grimy London dirt to the original pink, when I became aware of the chattering again. The tapes this time bore words, miles and miles of words, unreadable but urgent and angry. I hurried away, looking down to see if I'd got any of the paper wound around my legs. I all but fell down the steps of the pier and seemed to be carried along with the people onto the steamer waiting there.

The river noises began: engine, loud speaker and talk, and my eyes saw the bankside strangeness of London's back doors. Picking out and recognising the buildings, I began to enjoy myself. The end of the journey came quickly and I found myself walking towards Hampton Court Palace, for the very first time.

I was again looking at my castle in Cornwall. Could it have been built by the same man? Wolsey and the King would strike some such bargain. I passed into the kitchens, and being confronted with the huge fireplace was again conscious of the computer throwing out its tapes. It filled the hearth and over the spit; under the huge tables it wound around and then coiled over the top. I became scared and, turning, started to run. People were staring at me: they evidently could not see the strips of ticker tape trailing from me. I jumped on the first bus that came near to me, and the conductor stood over me, asking, 'Where to?' I said, 'End of journey'. The ticket read Hampstead Heath. I needed a good stiff drink and a sympathetic ear. I had a friend at Hampstead. Coincidence? I don't begin to know.

When I had finished telling my friend the tale he looked pretty disturbed and suggested a doctor. That's if I was sure I hadn't been indulging in hallucinating drugs. I tried to sound logical about it all. Neither of us could get the connection between a computer running wild and a castle's ruins in Cornwall, yet the computer always started up whenever I saw anything like a castle or something historical. The connection between Hampton Court was easy, but Cleopatra's Needle had conveyed only dates. Dates! That was it! I'd been searching around for the castle's history and the computer could give me it. My friend was quite excited and began to jot down some facts to start with. I had the office keys and he had a fast car. In no time we were on our way.

The machine had been installed in the basement, and it filled the large area. I brought down some well-upholstered chairs as we were likely to have a long session down there, and then we began to feed into it those facts we knew. It began to tick and we made jokes about its digestion. Would it be able to lay bare something that had been hidden for ages? I felt a little guilty that I was using a computer to find out about the past. We went out to tea. This mechanised brain could function alone. When we returned nothing had happened. We both stretched out in the chairs, relaxed and waiting, each with his own thoughts.

My neck was hurting, and it was dark, very dark. I could not move my head. I reached out, trying to touch something that would convey where I was. My hand encountered another, cold and wet. I shouted, then remembered and groped my way towards the switch. My friend looked dreadful; his hair literally standing on end. He was very pale and kept repeating, 'I saw it all! I saw it!' I looked at the computer. It was still a blank. We must have fed it the wrong sequence. I looked at my watch: three o'clock. We would have to stay here awhile. My friend was in no shape to travel anyway, yet I felt elated and free, and the uneasy restlessness had gone.

I drove back to Hampstead and insisted that I should call a doctor. We both thought that perhaps something at tea had disagreed with him, yet I was all right. The doctor made an examination and asked if we had been involved in an accident, as my friend showed all the classical signs of shock. The doctor prescribed a sedative and said he would call again that evening. I rang up my friend's firm and mine, to tell them we were unable to be there for a day or two. The poor chap looked ghastly and was reluctant to talk on the doctor's next visit. The following evening the doctor had time to listen to all that had transpired. I told him everything, from the day I made a bid for the castle, and the dreams of what you will, that had happened since that time, up to the feeding of data to the computer. He was intrigued and, judging by my own demeanour, now suggested that somehow I had transferred my turmoil to my friend, who was still very reluctant to say what it was he saw.

After much questioning and probing, and a great deal of hesitating, the words came tumbling out. He said that he, too, had seen the ticker tape writhe into the sea, but that he was unable to extricate himself from the coils. He was gradually being drawn towards the sea until the sea itself covered him and he floated down to the seabed. He was conscious of being pulled into a cave; he could make out the sides of rock which began to grow very narrow until he could feel the sides rubbing his shoulders. He became motionless with just his head resting on something hard. He could move only his eyes, and they became aware of a dim flickering light. He heard ropes straining and the dull sound of wood on wood, and then the screams, such screams of extreme agony. He turned a little and saw they came from a tied body on a wooden rack. He prayed for oblivion from the horrors going on all around him. He found he too was going to be a part of this macabre scene, for his head was on a block and about to be severed. His head was being carried past the foetid black holes, each emitting human cries of pain and suffering, out into a great courtyard. There it was placed with many others on the spikes.

Now he had never seen the castle. We were all pretty quiet when he had finished speaking, not daring to offer explanations or theories.

When, after deliberating, the board turned down my plans I think I was relieved. Somehow the castle had lost the glamour of being used as a new building. Those towers would always be present, reminding me of my friend's ordeal. I was lumbered with it for a while, but decided at the first opportunity to re-sell it.

A letter from Cornwall arrived some weeks later. I felt myself colouring as though I was about to reopen something I had been trying very hard to forget. It was from Willie, who hoped I was well and thought I might like to know what he had found out. He had heard tell that way back there were some pretty funny old stories about that old ruin I'd bought. Murder had been done more than once, and 'they do tell of a passage that led down to the sea used by smugglers and such. The Excise chaps had surprised many at one time using the great hall between the towers, and a real bloody battle took place ending in a fire that gutted it. People said that you could hear the screams some nights of certain tides, but of course everyone would swear the castle was haunted after a lot of killings there, No one seemed to want it, anyway, until you came along.'

Had the castle a spirit that rejected all I had been going to do?

No more questions. I didn't want to know the answers any more. I reached for the phone and placed the castle once more into the hands of the agents. My friend ? I haven't seen him for a long time. He only nodded the last time we met.

IX

Christmas Honeymoon

Howard Spring

We were married on 22nd December, because we had met on the 21st. It was as sudden as that. I had come down from Manchester to London. Londoners like you to say that you come up to London; but we Manchester people don't give a hoot what Londoners like. We know that we, and the likes of us, lay the eggs, and the Londoners merely scramble them. This gives us a sense of superiority.

Perhaps I have this sense unduly. Certainly I should never have imagined that I would marry a London girl. As a bachelor I had survived thirty Manchester summers, and it seemed unlikely to me that, if I couldn't find a girl to suit me in the north, I should find one in London.

I am an architect, and that doesn't make me love London any more. Every time I come down to the place I find it has eaten another chunk of its own beauty, so as to make more room for the fascias of multiple shops.

All this is just to show you that I didn't come to London looking for a bride; and if I had been looking for a bride, the last place I would have investigated would be a cocktail party. But it was at a cocktail party in the Magnifico that I met Ruth Hutten. I had never been to a cocktail party in my life before. We don't go in for much of that sort of thing in Manchester: scooping a lot of people together and getting rid of the whole bang shoot in one do. It seems to us ungracious. We like to have a few friends in, and give them a cut off the joint and something decent to drink, and talk in a civilised fashion while we're at it. That's what we understand by hospitality. But these cocktail parties are just a frantic St Vitus gesture by people who don't want to be bothered.

I shouldn't have been at this party at all if it hadn't been for Claud Tunstall. It was about half-past six when I turned from the lunatic illumination of Piccadilly Circus, which is my idea of how hell is lit up, and started to walk down the Haymarket. I was wondering in an absent-minded sort of way how long the old red pillars of the Haymarket Theatre would be allowed to stand before some bright lad thought what fun it would be to tear them down, when Claud turned round from reading one of the yellow playbills, and there we were grinning and shaking hands.

Claud had something to grin about, because the author's name on the playbill was his. It was his first play, and it looked as though it wouldn't matter to Claud, so far as money went, if it were his last. The thing had been running for over a year; companies were touring it in the provinces and colonies; and it was due to open in New York in the coming year. No wonder Claud was grinning; but I think a spot of the grin was really meant for me. He was the same old Claud who had attended the Manchester Grammar School with me and shared my knowledge of its smell of new exercise books and old suet pudding.

Claud was on his way to this party at the Magnifico, and he said I must come with him. That's how these things are: there's no sense in them; but there would have been no sense either in trying to withstand Claud Tunstall's blue eyes and fair hair and general look of a sky over a cornfield.

That's going some for me, and perhaps the figure is a bit mixed, but I'm not one for figures at any time. Anyway, it explains why, five minutes later, I was gritting my teeth in the presence of great boobies looking like outsizes in eighteenth-century footmen, yelling names and looking down their noses.

We stood at the door of a room, and I was aware of the gold blur of chandeliers, and a few dozen apparent football scrums, and a hot blast of talk coming out and smacking our faces, so I deduced this was the party all right. One of the boobies yelled: 'Mr Claud Tunstall and Mr Edward Oldham,' and from what happened it might just as well have been 'The Archangel Gabriel and one Worm.' Because the moment we were over the threshold all the scrums loosened up and girls descended on Claud like a cloud of bright, skittering, squawking parakeets, flashing their red nails at him, unveiling their pearly portals in wide grins, and bearing him off towards a bar where a chap in white was working overtime among all the sweet accessories of sin. I never saw him again.

Well, as I say, I might have been a worm, no use at all to parakeets, but that lets in the sparrows. I was just turning slowly on my own axis, so to speak, in the space that was miraculously cleared round me, when I saw a girl looking at me with an appreciative gleam in her brown eyes. She was the brownest girl I ever saw – eyes, skin and hair – homely as a sparrow, and just as alert.

As our eyes met, there came fluting out of one of the scrums a high-pitched female voice: 'No, Basil, I'm teetotal, but I can go quite a long way on pahshun fruit.'

The pronunciation of that *pahshun* was indescribable; it seemed the bogus essence of the whole damn silly occasion; and the brown girl and I, looking into one another's eyes, twinkled, savouring towards one another, the twinkle widening to a smile, and I found myself getting dangerously full of smiles again, for when she smiled the teeth in her brown face were like the milky kernel of a brown nut.

We sat together on a couch at the deserted end of the room, and I said: 'Let me get you something to drink. What would you like? Though whatever it is, it would taste nicer in civilised surroundings.'

'I agree,' she said simply. 'Come on.'

And so, ten minutes after I had entered the Magnifico, I was outside again, buttoning my overcoat warmly about me, and this girl was at my side. It was incredible. This is not the sort of thing I usually do; but it had happened so spontaneously, and to be out there in the street, with a little cold wind blowing about us, was such a relief after the gaudy Bedlam, that the girl and I turned to one another and smiled again. I could see she was feeling the same about it as I was.

Our eyes were towards the dazzle of Piccadilly Circus, when she turned and said, 'Not that way', so we went the other way, and down those steps where the Duke of York's column towers up into the sky, and then we were in the park. To be walking there, with that little wind, and the sky full of stars huddling together in the cold, and the bare branches of the trees standing up against the violet pulsing of the night – this was indescribable, incredible, coming within a few minutes upon that screeching aviary.

Ruth Hutten was a typist – nothing more. Her father had been one of those old fogies who rootle for years and years in the British Museum to prove that Ben Jonson had really inserted a semi-colon where the 1739 edition or what not has a full-stop. Things like that. Somehow he had lived on it, like a patient old rat, living on scraps of forgotten and unimportant meat. Ruth had lived with him – just lived, full of admiration for the old boy's scholarship, typing his annual volume, which usually failed to earn the publisher's advance.

When he died, the typewriter was all she had; and now she typed other people's books. She had been typing a long flaming novel about Cornwall by Gregoria Gunson; and Gregoria (whom I had never heard of before but who seemed a decent wench) had said:

'I'll take you along to a party. You'll meet a lot of people there. Perhaps I can fix up some work for you.'

So there Ruth Hutten was, at the Magnifico, feeling as much out of it as I did, and as glad to escape.

She told me all this as we walked through the half-darkness of the park, and I, as naturally, told her all about myself. She was hard up, but I had never known anyone so happy. And I don't mean gay, bubbling, effervescent. No: you can keep that for the Magnifico I mean something deep, fundamental, something that takes courage when you're as near the limit as Ruth was.

To this day I don't know London as well as Londoners think everyone ought to know the place. I don't know where we had supper; but it was a quiet place that everybody else seemed to have forgotten. There was a fire burning, and a shaded lamp on the table. The food was good and simple, and no one seemed to care how long we stayed. I wanted to stay a long time. I had a feeling that once Ruth got outside the door, shook hands and said 'Good night', I should be groping in a very dark place.

I crumbled a bit of bread on the table, and without looking at her I said: 'Ruth, I like you. I've never liked anyone so much in my life. Will you marry me?'

She didn't answer till I looked up, and when our glances met she said: 'Yes, if you and I can't be happy together, no two people on earth ever could.'

This was five years ago. We have had time to discover that we didn't make a mistake.

We were married at a registry office the next morning. The taxi-driver, who looked like one of the seven million exiled Russian princes, and the office charwoman, who had a goitre and a hacking cough, were the witnesses. I tipped them half a sovereign each. I cling to these practical details because I find them comforting in view of the mad impracticality of what was to follow. Please remember that I am an unromantic northerner who couldn't invent a tale to save his life. If I tried to do so, I should at once begin to try it with this and that – in short, with Something.The remarkable thing about what happened to me and Ruth was simply that Nothing happened. If you have never come up against Nothing you have no idea how it can scare you out of your wits. When I was a child I used to be afraid of Something in the dark. I know now that the most fearful thing about the dark is that we may find Nothing in it.

It was Ruth's idea that we should spend the few days of our honeymoon walking in Cornwall. Everything was arranged in a mad hurry. Not that there was much to arrange. We bought rucksacks, stuffed a change of underclothing into them, bought serviceable shoes and waterproofs, and we were ready to start.

Walking was the idea of both of us. This was another bond: you could keep all the motor cars in the world as far as we were concerned, and all the radio and daily newspapers too; and we liked walking in winter as much as in summer.

Cornwall was Ruth's idea. She had Cornwall on the brain. Her father had done some learned stuff on Malory; and her head was full of Merlin and Tintagel and the return of Arthur. Gregoria Gunson's novel helped too, with smugglers and romantic inns and the everlasting beat of surf on granite coasts. So Cornwall it was – a place in which neither of us had set foot before.

We made our first contact with Cornwall at Truro. Night had long since fallen when we arrived there on our wedding day. I have not been there since, nor do I wish ever to return. Looking back on what happened, it seems appropriate that the adventure should have begun in Truro. There is in some towns something inimical, irreconcilable. I felt it there. As soon as we stepped out of the station, I wished we were back in the warm lighted train which already was pulling out on its way to Penzance.

There was no taxi in sight. To our right the road ran slightly uphill; to our left, downhill. We knew nothing of the town, and we went to the left. Soon we were walking on granite. There was granite everywhere: grey, hard and immemorial. The whole town seemed to be hewn out of granite. The streets were paved with it, enormous slabs like the lids of ancestral vaults. It gave me the feeling of walking in an endless graveyard, and the place was silent enough to maintain the illusion. The streets were lit with grim economy. Hardly a window had a light, and when, here and there, we passed a public house, it was wrapped in a pall of decorum which made me wonder whether Cornishmen put on shrouds when they went in for a pint.

It did not take us long to get to the heart of the place, the few shopping streets that were a bit more festive, gay with seasonable things; and when we found an hotel, it was a good one. I signed the book, 'Mr and Mrs Edward Oldham, Manchester', and that made me smile. After all, it was something to smile about. At this time last night, Ruth and I had just met, and now we were 'Mr and Mrs Edward Oldham'.

Ruth had moved across to a fire in the lounge. She had an arm along the mantelpiece, a toe meditatively tapping the fender. She looked up when I approached her and saw the smile. But her face did not catch the contagion. 'Don't you hate this town?' she asked.

'I can put up with it,' I said, 'now that I'm in here and now that you're in here with me.'

'Yes,' she answered, 'this is all right. But those streets! They gave me the creeps. I felt that every stone had been hewn out of a cliff that the Atlantic had battered for a thousand years and plastered with wrecks. Have you ever seen Tewkesbury Abbey?'

The irrelevant question took me aback. 'No,' I said.

'I've never seen stone so saturated with sunlight,' said Ruth. 'It looks as if you could wring summers out of it. The fields about it, I know, have run with blood, but it's a happy place all the same. This place isn't happy. It's under a cold enchantment.'

'Not inside these four walls,' I said, 'because they enclose you and me and our supper and bed.'

We fled from Truro the next morning. Fled is the word. As soon as breakfast was over we slung our rucksacks on to our backs and cleared out of the granite town as fast as our legs would take us. December 23rd, and utterly unseasonable weather. The sky was blue, the sun was warm, and the Christmas decorations in the shops had a farcical and inappropriate look. But we were not being bluffed by these appearances. We put that town behind us before its hoodoo could reimpose itself upon our spirits.

And soon there was nothing wrong with our spirits at all. We were travelling westward, and every step sunk us deeper into a warm enchantment. Ruth had spoken last night of a cold enchantment. Well, this was a warm enchantment. I hadn't guessed that, with Christmas only two days ahead, any part of England could be like this. We walked through woods of evergreens and saw the sky shining like incredible blue lace through the branches overhead. We found violets blooming in a warm hedge bottom, and in a cottage garden a few daffodils were ready to burst their sheaths. We could see the yellow staining the taut green. We had tea at the cottage, out of doors! I thought of Manchester, and the fog blanketing Albert Square, and the great red buses going through it, slowly, like galleons, sounding their warning horns. I laughed aloud at the incredible, the absurd things that could happen to a man in England. One day Manchester. The next London. The next marriage, Truro, and the cold shudders. The next - this! I said all this to Ruth, who was brushing crumbs off the table to feed the birds that hopped tamely round her feet. 'It makes me wonder what miracle is in store for tomorrow,' I said.

'And anyway, what is Cornwall? I always thought it was beetling cliffs and raging seas, smugglers, wreckers and excisemen.'

We entered the cottage to pay the old woman, and I went close up to the wall to examine a picture hanging there. It was a fine bit of photography: spray breaking on wicked-looking rocks. 'That's the Manacles,' the old girl said. 'That's where my husband was drowned.'

The Manacles. That was a pretty fierce name, and it looked a pretty fierce place. The woman seemed to take it for granted. She made no further comment. 'Good-bye, midear,' she said to Ruth. 'Have a good day.'

We did, but I never quite recaptured the exultation of the morning. I felt that this couldn't last, that the spirit which had first made itself felt in the hard grey streets of Truro had pounced again out of that hard grey name: the Manacles. It sounded like a gritting of gigantic teeth. We were being played with. This interlude in fairyland, where May basked in December, was something to lure us on, to bring us within striking distance of – well, of what? Isn't this England? I said to myself. Isn't Cornwall as well within the four walls of Britain as Lancashire?

We breasted a hill, and a wide estuary lay before us, shining under the evening sun. Beyond it, climbing in tier upon tier of streets, was Falmouth. I liked the look of it. 'This is where we stay tonight,' I said to Ruth. 'We shall be comfortable here.'

A ferry took us across the harbour. Out on the water it was cold. Ruth pointed past the docks, past Pendennis Castle standing on the hill. 'Out there is the way to Land's End,' she said.

I looked, and low down on the water there was a faint grey smudge. Even a Manchester man would know that that was fog, creeping in from the Atlantic.

All night long we heard the fog-horns moaning, and it was very cold.

I hate sleeping in an airless room, but by midnight the white coils of fog, filling every crevice, and cold as if they were the exhalation of icebergs, made me rise from bed and shut the window. Our bedroom hung literally over the sea. The wall of the room was a deep bay, and I had seen how, by leaning out of the window, one could drop a stone to the beach below. Now I could not see the beach. I could not see anything. If I had stretched my arm out into the night the fingers would have been invisible. But though I could not see, I could hear. The tide had risen, and I could hear the splash of little waves down there below me. It was so gentle a sound that it made me shudder. It was like the voice of a soft-spoken villain. The true voice of the sea and of the night was that long, incessant bellow of the fog-horns. The shutting of the window did nothing to keep that out.

I drew the curtains across the window and, turning, saw that a fire was laid in the grate. I put a match to it. Incredible comfort! In ten minutes we felt happier. In twenty we were asleep.

There seemed nothing abnormal about Falmouth when we woke in the morning. A fairly stiff wind had sprung up. The fog was torn to pieces. It hung here and there in isolated patches, but these were being quickly swept away. There was a run on the water. It was choppy and restless, and the sky was a rag-bag of fluttering black and grey. Just a normal winter day by the seaside; a marvellous day for walking, Ruth said.

At the breakfast table we spread out the map and considered the day's journey. This was going to be something new again. There had been the grey inhospitality of Truro; the Arcadian interlude; the first contact with something vast and menacing. Now, looking at the map, we saw that, going westward, following the coast, we should come to what we had both understood Cornwall to be; a sparsely populated land, moors, a rock-bound coast. It promised to be something big and hard and lonely, and that is what we wanted.

We put sandwiches into our rucksacks, intending to eat lunch out of doors. We reckoned we should find some sort of inn for the night.

A bus took us the best part of ten miles on our journey. Then it struck inland, to the right. We left it at that point, climbed a stile, walked through a few winter-bare fields, and came to a path running with the line of the coast.

Now, indeed, we had found traditional Cornwall. Here, if anywhere, was the enchanted land of Merlin and of Arthur – the land that Ruth dreamed about. Never had I found elsewhere in England a sense so overpowering both of size and loneliness. To our left was the sea, down there at the foot of the mighty cliffs along whose crest we walked. The tide was low, and the reefs were uncovered. In every shape of fantastic cruelty they thrust out towards the water, great knives and swords of granite that would hack through any keel, tables of granite on which the stoutest ship would pound to pieces, jaws of granite that would seize and grind and not let go. Beyond and between these prone monsters was the innocent yellow sand, and, looking at the two – the sand and the reefs – I thought of the gentle lapping of the water under my window last night, and the crying of the fog-horns, the most desolate crying in the world.

Southward and westward the water stretched without limit; and inland, as we walked steadily forward all through the morning, was now a stretch of cultivation, now the winter stretch of rusty moor with gulls and lapwings joining their lamentations as they glided and dropped across it, according to their kind. From time to time a cluster of trees broke the monotony of the inland view, and I remember rooks fussing among the bare boughs. Rooks, lapwings and gulls: those were the only birds we saw that day.

It was at about one o'clock that we came to a spot where the cliff path made a loop inland to avoid a deep fissure into which we peered. In some cataclysm the rocks here had been torn away, tumbling and piling till they made a rough giant's stairway down which we clambered to the beach below. We ended up in a cove so narrow that I could have thrown a stone across it, and paved with sand of an unbelievable golden purity. The sun came through the clouds, falling right upon that spot. It was tiny, paradisial, with the advancing tide full of green and blue and purple lights. We sat on the sand, leaned against the bottom-most of the fallen granite blocks, and ate our lunch.

We were content. This was the loveliest thing that we had found yet. Ruth recalled a phrase from the novel she had typed for Miss Gregoria Gunson. 'And you will find here and there a paradise ten yards wide, a little space of warmth and colour set like a jewel in the hard iron of that coast.' Far-fetched, I thought, but true enough.

It was while we were sitting there, calculating how long that bit of sun could last, that Ruth said, 'We wanted a lonely place, and we've found it, my love. Has it struck you that we haven't seen a human being since we got off the bus?'

It hadn't, and it didn't seem to me a matter of concern. I stretched my arms lazily towards the sun. 'Who wants to see human beings?' I demanded. 'I had enough human beings at the Magnifico to last me a very long time.'

'So long as we find some human beings to make us a bit of supper tonight. . . .'

'Never fear,' I said. 'We'll do that. There! Going, going, gone.'

The sun went in. We packed up, climbed to the cliff top, and started off again.

At three o'clock the light began to go out of the day. This was Christmas Eve, remember, We were among the shortest days of the year. It was now that a little uneasiness began to take hold of me. Still, I noticed, we had seen no man or woman, and though I kept a sharp lookout on the country inland, we saw no house, not a barn, not a shed.

We did not see the sun again that day, but we witnessed his dying magnificence. Huge spears of light fanned down out of the sky and struck in glittering points upon the water far off. Then the clouds turned into a crumble and smother of dusky red, as though a city were burning beyond the edge of the world, and when all this began to turn to grey ashes I knew that I was very uneasy indeed.

Ruth said: 'I think we ought to leave this cliff path. We ought to strike inland and find a road – any road.'

I thought so, too, but inland now was nothing but moor. Goodness knows, I thought, where we shall land if we embark on that.

'Let us keep on,' I said, 'for a little while. We may find a path branching off. Then we'll know we're getting somewhere.'

We walked for another mile, and then Ruth stopped. We were on the brink of another of those deep fissures. like the one we had descended for lunch. Again the path made a swift right-hand curve. I knew what Ruth was thinking before she said it. 'In half an hour or so the light will be quite gone. Suppose we had come on this in the dark?'

We had not found the path we were seeking. We did not seek it any more. Abruptly, we turned right and began to walk into the moor. So long as we could see, we kept the coast behind our backs. Soon we could not see at all. The night came on, impenetrably black, and there would be no moon. It was now six o'clock. I know that because I struck a match to look at the time, and I noticed that I had only three matches left. This is stuck in my mind because I said, 'We must be careful with these. If we can't find food, we'll find a smoke a comfort.'

'But, my love,' said Ruth, and there was now an undoubted note of alarm in her voice, 'we *must* find food. Surely, if we just keep on we'll see a light, or hear a voice, or come to a road –'

She stopped abruptly, seized my arm, held on to prevent my going forward. I could not see her face, but I sensed her alarm. 'What is it?' I asked.

'I stepped in water.'

I knelt and tested the ground in front of me with my hands. It was a deep oozy wetness; not the clear wetness of running water. 'Bog,' I said: and we knew we could go forward no longer. With cliff on the one hand and the possibility of stumbling into a morass on the other, there seemed nothing for it but to stay where we were till heaven sent us aid or the dawn came up.

I put my arm round Ruth and felt that she was trembling. I want to put this adventure down exactly as it happened. It would be nice to write that her nerves were as steady as rock. Clearly they weren't, and I was not feeling very good either. I said as gaily as I could. 'This is where we sit down, smoke a cigarette, and think it out.'

We went back a little so as to be away from the bog, and then we plumped down among the heather. We put the cigarettes to our lips and I struck a match. It did not go out when I threw it to the ground. In that world of darkness the little light burning on the earth drew our eyes, and simultaneously we both stood up with an exclamation of surprised delight. The light had shown us an inscribed stone, almost buried in the heather. There were two matches left. Fortunately we were tidy people. We had put our sandwich papers into the rucksacks. I screwed these now into little torches. Ruth lit one and held it to the stone while I knelt to read. It seemed a stone of fabulous age. The letters were mossy and at first illegible. I took out a penknife and scraped at them. '2 miles – we made out, but the name of the place two miles off we do not know to this day. I scraped away, but the letters were too defaced for reading, and just as the last of the little torches flared to extinction the knife slipped from my hand into the heather. There was nothing to do but leave it there.

We stood up. Two miles. But two miles to where, and two miles in what direction? Our situation seemed no happier, when suddenly I saw the stones. I had seen stones like them on the Yorkshire moors, round about the old Brontë parsonage. But were they the same sort of stones and did they mean the same thing? I was excited now. 'Stay here,' I said to Ruth, and I stepped towards the first stone. As I had hoped, a third came into view in line with the second, and, as I advanced, a fourth in line with the third. They were the same: upright monoliths set to mark a path, whitewashed half-way up so that they would glimmer through the dark as they were doing now, tarred on their upper half to show the way when snow was on the ground. I shouted in my joy: 'Come on! Supper! Fires! Comfort! Salvation!' Ruth came gingerly. She had not forgotten the bog.

But the stones did not let us down. They led us to the village. It must have been about nine o'clock when we got there.

Half-way through that pitch-black two-mile journey we were aware that once more we were approaching the sea. From afar we could hear its uneasy sound: the voice of a bell-buoy tolling its insistent warning out there on the unseen water. As the murmur of the sea and the melancholy clangour of the bell came clearer we went more warily, for we could not see more than the stone next ahead; and presently there was no stone where the next should be. We peered into the darkness, our hearts aching for the light which would tell us that we were again among houses and men. There was no light anywhere.

'We have one match,' I said. 'Let us light a cigarette apiece and chance seeing something that will help us.'

We saw the wire hawser: no more than the veriest scrap of it, fixed by a great staple into the head of a post and slanting down into darkness. I first, Ruth behind me, we got our hands upon it, gripping for dear life, and went inching down towards the sound of water.

So we came at last to the village. Like so many a Cornish village, it was built at the head of a cove. The sea was in front; there was a horse-shoe of cliffs; and snuggling at the end was a half-moon of houses behind a seawall of granite.

All this did not become clear to us at once. For the moment we had no other thought than of thankfulness to be treading on hard cobbles that had been laid by human hands, no other desire than to bang on the first door and ask whether there was in the place an inn or someone who would give us lodging for the night.

Most of the cottages were whitewashed; their glimmer gave us the rough definition of the place; and I think already we must have felt some uneasy presage at the deathly mask of them, white as skulls with no light in their eyes.

For there was no living person, no living thing, in the village. That was what we discovered. Not so much as a dog went by us in the darkness. Not so much as a cock crowed. The tolling from the water came in like a passing bell, and the sea whispered incessantly, and grew to a deep-throated threatening roar as the tide rose and billows beat on the sand and at last on the sea-wall; but there was no one to notice these things except ourselves; and our minds were almost past caring, so deeply were we longing for one thing only – the rising of the sun.

There was nothing wrong with the village. It contained all the apparatus of living. Bit by bit we discovered that. There was no answer to our knocking at the first door we came to. There was nothing remarkable in that, and we went on to the next. Here again, there was no welcome sound of feet, no springing up of a light to cheer us who had wandered so long in the darkness.

At the third house I knocked almost angrily. Yes; anger was the feeling I had then: anger at all these stupid people who shut down a whole village at nine o'clock, went to their warm beds, and left us standing there, knocking in the cold and darkness. I thudded the knocker with lusty rat-tat-tats; and suddenly, in the midst of that noisy assault. I stopped, afraid. The anger was gone. Plain fear took its place. At the next house I could not knock, because I knew there was no one to hear me.

I was glad to hear Ruth's voice. She said, surprisingly, 'It's no good knocking. Try a door.'

I turned the handle and the door opened. Ruth and I stepped over the threshold, standing very close together. I shouted, 'Is there anyone at home?' My voice sounded brutally loud and defiant. Nothing answered it.

We were standing at the usual narrow passageway of a cottage. Ruth put out her hand and knocked something from a little table to the floor. 'Matches,' she said; and I groped on the floor and found them. The light showed us a hurricane lantern standing on the table. I lit it, and we began to examine the house room by room.

This was a strange thing to do, but at the time it did not seem strange. We were shaken and off our balance. We wanted to reassure ourselves. If we had found flintlocks, bows and arrows, bronze hammers, we might have been reassured. We could have told ourselves that we had wandered, bewitched, out of our century. But we found nothing of the sort. We found a spotless cottage full of contemporary things. There was a wireless set. There was last week's *Falmouth Packet*. There were geraniums in a pot in the window; there were sea-boots and oilskins in the passage. The bed upstairs was made, and there was a cradle beside it. There was no one in the bed, no child in the cradle.

Ruth was white. 'I want to see the pantry,' she said, inconsequently, I thought.

We found the pantry, and she took the cloth off a bread-pan and put her hand upon a loaf. 'It's warm,' she said. 'It was baked today.' She began to tremble.

We left the house and took the lantern with us. Slowly, with the bell tolling endlessly, we walked through the curved length of the village. There was one shop. I held up the light to its uncurtained window. Toys and sweets, odds and ends of grocery, all the stock-in-trade of a small general store, were there behind the glass. We hurried on.

We were hurrying now, quite consciously hurrying; though where we were hurrying to we did not know. Once or twice I found myself looking back over my shoulder. If I had seen man, woman or child, I think I should have screamed. So powerfully had the death of the village taken hold of my imagination that the appearance of a living being, recently so strongly desired, would have affected me like the return of one from the dead.

At the centre of the crescent of houses there was an inn, the Lobster Pot, with climbing geraniums ramping over its front in the way they do in Cornwall; then came more cottages; and at the farther tip of the crescent there was a house standing by itself. It was bigger than any of the others; it stood in a little garden. In the comforting daylight I should have admired it as the sort of place some writer or painter might choose for a refuge.

Now I could make it out only bit by bit, flashing the lantern here and there; and, shining the light upon the porch, I saw that the door was open. Ruth and I went in. Again I shouted, 'Is anyone here?' Again I was answered by nothing.

I put the lantern down on an oak chest in the small square hall, and that brought any attention to the telephone. There it was, standing on the chest, an up-to-date microphone in ivory white. Ruth saw it at the same moment, and her eyes asked me, 'Do you dare?'

I did. I took up the microphone and held it to my ear. I could feel at once that it was dead. I joggled the rest. I shouted 'Hallo! Hallo!' but I knew that no one would answer. No one did.

We had stared through the windows of every cottage in the village. We had looked at the shop and the inn. We had banged at three doors and entered two houses. But we had not admitted our extraordinary situation in words. Now I said to Ruth. 'What do you make of it?'

She said simply, 'It's worse than ghosts. Ghosts are something. This is nothing. Everything is absolutely normal. That's what seems so horrible.'

And, indeed, a village devastated by fire, flood or earthquake would not have disturbed us as we were disturbed by that village which was devastated by nothing at all.

Ruth shut the door of the hall. The crashing of the sea on granite, the tolling of the bell, now seemed far off. We stood and looked at one another uneasily in the dim light of the hurricane lamp. 'I shall stay here,' said Ruth, 'either till the morning or till something happens.'

She moved down the hall to a door which opened into a room at the back. I followed her. She tapped on the door, but neither of us expected an answer, and there was none. We went in.

Nothing that night surprised us like what we saw then. Holding the lantern high above my head, I swung its light round the room.

It was a charming place, panelled in dark oak. A few fine pictures were on the walls. There were plenty of books, some pieces of good porcelain. The curtains of dark-green velvet fringed with gold were drawn across the window. A fire was burning on the hearth. That was what made us start back almost in dismay – the fire.

If it had been a peat fire – one of those fires that, once lit, smoulder for days – we should not have been surprised. But it was not. Anyone who knew anything about fires could see that this one had been lit within the last hour. Some of the coals were still black; none had been consumed. And the light from this fire fell upon the white smooth texture of an excellent linen cloth upon the table. On the table was supper, set for one. A chair was placed before the knife and fork and plates. There was a round of cold beef waiting to be cut, a loaf of bread, a jar of pickles, a fine cheese, a glass, and a jug containing beer.

Ruth laughed shrilly. I could hear that her nerves were strained by this last straw. 'At least we shan't starve,' she cried. 'I'm nearly dying of hunger. I suppose the worst that could happen would be the return of the bears, demanding "Who's been eating my beef? Who's been drinking my beer?" Sit down. Carve!'

I was as hungry as she was. As I looked at the food the saliva flowed in my mouth, but I could as soon have touched it as robbed a poor-box. And Ruth knew it. She turned from the table, threw herself into an easy chair by the fire, and lay back, exhausted. Her eyes closed. I stood behind the chair and stroked her forehead till she slept. That was the best that could happen to her.

That, in a way, was the end of our adventure. Nothing more happened to us. Nothing *more?* But, as you see, nothing at all had happened to us. And it was this nothingness that made my vigil over Ruth sleeping in the chair the most nerve-racking experience of all my life. A clock ticking away quietly on the chimney-piece told me that it was half-past nine. A tear-off calendar lying on a writing-table told me that it was 24th December. Quite correct. All in order.

The hurricane lamp faded and went out. I lit a lamp, shaded with green silk, that stood on the table amid the waiting supper. The room became cosier, even more human and likeable. I prowled about quietly, piecing together the personality of the man or woman who lived here. A man. It was a masculine sort of supper, and I found a tobacco jar and a few pipes. The books were excellently bound editions of the classics, with one or two modern historical works. The pictures, I saw now, were Medici reprints of French Impressionists, all save the one over the fireplace, which was an original by Paul Nash.

I tried, with these trivial investigations, to divert my mind from the extraordinary situation we were in. It wouldn't work. I sat down and listened intently, but there was nothing to hear save the bell and the water – water that stretched, I reminded myself, from here to America. This was one of the ends of the world.

At one point I got up and locked the door, though what was there to keep out? All that was to be feared was inside me.

The fire burned low, and there was nothing for its replenishment. It was nearly gone, and the room was turning cold, when Ruth stirred and woke. At that moment the clock, which had a lively silver note, struck twelve. 'A merry Christmas, my darling,' I said.

Ruth looked at me wildly, taking some time to place herself. Then she laughed and said, 'I've been dreaming about it. It's got a perfectly natural explanation. It was like this. . . . No. . . . It's gone. I can't remember it, but it was something quite reasonable.'

I sat with my arm about her. 'My love,' I said, 'I can think of a hundred quite reasonable explanations. For example, every man in the village for years has visited his Uncle Henry at Bodmin on Christmas Eve, taking wife, dog, cat and canary with him. The chap in this house is the only one who hasn't got an Uncle Henry at Bodmin, so he laid supper, lit the fire, and was just settling down for the evening when the landlord of the Lobster Pot thought he'd be lonely, looked in, and said: "What about coming to see *my* Uncle Henry at Bodmin?" And off they all went. That's perfectly reasonable. It explains everything. Do you believe it?'

Ruth shook her head. 'You must sleep,' she said. 'Lay your head on my shoulder.'

We left the house at seven o'clock on Christmas morning. It was slack tide. The sea was very quiet, and in the grey light, standing in the garden at the tip of the crescent, we could see the full extent of the village with one sweep of the eye, as we had not been able to do last night.

It was a lovely place, huddled under the rocks at the head of its cove. Every cottage was well cared for, newly washed in cream or white, and on one or two of them a few stray roses were blooming, which is not unusual in Cornwall at Christmas.

At any other time, Ruth and I would have said, 'Let's stay here.' But now we hurried, rucksacks on backs, disturbed by the noise of our own shoes, and climbed the path down which we had so cautiously made our way last night.

There were the stones of black and white. We followed them till we came to the spot where we found the stone with the obliterated name. 'And behold, there was no stone there, but your lost pocket-knife was lying in the heather,' said a sceptical friend to whom I once related this story.

That, I suppose, would be a good way to round off an invented tale if I were a professional story-teller. But, in simple fact, the stone *was* there, and so was my knife. Ruth took it from me, and when we came to the place where we had left the cliff path and turned into the moor, she hurled it far out, and we heard the faint tinkle of its fall on the rocks below.

'And now,' she said with resolution, 'we go back the way we came, and we eat our Christmas dinner in Falmouth. Then you can inquire for the first train to Manchester. Didn't you say there are fogs there?'

'There are an' all,' I said broadly.

'Good,' said Ruth. 'After last night, I feel a fog is something substantial, something you can get hold of.'

X

Episode

Nigel Tangye

First, let me declare my interest. I am an incurable romantic. I see romance behind the most ordinary façade, and to such an extent, I may say, that my imagination consumes the object of my attention, so that it is obscured in itself.

Sometimes, my imagination is such that a work of art takes on a new dimension as I add to it the pain and tension to an unbearable degree that the artist has put into it. For instance, the climax of Wagner's Ring for me is in the last three minutes of Gotterdämmerung, those final three minutes of the whole immense cycle, which is not what Wagner intended my emotion to be at all. But I always hear, superimposed, the terrible silence between Wagner and his wife, a monumental misunderstanding dividing them and debasing what, after the completion of twenty years of superhuman creative struggle, should have exploded into a paean of thanksgiving and celebration.

I confess to this because you might conclude, on hearing my story, that I had imagined it all. The fact that, on the contrary, I am convinced of its curious reality is surely a view the more to be respected.

I am Cornish, and I live virtually on top of a cliff on the West coast.

At the time of this story I was living alone in my old family house, an abode of some twenty rooms and a relic of more spacious days. I had returned after the Second World War to live here. Though she was not Cornish, my life loved our home passionately, and we hoped to earn enough money by a combination of writing and running a market garden to keep the place for the family we hoped to have.

Although the house was big it was built in an ancient disused quarry so that, except for northerly winds, the gales swept along above the roof. It was well built, the view northward up the coast was stupendous, and from just in front of the house winding steps dropped a hundred feet to the cove.

We were, I thought, very happy, and so it was for a few years; but my romantic viewpoint of life clouded reality, and I failed completely to realise the burden my wife was suffering from our childlessness.

My wife left me for another man. I was alone.

For many months I struggled beneath the surface of existence. Continued disbelief of the reality retarded what might otherwise have cleared sooner. But gradually I came to the surface, and the sun on the primroses and the spring breeze stirring among the daffodils brought my senses gently alive again, and the future beckoned.

I began to circulate and worked hard on the land. I had friends round and began to feel again the stirring of the need for companionship, the sweet taste for intimacy with someone special. I was alive again.

For as long as I remember a favourite walk in my family was along the cliff path to the boundary of our property a few hundred yards along. Walking on the deep soft turf was as if you were weightless. You moved away from reality into a place where you were an intruder into the lives of rabbits, oyster catchers, rock pigeon and gulls on the wing.

At the end of this walk the cliff protruded some fifty yards seaward, thus making a small promontory which we called the Point. At its tip, pointing with a seeming defiance out to sea, was a six foot long cannon which had been lifted from the wreck of a Spanish Armada ship which came to grief in the course of the long voyage of escape around the north coast of Scotland. This cannon was recovered on some unknown occasion, in fine condition, and was the only one retrieved. The remains of the luckless ship lie now beneath the sands below the Point.

I have often stood on the edge, looking down 100 feet on to the black rocks below and imagined the terrible moment when the final huge wave lifted the ship and smashed her against the solidity of a million years. The cliff is not quite sheer there, and I sometimes wondered if any survivor might have managed to escape the raging ocean and climbed to the top.

Most days I would walk along the cliff edge, or across the expanse of green soft turf to the Point. I was never without my field glasses. There was so much to observe. The wide expanse of Atlantic Ocean never failed to be spectacular whatever its mood of the moment happened to be. Inshore there would be fishing boats and tourist launches to look at, while out to sea were ships, from coasters to big tankers, plying to and from ports northward. And inland, on the cliff face and the rocks below was the wild life that flatteringly chose me as their host.

I would lie on my stomach at the Point, looking at all this. And the cannon too, never failed to attract my attention. A beautifully made weapon outliving generations of men, and with a little furbishing as lethal now as when the craftsmen rolled it out from the foundry on to the white dust of Spain more than four hundred years ago. The work of craftsmen of past generations which still bears the freshness of youth is a splendid mockery of man and a salutary reminder of our frailty. No harm is done to man by having his pride humbled by his own works that outlive him, but, nevertheless he may be excused a moment of melancholy.

It was not long after my re-awakening to life, to the warmth of the sun and the scent of the primrose, that I resumed the stance of the normal male and hoped for the magic encounter with a girl, that someone special who is a dream in a man's life, and then, after he meets her and loves her, remains a dream by his side forever.

I thought back to the catastrophe of the end of my marriage two years ago and was reminded of a glimpse of how I felt when I found this in my notebook:

The world is spanned by shadowed lives
  That keep the sun from me,
Or is it that my own despair
  Forbids my eyes to see?

All unfolds, as my mother used to say, and now, I thought, those lines do not relate to me at all. God be praised.

My idle thoughts were interrupted by the maroons being fired for the launching of the inshore lifeboat. Someone in trouble. I glanced out and looked at the weather. Force four to five wind. I should say, good visibility, fine.

I ran outside and scanned the sea with my glasses. No sign of anything from where I stood. I started walking along the cliff top toward the Point. The gulls were soaring restlessly above me, still alarmed by the two bangs of the maroons.

Unlikely to be a boat in trouble then. Must be holiday-makers caught by the incoming tide.

From the harbour a mile across the Bay I could see the white teeth of the speeding lifeboat coming northward towards us. Those stranded could be anywhere of a dozen places. So easy to do. A snooze on a deserted beach, the sea far out, and an hour later the sea still several yards out but no escape around the now submerged spurs on either side. Cliffs too steep to climb, though many try, nothing to do except hope someone, somehow, was going to see you.

The lifeboat bouncing proudly in the swell, was approaching my section of the coast. I raised my glasses to it and could see the bowman and the other crew members looking towards the base of what seemed my cliff.

As I turned away, my eye caught an unusual contour on the cannon, now some four hundred yards from me. I stopped and shielded my eyes from the sun as I looked against the glare at its black silhouette.

There was someone sitting on the cannon, sitting astride it, leaning forward, hands on the barrel rim.

At this moment, my attention was drawn to a car driving across the rough turf. It was the vehicle the Fire Brigade use for cliff rescues. It stopped twenty yards or so short of the cliff edge between me and the Point. I ran towards it. By the time I reached it two uniformed men had jumped out and were at the cliff edge peering over. A third man was taking out the equipment – rope, stakes, sledgehammer – and laying it neatly on the grass.

'Hullo m'dear,' I said to him, 'What are you after today?'

''Tis they tourists again. 'Tis always tourists. Two down there, they say.'

I helped him to lug the gear a little nearer the cliff. The other two approached with confident, unhurried step. The prospect of dropping down a rope for a hundred feet down a cliff face would have scared me stiff, but they showed professional indifference.

The three now conferred together. The ambulance arrived looking grotesquely out of place in this nature reserve. The group was joined by the ambulance crew as they looked over the edge and assessed the situation.

It was a girl on the gun! I had been so wrapped up in what the rescue team was doing that I had not noticed. It was a girl on the gun, astride it, leaning forward on her hands like a ship's figurehead and gazing straight ahead, out to sea. The excitement of the rescue failed to draw her attention. The breeze from behind her blew her long black hair forward, a dark waving streamer in the sunshine.

I rejoiced in a quickening of my senses. I was sure that she must be entrancing, adorable, someone special. I started to walk to close the fifty yards that separated me from her when I was hailed by the rescue leader. Apparently the configuration of the cliff in relation to the stranded couple was awkward for rescue. It would help if they could make fast one line to the carriage of the cannon. Would I mind? The ground is much too hard there to take a stake. Of course not. He looked towards the Point and the cannon. 'I'll go and check it. Must weigh nearly a ton. Should be all right,' he said, almost to himself.

The ambulance man called me. I turned back, leaving the officer to go to the cannon alone. What of the girl, I thought. She mustn't go away. She mustn't leave now.

I was impatient to know why I had been called. Had I a spare blanket in the house? Of course. Could he borrow it? Yes. 'Do you want it now?' I asked, my heart sinking at the delay if I had to go and fetch it. 'Please.' So that was it. No remonstrance was seemly under these circumstances. I glanced back at the girl. The nape of her neck, renounced by her waving black hair now over her face, gleamed in the sun. I turned and ran back to the house.

By the time I returned to the scene, the line had been rigged to the cannon and a man was half way down the cliff on the rescue. The remaining two were making arrangements for manning the line to haul up the load.

Although I wanted very much to speak to the girl, my natural shyness and invariable fear of a rebuff were such that I was glad when I was asked to join the crew on the haul, and would I stand just here? I was able freely to study her, shielded as I was by my anonymity in the group.

I was now standing slightly in front of her and could see her features for the first time. As though aware of my interest she tossed her head so that all her hair streamed by the other side of her face.

What I saw puzzled me, and unaccountably drew compassion from me. She was smiling, still looking seaward, still astride the cannon, and apparently not in the least inconvenienced by the turn of ropes beneath. But in her smile there was a haunting wistfulness, a sort of reaching out for something beautiful she knew she would never attain again. Or so my heart told me.

For a moment our eyes met, great deep, dark eyes that fixed me long enough for me to catch my breath. She was wearing one earring that I could see, like a thick Victorian wedding ring. I could see the top of a gold cross on a fine chain lying in the valley of her breasts. Her cheeks were brown and glowing, and her colour was set off by the sombrely woven woollen shirt and full skirt she wore. Her legs and feet were brown and bare. I wanted her. I wanted her for keeps. She was vulnerable and I could protect her.

There was a shout of 'Heave!' and my attention and strength were concentrated on the rescue. For several minutes I responded impatiently to the orders and exhortation of our leader, until with a final heave there emerged over the lip of the cliff a frightened youth, still cradled in the arms of the officer who kept with him so that he would not lose his head.

It appeared that it was a false alarm that there were two stranded people. I was glad I wasn't going to be put to the same treadmill again. Out to sea I could see the little inshore lifeboat amid a flurry of spray explosions, rushing its crew home to tea. And now I could devote my attention to the girl.

She had gone! She wasn't there any more. I looked madly up, down and across the open ground. Nothing. I could see no cover which she could have reached in the brief time involved. The ambulance. She must be in there. I ran to it. The driver was leaning against the big door, relaxed knowing there was no casualty. Where is the girl, I asked, is she in here? He looked at me blankly. The girl, I repeated, the girl on the cannon. He hadn't seen a girl.

Two hundred yards away a hedge formed the boundary of my property. I rushed to it, breathless as I looked over across the neighbouring field. Nothing. Then, Christ, the cliff. She's over the cliff!

A minute later I was peering over the cliff, as fearful and anxious as though I were looking for my own daughter.

'What's the matter? What are you looking for?' It was the team leader speaking to me. The expression on his face told me that I must have been looking pretty harassed.

'The girl. The girl on the cannon. She's disappeared!'

He looked quizzically at me, imperceptibly shaking his head.

'The girl,' I went on, 'with the long dark hair and the gold earring.'

'Didn't notice any girl,' he said, doubtfully.

'Ye gods!' I cried. 'Didn't *notice* that girl? She was sitting on the gun when you tied your rope round it.'

He didn't answer but kept looking at me, puzzled. 'For God's sake! I'm not mad. You *must* have seen her. She was in your way!'

'We didn't see any girl.'

I turned away and started walking slowly back across the green turf. A group of gulls, resting in the sunshine and disturbed by my approach rose with a commotion into the air circling higher and higher and filling the heavens with their golden cry.

I felt utterly deflated.

She was real. She must have been there.

My mind was filled with concern and conjecture that night as to how I might find her. Who could she be? Her face and colouring – the deep dark eyes, and jet black hair, the high cheek bone – these were to be seen among the Cornish, arising from union between local girls and shipwrecked seamen.

There is belief that many progeny stemmed from seamen of the Spanish Armada. My heart missed a beat. No, it couldn't be – but the Spanish . . . the Armada wreck at the foot of the cliff . . . the phallic cannon . . . no, no . . . but –

A seed of doubt was sown in my mind.

I pursued a different line. I recalled, out of the blue, some entries in my great grandfather's diary which might be relevant. From a cabinet I drew the manuscript out. I found what I was looking for, but it was tantalisingly incomplete. Just:

The maid was there again today.

The date May 5th, 1821.

There were five more similar, unexplained entries like that in the next few months, and then no more.

One other thing. I thought I would have a look at local Church Registers. In St Mawgan church I saw that Seraphin Valiente married a Katherine Tregone on May 1st, 1589.

None of this leads to much. But there's a link of sorts between each fact.

A month or so later I had a buyer for the house. It was an offer I could not refuse so that I resolved to forsake the old place and go and live in the Lodge at the head of the Drive, an arrangement which I made a condition of the sale.

Of course I took with me as many items representing past family life as I could – pictures, the grandfather clock, the chest from the hall, that sort of thing.

I also decided to take the cannon and place it by the Drive gates.

It was a major operation to move it. A huge lorry with a crane arrived and trundled across to the Point. I watched as the two men, skilled in manhandling heavy weights, went calmly and surely about their task. The cannon was lifted, and gently lowered on to the vehicle, leaving a brown scar where it had rested on the ground for heaven knows how long.

For me the scene was permeated by the vision of the girl, the girl so vivid and warm and yet unseen by anyone but me. Before me was her face, the eyes and glow of her cheek, the wistful smile and gold cross hanging from her neck.

My toe was idly rubbing along the brown scar when I thought of the gold earring, the single earring. And there, rubbed free of the dead grass roots by my toe, lay a ring, not a gold one, but a blackened, roughened one. I sensed a thrill of significance and stooped to pick it up. It had been there a very long time, no doubt about that.

I took it up to the Lodge and studied it under a glass. It couldn't have any meaning. I recalled that gold always glittered, so this could have no connection.

My feelings were in conflict. I held the ring in my hands and willed and willed desperately that it should be the key to unlock the mystery of she who had barely left my thoughts for an hour; but no release was forthcoming.

I spoke to no one of all this until years later when I related my experience to a close friend who was a chemist.

He listened attentively. When I had related to him the momentary flash of truth I experienced on finding the earring followed by my dismay it was not of gold, he said to me,

'Why are you so sure the ring she wore was gold?'

'Well, what do you mean? It *was* gold.'

He said, 'More likely to have been brass. And that would have paired with the weathered one you found.'

XI

Window in the Attic

J. C. Trewin

Over on the southern horizon, where Cornish sky met Cornish sea, the lighthouse was flashing. It had begun an hour or so earlier, for this was deep now in an October evening, its grey and umber lost in the all-embracing dark.

As the car approached St Rumon, its driver saw with a pang of memory a long beam that fanned across the peninsular coast and the half-mile of bare down behind. Transiently the beam rested on an isolated building that stood a few hundred yards off the Meriol road. Then it fanned back across rocks and sea, its own lime-washed tower, and the distant curve of the eastern cliffs.

It was a cold, dampish night in the early nineteen-sixties. There was no one on the plateau-road from Meriol; at this time of year there seldom was. As he stopped his car at the head of a muddy, brambled track, the man asked again – and a shade petulantly – why he had come. By now it must be getting on for seven o'clock; half an hour ago he had been sitting with the local paper in the lounge of Meriol's single hotel, wondering how to waste the remainder of a drab evening. Then this inexplicable wish possessed him; he must get back to St Rumon, and at once.

At the moment it had appeared to him less of a wish than a summons, almost a peremptory call. Nonsense, of course: he realised that. But he yielded, arguing with himself that there were worse things than a quick run, ten, eleven miles down the southern road.

All these years away from it, he had had comfortably romantic ideas about the place where his ancestors were bred. Until that morning he had not seen it since he was a young child, and in the drizzle it had hardly excited him: the upper barrens, the church-town cottages bunched in their cup beside a granite tower, the lighthouse white on the cliff-edge. It was not a friendly hamlet; it had never powerfully wanted visitors, and it did not try to help them. The summer cars from Meriol soon turned back.

He could turn back himself once he had had a look at the old place in the darkness. Here, anyway, he was; and here again was the house he had owned since his brother's death a month ago. Frank, a wealthy, amiable bachelor, had not troubled about it in a quarter of a century. There had been some hit-or-miss caretaking, but the man had died, and (so Hocking, the solicitor, had said that afternoon) no one seemed eager to take on the job. They had other things to do at St Rumon.

A thankless job, Edward Paynter thought, as he loitered now in the mouth of the lane. The wheeling light had hesitated upon the façade of Tree, and upon a broken, jagged window on the attic storey, the window (he supposed) that Hocking had talked about. An odd tale, but it was an odd enough house. In the alternation of darkness and phantasmal light it looked dangerously insubstantial: a thin steel engraving; a stage-set with nothing behind it. Even the name, Tree House, was false. Few trees survived on the upland. In the cleft of the church-town valley, yes; but the house was square to every gale that attacked the flat, shorn downs. Behind it were a pair of stunted Cornish elms, wind-bent. Someone had endowed the place with the usual monkey-puzzle, a 'bristly' to St Rumon children, and through the years an embarrassed stranger.

Nothing else rose from the jungled lawns; the last caretaker had had to scythe a path through to the front door. Beyond the loose stone wall, the swishing tamarisk feathers, the rank grasses, Tree stood roughly as it had done since the ebb of the eighteenth century. Its period meant nothing whatever. There were unimaginative builders then, as now; and Tree had little to grace it. Its front door was pleasantly canopied; otherwise it was a plain stone structure, ridiculously large. Above the ground floor were three tiers of shuttered windows; over these the low sprawl of the attic floor, unshuttered, and with that one hole, a jagged gash, through which the winter winds would drive. Useless to repair it, Hocking had said; no sooner was it re-glazed than it splintered into fragments.

By this time it scarcely mattered; not much did. There had never been any pilgrimage to Tree. Not a guide-book named it; no one had hurried to the village to say that it must be preserved at any cost, its plaster scrolls, the carved cedar screen in its dining-room. It had neither screen nor plaster: nothing but its range of empty rooms and the attics where the 'girls' had lived, the maids, the Lidgeys, who had staffed the place, generation by generation, for over a century. Since the coastguards had left it after the second world war, it had simply waited for the end. Occasionally a District

Councillor was inquisitive; but that was all. St Rumon kept its affairs to itself.

Edward stepped carefully towards a gap in the boundary wall where the stones had toppled. He must not be late, he repeated to himself. Late? For what? Why this silliness? He shook himself and paused in the middle of the jungle path as the fanning beam returned. He noticed how still the evening was; so still that he feared to disturb with any footfall a world that was poised and listening.

Well, the old house must go. Obviously it would be simpler to clear the site. To build again? To sell the land? As yet he was unsure; he would have to consider. Who would want a house the size of Tree, and on the edge of the beyond? It had been reasonable in his grandfather's Edwardian time. Size was not worrying then, and the Lidgey girls had 'belonged', an endless supply of daughters, nieces, cousins, from the fishermen's, labourers' families that lived in St Rumon church-town. Emma, Mildred, Jenny; Eva and Margaret, Mary and Lucy and Alice; the house had been their natural work: Paynters at Tree, Lidgeys from the village. One or two, older and unmarried, had been in service for most of their lives. Laura, the last and dominant parlourmaid, was over seventy: she had been in control when Edward stayed, as a child, with his grandparents, and she was in a sheaf of pictures in the family album – wherever that was now; one day he must search for it.

The good years were far back. The Lidgey girls had gone; today the only pair of that name from St Rumon were teaching up-country, towards Plymouth or farther. The feudal system was just a village legend, though there might be someone in the pub at night to revive an old tale.

Way back – it would be before the first world war – Alice, an eighteen-year-old Lidgey, had fallen sheer from her window. What business, they asked in the village, had young William Paynter to be in the attics on an October midnight? He told the Coroner that he had heard a scream and run up to find the room empty and the window smashed. They called it accidental death, but presently the young man left Tree and few Lidgey girls went there again. That was the beginning of the end; the closing of parts of the house, the family's dispersal, the old people left with only Laura to watch them. All were dead: since then (after that brief period of a second war) simply solitude and decay.

A glum affair, Edward reflected. William Paynter had been his father: not, he would have said, given to any kind of melodrama.

Still, after all, this was Edwardian, a primeval period when practically anything could have happened, and did. During the early nineteen-twenties his parents had sent him, with Frank to stay at Tree, but they never came themselves and the house was not left to them: significantly it missed a generation.

Pacing down the muddy path, Edward had a blurred memory of the place as it used to be, the grandfather clock in the hall, Old Testament oil-paintings in the dining-room, upstairs a range of closed doors, in the kitchen Laura and another starched and silent maid, her younger sister Milly, who married the St Rumon carpenter. Not much to do or to see; for a child (and he had to admit it) those days had dragged.

From a distance tonight he could hear, very faintly, the flat wash of the tide: not a flutter in the grass and heather, not a quiver in the monkey-puzzle branches. He heard his own too anxious breathing. Why in the world had he come?

It was then that, with a sudden whirring, a clearing of its throat, a grandfather clock struck seven.

Startled, Edward halted in mid-stride, mechanically counting the beats until the last stroke faded. It could have come only from the house, but the house was bare and dead.

The clock had been gone for twenty-five years. Frank had sold it with the other things at Lutton's before the war: the clock, the huge gong of Benares brass, the inlaid mahogany dining-table, the paintings (which brought next to nothing, even the descent from Sinai), the deep sitting-room carpet, the billiards-table, a dozen beds: he recalled the auctioneer's slightly ghoulish catalogue. For himself he had bought one of the stray lots, half-a-dozen shell candlesticks, and an oil-lamp on a veined serpentine base that used to shimmer in its dull red and a mottled green.

Edward was shivering a little; for no reason (he insisted) his hands were clenched. Seven o'clock: then he was late. Someone in this house was waiting for him, but need he go in? Relief overwhelmed him. Even if he wanted to, he could not; that afternoon he had left the key at Hocking's office and the house was safely locked. He would do no more than drive back to Meriol; dinner at the hotel, what sleep he could get, a word with Hocking in the morning, a final decision. He twisted on his heel; and, as he did so, the light flickered across the doorway.

Beneath its curved canopy the door stood wide open.

He was late. He knew without question that he had to keep his word, and he hurried forward up the three steps and into a square hall where once the grandfather clock had filled its alcove.

Darkness was profound until the lighthouse ray slipped across the dusty spaces, a few lank trails of cobweb, a floor where uneven boards squeaked to his tread.

Vaguely now he imagined that he heard a rustle of starched skirts, saw a pallid glimmer, even felt a hand on his arm. But nothing stirred and the swinging ray did not return. Someone had shut the door.

He moved instinctively to his left, groping along the wall until the china knob he wanted turned smoothly in his grasp and he was in what had been the western sitting-room. It was his grandparents' room; long ago the family would have gathered there before dinner. Shutters blocked both windows, but the fanning light still flickered eerily through any crack. Remembering a torch in his overcoat pocket, he felt for it vainly. He was not wearing an overcoat, yet he had been when he entered the house. For a moment he stood irresolute. Then the recurring gleam showed to him, beside the dark hearth, the tasselled, knotted length of a dull crimson bell-rope. Edward reached across and pulled at it: a long, hard tug.

Out in the recesses of the house a bell jangled.

Half a minute passed as Edward waited. There came a tap on the door, a discreet two-fingered tapping, and the door creaked open along a furrow in the dust. Striding to the window, Edward tore at its shutter-bolt and pushed the panel aside. Briefly the next beam revealed a motionless figure: a woman who wore with a dignity of her own the starched, heavy apron of an Edwardian parlourmaid. Beneath the cap her face, with its sunken eyes, was pale and prim. He recognised her from many album pictures. She was younger than when he had known her, but he could not mistake Laura Lidgey who had been in St Rumon churchyard for nearly thirty years.

Now she bobbed ritually and held back the door while the house seemed to shake to the thudding of a brass dinner-gong.

Edward had tried to speak, but the words did not come, and what was there to say? He found himself walking diagonally across that mustily forsaken hall to a long room at the back; the former dining-room where in the cold light of midday he had seen only a battered Windsor chair.

There was some dim illumination now, though where it came from he had no idea. He seemed to be suffering from double vision, for the room as it had been that morning was overlaid by the room as it used to be: on flaking, damp-blotched walls the pictures

(Moses after Sinai, and the rest) in shadowy gilt frames; on the mahogany table – only one place was set – glass and silver that showed no sparkle in the light; round the table a ceaseless coming-and-going, a soft crackle of skirts, a quick murmur; no word he could distinguish and no person he could see but Laura Lidgey as she passed by him or stood, with her sunken brown eyes on his, a silver dish in her hand.

He could not tell how long he sat there or what he did, but certainly he heard the chimes of nine o'clock and knew he must rise from the table. The door had opened before he could touch it, and he was in the hall, wondering why he had not seen the gong, with its padded stick upon the tray; the grandfather clock by Rowe of Falmouth; the wall mirror, which reflected precisely nothing; the bookcase with its calf folios behind the glass; and a great Hungarian rug on the polished floor.

Somewhere he could hear what sounded like the repeated click of billiard-balls. No time to speculate; he was back in the western sitting-room, treading on the pile of a carpet, florally Victorian, that he remembered in the sale at Lutton's. The hearth was alive with the bluish flame of driftwood, though whenever light flickered through the unboarded window the room was derelict and the hearth was dead.

Edward was aware of a younger maidservant, clearly one of the Lidgeys, a girl with a carriage as upright as Laura's, the same curiously sunken brown eyes, and a drift of brown hair beneath the absurd and repressive cap. Putting down what she carried, she lingered there, gazing at him boldly; and he realised what he must do. It was not yet time. Twice he heard the clock strike the hour. At eleven the girl entered again to place a candlestick beside him. He could have cried aloud, for that painted, hollowed rod, springing from the shell at its foot, was one of those above his bed in the London flat a world away. Once more the girl paused to watch him. Then the door closed and Edward knew that the night was deadly cold. The room he stood in was in dark decay: no fire, no carpet, merely an ancient milking-stool, the floor's dirty planking, and the walls peeling and cracked.

Yet there by the hearth was his candlestick, filmed with dust. It held no candle, but he reached down for it. Time to go upstairs.

Pulling the door towards him, he walked cautiously into the blackness of a hall empty of furniture, emptied of any sound. He fumbled his way across to the dining-room, a frigid vault; within it he tripped over the shafts of a broken Windsor chair. He was conscious suddenly of a light over his shoulder, the faintest sheen;

as he retreated into the hall he saw Laura Lidgey's face gazing down at him from the bend of the staircase and whiter than ever in the glow of the oil-lamp she carried on a mottled serpentine base. She vanished round the curve; and, dropping his candlestick with a clatter, he followed her up the uncarpeted treads that creaked and sighed beneath his weight.

Her light had gone. On the bleak landing he passed room by room, some fast-locked, others shuttered and dustily unused. He climbed to the next floor. Here there seemed to be a scurrying, a mutter, a bustle sensed rather than heard. He thought that there was laughter; and, with the thought, the young maid looked questioningly at him across the trembling wick of a candle. He leapt forward; the candle went out; every sound had fallen away.

Somehow he got up to the next floor, a copy of the others. The landing window was only half-shuttered: from it he could see the plateau blanched by a risen moon that dimmed the swinging beam. Thin in the distance, just visible over the cup of the church-town, were the spiked pinnacles of St Rumon tower. A wind, blowing harshly in from the sea, fretted about the eaves above him; he heard from below the noise of a clock collecting its strength before breaking into the twelve midnight chimes.

Halfway down that corridor a spiral ladder rose to the attic rooms of Tree. By it, holding her lamp, waited Laura Lidgey. For a last time he saw her, her face whiter than her apron. Then she had gone; and desperately, in the fading strokes of midnight, he clambered to the cramped passage below the roof where every door was shut but one.

This he pushed open. Within, the younger Lidgey girl rose to face him in a haze of moonlight, her back to the uncurtained window. She wore a nightgown; her hair was free; she stretched her arms in greeting. But, as he advanced, she slipped aside in the narrow space. Again, without speech or sound, she eluded him; and yet again. Then, so he imagined, and strangely, she began to fade: he cried out, bending urgently towards her, and in that moment a cold hand pressed his back and thrust him steadily to the low, unguarded window.

He could not check himself. Hurled against the starred and shattering glass, he lost his balance and dived headlong, a sheer drop into the night. Overhead, the wind was driving through the gap into a forlorn, dusty room; and on the southern horizon, where sky met sea, the lighthouse flashed.

*

They discovered Edward's body next morning. A hedger, who saw the car by the top of the lane, had walked down to Tree to find its owner. Dr Lanyon, hurrying from the church-town, shook his head.

'Who was he? Why was he here?'

He stared up at a broken attic window and turned to the man with him.

'Too late, Lidgey, but you had better ring for the ambulance. Meriol four-five.'

XII

The Wheel

James Turner

They all saw it. Philip, James, Mary and Annabel. It came out of the sandhills at the point where the stream broke the dunes and flowed across the beach to join the sea. It was late summer and the sea in the bay was low. But, because of an offshore wind whipping the dunes into tiny flurries of sand, the waves were crashing far out and making a considerable thunder.

James, a small, black-haired man, a TV script writer, was the first to speak after it passed. 'God,' he said, his eyes still on the sea where it had disappeared, 'How horrible! What the hell do you think it was?'

The two girls and two young men were standing absolutely still beside the edge of the shallow sand-river. Mary was shivering. She had put her arms about her body inside the yellow cardigan she was wearing as if to protect herself. In her white summer dress. the cardigan toning in with the colour of the sand, and in this position she looked very small.

'We'd better go back, Annabel,' she said and turned. Then, quickly, she put her right hand on the other girl's arm and went on. 'There's nothing to be afraid of now, I'm sure there isn't. Really, it's over.'

Annabel was already weeping. 'I can't bear it,' she got out, feeling the comfort of Mary's hand. 'I've never liked this beach. And now. . . .' She turned her back on the mass of rocks ahead of them which was called the 'Island' because it jutted into the sea and formed the edge of the long bay to which the sand dunes created the background. She began to walk away, ashamed of her tears, the last light of the red-falling sun catching her golden hair. Mary, still conscious that she needed protection, followed her.

Philip, however, had run after whatever 'it' was which had so frightened all of them and now returned to announce that he had seen the great black ball 'disintegrate' as he put it, 'like the ash of some huge coal, when it hit the sea, I distinctly saw the steam.'

Only James seemed to be aware of the light hovering over this end of the bay, emanating from the sand dunes themselves. 'Whatever it was,' he said, 'it was moving at colossal speed. It looked like a hoop to me. Some white-hot iron wheel. But what the hell was driving it?'

'No,' Philip, who did not seem to have missed the girls, was sitting on the sand, his long legs stretched out before him, waiting in case anything further happened. 'It was definitely a huge black wheel – not white at all – like a mill-stone. Did you hear the high-pitched whine? When it passed us? Like the whistle of an express train. Come to think of it, now, it was much more like a train wheel than a mill-stone.'

'Yes,' James lit his pipe, half because he wanted it, half because he had the absurd idea that the girls would see his match and know that everything was all right with them. 'Yes, I heard the whining when it came out of the dunes just where the stream emerges. Only not so loud when it reached us. And then the hissing when it reached the sea.'

'Let's go and look at the dunes. It will be too late tomorrow. All clues will have gone with the next tide.'

They walked along the stream's edge to the mouth of the dunes looking at the sand. Not even a footstep broke the even surface and the great hills of dry sand were now too dark, in their own shadow, to show them anything. A silver thread of light did penetrate the mouth, like a cavern, from which the stream emerged. It was the last of the sun reflected off the water and looked like a thin trickle of blood.

They gave up. 'It's no good stopping here any longer. We'd better run and catch the girls. Annabel was really frightened. We don't want the holiday spoilt, do we?'

'It's odd all the same,' Philip said, 'You know, my impression was that it was a very old piece of machinery, something off an old ship, I'd say.'

They had, the four of them, only arrived in the bay that afternoon from London, though Annabel had known the place for years. In fact, the cottage was borrowed from her brother who, for the rest of the year, let it to strangers and only came himself during the winter. A Mrs Brenton came in daily to keep it clean.

While Mary got the supper from the hampers they had brought with them, the others sat on the open veranda and discussed what had happened. They seemed unwilling to let the subject drop. The tide had, by now, ridden in and was banging away at the concrete sea-wall which, in effect, held up the cottage garden. Now, in the safety of the cottage, with Mary clattering dishes and knives and forks behind them, the subject took on all the attraction of an abstract problem in mathematics or philosophy. They were playing with possibilities as if, in fact, any answer to the problem was to be avoided at all costs.

'There is never any answer,' James said, 'It's got something to do with our states of mind, I'm sure. Or, else, it must have been some odd electrical discharge. I mean it didn't appear in any way malevolent, did it?'

'Oh, no,' Annabel said, firmly, 'it seemed horribly malevolent to me. I can't explain it but it was evil. It was against us and it had a kind of face, or I thought it did.' It was plain that she had not fully overcome her fright. 'I shall dream about it, something out there, alone, evil, in the sand. My brother always says that beach is haunted. He's right.'

'But, Annabel, what is there to dream of? A kind of wheel thing? And it didn't do you any harm, did it? It merely passed us and rushed into the sea. It was come and gone almost before any of us was aware of it.'

'It might have hurt us if we'd got in its way. Another step or two. And, anyway, who can tell if it did any harm or not? Fear always leaves traces. I wish we hadn't come to the cottage, it's too near the sea, you never get away from the sound of it.'

'Rubbish,' Philip said. When not on holiday he was a marine engineer. 'There are hundreds of other beaches we can go to. It's going to be fun here. The sound of the sea is going to make all of us content. And you couldn't ask for better weather, could you?'

'I love it here, too,' James pulled the cork out of a bottle of wine. 'The sound of the waves and the gulls screaming. The souls of all drowned men looking for a home.'

'Don't, James, please,' Annabel pleaded. 'That thing in the dunes was bad enough. I know we'll never be able to explain it. I shan't go up that end of the bay again, not on the sand anyway!'

'Oh, I don't know.' Philip turned from the window. The lighthouse on Trevose Head was winking silently, regularly, remorselessly. 'We might find an explanation. Who knows, it may be something to do with that place, what's it called, Nanskuke.'

'You mean a kind of secret weapon?' James asked, with the cork half out of the bottle. 'My God, I never thought of that.

Might make a good TV play. Wonderful setting, anyway.'

'But they only make poison gases up there, don't they?' Mary asked, 'And it's miles away from here.'

'Who knows what else they make? It's all bloody secret. And this long sandy beach might be just the place for a try-out.'

'Don't be so damned silly! In that case people would have been warned to keep away. We'd never have got near the beach, nor into this cottage, I wouldn't wonder.' Mary put the eggs and bacon on the table and a large yellow melon. 'It's absolutely ridiculous to talk like that.'

'Well, we're on holiday. When else can you be ridiculous?'

'No,' Annabel said. She had recovered enough to relish the food. 'It was supernatural. I'm sure it was. And, what's more, it's going to thunder. You always get things like this, supernatural I mean, when there's thunder about.'

'I don't know,' James cut the bread, 'what is really meant by the supernatural. Ghosts and that kind of thing, I suppose. How can a round object, moving at great speed, hot and perhaps dangerous, be referred to as a ghost?'

'It could be a sort of time trace of something years ago. It could be an elemental, couldn't it? And, you know, there's an ancient village site over behind the dunes. They'd have had a smithy, wouldn't they?'

'But none of us know if it was solid or not,' Philip put in. He was already bored with the subject on which none of them could come to any definite conclusion and wanted to be out. 'I mean none of us touched it, did we? We only thought we saw it, though, I suppose, we all heard it. And if it were a ghost, then it can't have been anything solid, like a human being. I thought actually, only once sentient beings became ghosts – not wheels.'

'I don't see why anything couldn't leave traces of itself, if it had a mind to,' Mary said, 'Wasn't there a case once of someone seeing a ghostly chess set? And, at least, whatever it was, it was red and alive. Some force was driving it, like the wheel of a waggon, careering over the sand.'

'You said, "if it had a mind to".' Philip laughed. 'That's the whole point, isn't it? This thing, whatever it was, didn't have a mind. Come on, James,' he said impatiently, 'I'm going out again, it's too hot in here.'

'Oh, don't,' Annabel pleaded, 'Don't go looking for it again. Not at night, please, I'm sure it's dangerous.'

'Oh, we'll go the other way. Into Treyarnon Bay. It'll be quite safe there and full of holiday-makers and late bathers. Besides there's a storm coming up and we shan't be long.'

The storm blew away by morning after a night of brilliant pyrotechnics over the sea. But still Annabel didn't seem able to drop the subject of what they had seen the evening before. She even mentioned it to Mrs Brenton when she came in, after breakfast, to clear up. The others were in the sea and she was alone. Mrs Brenton took her seriously. 'It's always been known as the haunted beach,' she said, 'Your brother saw something once.'

'What?'

'I'm not sure. A dark figure by the rocks I think he said. I think, myself, it's due to the ancient people who lived here-abouts once, miss.'

'What ancient people?'

'Well, I'm not any good at that sort of thing, living people are bad enough, I say, without those who've been dead for centuries. But they do say the "Island" was once lived on by them neolithists. Little, shaggy men they say who lived by fishing and making pots. Very likely! And there used to be a village of 'em by the ruined church in the dunes by the holy well. All sorts of things have been seen up that end of the beach.' She pointed out of the windows across the bay.

'What sort of things?' Annabel asked again, thinking of her brother.

'Black dogs,' Mrs Brenton laughed, 'Great monstrous black dogs with red fangs and blood coming from their mouths. I reckon it's due to drinking too much rough cider.'

'But this wasn't a dog, Mrs Brenton. It was some kind of wheel.'

'Fancy!' Mrs Brenton pressed the knob of the hoover and obliterated any idea of ghosts in its noise. A moment later she switched it off to add, 'I'd be careful up there, miss, if I was you. You're different from your brother. Women are, and I never liked that beach at all.'

She switched on the machine again and went to work without explaining exactly what women were. But Annabel knew.

James was walking a little ahead of the girls. In the perfect weather, after the storm of last night, the sea was blue, tipped with white of the wavelets. In fact, it was a day from an Academy picture, a blazing summer's day. A great oil ship on the horizon, like a distant castle, was making its way towards Pembroke Docks.

For Mary the walk was almost an exploration. She had never

been in Cornwall before and she was excited. The sand dunes rising high above the beach and covered thickly with marram grass had the attraction of all unknown places. They had been raised and planted as a protection for the low lying land beyond the sea. From the deep cuttings and paths in the sandhills it was possible to take in both the sea and the whole countryside, which on a fine day like this ran almost to the edges of Dartmoor.

A mirage of heat waves, like a silver veil, was rising from the dry sand and the paths through the dunes rose and fell, switchbacks where high winter winds had scored and driven the sand against the holding grass. The voices of children could be heard playing hide-and-seek and other games. Occasionally a small head would appear above the spiney grass. Because of the height and thickness of this grass the head would seem almost to be floating on the grey-green carpet. A curious dry smell was coming from the land.

James struck inland at a spot just this side of the stream from which, the night before, the 'thing', as they now referred to it, had come out upon them. Almost as soon as they took the sandy path down to the low lying land, Annabel began to feel uneasy. A slight breeze was beginning to whistle through the wire-like grass, making the hot day more pleasant but increasing her uneasiness. She said nothing to James or Mary and Philip, who had walked into the village for shopping, was not here to help her. She didn't know for certain but she felt that he would have sympathised with her fears.

'We'll go down and have a look at the ruined church and the holy well.' James called back to the girls. He was already ahead of them and Annabel, following Mary, could see the ruins of the church ahead and the three tiny stone bridges over the stream which poured out, between the dunes, to the sea.

In fact, when they came to the church ruins they were not impressive at all, being no more than the fragment of a heavy arched doorway, the six-foot tall walls of the nave and a sketch or two of a window. Although the arched doorway stood out from the land on which the church was built, the rest of the ruins were smothered in brambles and sloe bushes, the fruit of which was already purple. At the east end of the church a fine growth of the wild flower himalayan balsam gave colour to an otherwise grey-green scene, its pink and white orchidaceous bloom already making seed and about to pop off like a gun when fully ripe.

James was standing against the ruined arch when the girls caught up with him. 'It's fascinating,' Mary said, 'Though I had hoped for something more substantial. Where's the holy well, by the way?'

James pointed. Three or four late-hatched red admirals suddenly alighted from nowhere on a nettle bed before him. Annabel clapped her hands at their pure beauty. 'Down there to the north. Over that slight rise. You can just see the top of the roof put on to protect it. We'll go down in a minute and you can cure all your ills at one go.' He moved among the tall weeds and the girls followed him.

'Those people over there,' Annabel asked, 'What on earth are they doing?' The hot sun was now burning her bare arms. Both girls were wearing floppy white sunhats and rather brilliantly coloured summer dresses.

'Digging.'

'In this heat?' Mary asked.

'Not that kind of digging. They're on the site of the neolitic village.'

'What Mrs Brenton calls the "neolithists".'

'Actually there was a village on that spot for centuries after those early people. They must have dug through that already. And there is even supposed to have been a Druid's temple on the site of the church originally.'

'What, just here?' Annabel asked. She had hardly moved from the ruins and, as she asked the question she touched a large stone with her foot. It rolled away from her. It must once have been part of the walls. She gasped. Her action uncovered a great green toad. It looked up at them with sleep-ridden eyes, reproachfully. 'Oh, James,' she called him back, 'I'm sure it's unlucky to uncover a toad. Poor thing! Do cover him again, this heat will kill him. Look he's panting terribly already.'

James bent down to replace the stone.

'No, not with that, you'll crush him. Look he's moved a little. Put some grass over him. Perhaps he'll forgive me for disturbing him.'

'We ought to catch it and extract the precious stone from its brain,' James said, pulling grass and weeds to keep the sun from it.

'Oh, how could you!' Mary turned away, 'I think you're horrid.'

'Well, that's what the ancients thought. Pliny, wasn't it?' James laughed and added, 'You know, Annabel, one of those old Cornish saints built his church on top of the Druid temple. He'll protect you, even if his church did fall into ruin. Then, in 1390, it was rebuilt and again fell into this ruin we see today. What with the village on the top of those excavations they're digging, there must have been, in this one small area, quite a community worshipping in the church, taking miraculous cures in the holy well and testing their good luck from the water itself before they went fishing in the still dangerous seas to the west.'

'Do you think,' Mary asked, as they walked on, 'that what we all saw and heard last night could have been anything to do with the ancient people and their settlement? I mean anything to do with the site being disturbed by those diggers?'

'Of course not,' James said and they ran, hand in hand, down the shallow meadowland towards the figure of Annabel which, they saw, had just reached the holy well.

Annabel had been apprehensive at the beginning of their walk. Now, both in the ruined church and at the holy well, she was completely at peace. And Mary, when she and James joined her said an odd thing. She was sitting on the long stone seat where pilgrims sat to bathe their eyes and feet in the well water. She looked up through the stone arches of the ruined well-chapel and said, as if to herself, 'Whatever it was that frightened us last night, it didn't come from here or the church, or, I think, the ancient village. I feel completely happy.'

And Annabel, when they walked to the village dig and stood looking down at the traces of the round huts and the trays of finds in the shed nearby, agreed. 'I feel as if a weight had been lifted from me,' she said, 'I'm so happy. I'm sure we'll enjoy our holiday. And we really must go and bathe. I suppose that's where Philip's gone?'

'No. He'll still be doing the shopping and getting the papers. I did say we'd meet him in the pub at noon. Only it's that now.'

When they left the ancient village they followed the little stream back towards the sea.

'It's odd, though,' James said, 'But whatever it was, was coming from the direction of the land, from, more or less, here. Which rather goes against your feelings of peace and happiness.'

'Oh shut up, James,' Mary said, 'I'm getting bored with the subject. It was probably nothing but a trick of the light.'

The ruined church was now on their left and the sandhills in front. They could hear the sea swishing and moaning. Over the edge of the hills they could see the tip of the 'Island' jutting out between the two bays.

'There's an old German wreck out there in the smaller bay,' James said, 'Beyond the "Island" which, incidentally was, also, the site of an ancient settlement'.

'A wreck,' Mary said excitedly, 'Oh, I must see that.'

'There isn't much to see now. And what there is you can only see at low tide. But come on, perhaps we shall be in time.'

When they reached the 'Island' they saw that a small crowd had gathered in the bay below them. Annabel began to shiver. 'No,' she said firmly, 'I'm not going down there. Something awful has happened, I know it has. Why all those people, otherwise? And they are all standing so still. I'm going back to the cottage to wait for Philip.'

Mary held her arm. She could feel the cold of her flesh. 'Sure you'll be all right?' she asked, and Annabel tore herself away and ran back into the dunes, her fair hair flying out behind her.

Mary and James crossed the stream. They went up the slope of the 'Island' and looked down into the bay. They could see the rusty fangs of the German wreck, all that was left of the ship which foundered here in 1917. The sea in the bay was so low 'you could almost walk to America,' Mary said, 'three thousand miles away.' The tide, actually, was unusually low; it had been, as it were, sucked from the land. Birds were already swallowing the low waters, diving into rock pools. Oyster-catchers were running in a flock from low rock to low rock, as if they were engaged in a quarter mile race. Mussel-bound rocks, razor-edged, were deep blue in the shadows cast by the sun. Things were being uncovered that were only uncovered at very low tides like today's. The old German wreck looked like some agricultural machine left in a stubble field after harvest. A hedge of sand, bright gold in the sunlight, was about it. From where they were standing they could look directly into the wreck.

'Someone's been drowned,' Mary said in a low voice. The body was lying huddled against the brown rusting iron of the wrecked ship. It seemed to be curled round the iron stays as if, dead, it was making a desperate effort for love and warmth. The body of the young man lay very still, the flesh grey, mottled here and there with the deeper purple of bruises. It hardly looked like flesh at all. Yet both Mary and James saw the circular weals on the back which, because they were still red, stood out. 'It looks as if the body has been burnt, branded or something like that.' James said.

'You don't suppose . . . ?' Mary began and stopped.

'I don't suppose anything,' James was abrupt. 'All I said was that the body looked as if it had been branded in some way.'

Only the shape of the curled thing – it could hardly be called more – made it at all human. That and the hair that was swinging back and forth in the pool of sea water left in the sand by the rusting iron staves.

'I suppose it's a holiday-maker who went out too far.' Mary said and turned away. 'Someone should do something.' She felt suddenly sick.

'They'll come soon,' James held her tightly in his arms. 'The police and ambulance men will come. It's not just happened, he's been in the water a few hours. Probably all night, poor chap.'

'That makes it all the worse,' Mary ran back into the sand-dunes. 'I don't think I can cross the stream, James, honestly I don't.'

'But why? It's daytime, and it was almost dark when we crossed last night.'

'I know, I know,' She was impatient with him.

'But that drowned man hasn't got anything to do with what we saw. How could he?'

Mary did not answer but went on, leaving James to cross the stream in the bay alone. She went the long way round through the dunes. He waited for her and they walked back to the cottage without a word.

'Someone was drowned in the bay,' James told Philip when he got back just before lunch, 'that's why we didn't come to the pub. We'd have been late, anyway.'

'I heard it in the village,' Philip put down a laden shopping basket on the table. 'God it's hot, I'll go for a swim before lunch, I think.'

There was no doubt that Mary and Annabel were upset. Mary because of what she had seen of the dead man and Annabel because of her supernatural fears.

'Oh, don't lets talk about him,' Mary said, 'not even think of him. He's dead and gone. At least, we're alive. And how you can go swimming in the bay at such a time, Philip, I can't imagine. In any case Annabel's got the lunch ready. You won't have time, if you want to eat.'

It was so hot, in the afternoon, that they merely sat in the garden overlooking the sea and read or slept until the evening. The sound of holiday-makers and dogs barking formed a pleasant background frieze to their half-dreams.

It was dusk when Philip suggested to James that they go for a walk before supper. They jumped over the garden wall and were on the sand before the girls were aware of it. The extensive line of sand across to the farther bay where the drowned man had been discovered was now half covered by the tide. The remains of the German wreck had disappeared under water.

'I've got to go, James,' Philip said, 'I have to see if it will come again. They told me, up in the village, that this beach is haunted by something, though they didn't say what.'

'They'd tell you anything. Taking the mickey out of you.'

'But I must make certain whether we actually did see and hear anything. I've got a theory that it's connected with that old wreck out there, and the fact that the tides are abnormally low at the moment.'

James smiled, looked at his feet which were crushing the white and pink shells into the sand as he walked. 'Oh, I've given up believing in it,' he said, 'if I thought it was connected with anything, I suppose I'd put it down to the ancient village up beyond the ruined church, where they're excavating.'

'In what way?'

'Well, there must have been a blacksmith's there. At least when the primitive people became less primitive, if you see what I mean? And, as smiths were always supposed to have unusual powers, it is part of their past image photographed on to today? After all, whatever it was did seem to be red-hot as if it had recently come off an anvil.'

The sun was very near the horizon. A pearl white light was hovering over sea and land when they first heard the call for help. They stopped, listening. The call came again, faintly, out from the sea. The waves were tipped crimson from the dying sun. They looked at each other and when the cry came once more, farther away this time, Philip began to take off his shirt and shorts.

'I'm going in,' he said, 'he's out there beyond the "Island" I can hear him. I'll probably be too late but I've got to try. You stay here.'

For James it was one of those clear moments when, as it is said, 'time stands still'. In fact, afterwards he considered that time had actually gone backwards and that what once had happened was happening again. It was a kind of Serial Time experience, if that had any validity at all. But now, at least, he knew. Now everything fitted into place.

The young man he and Mary had seen in the bay, dead, this morning must have been drowned last night at about this time when he and Philip and the girls had seen the 'thing'. Now he remembered that the sea was making so much noise that none of them could have heard the man crying for help. He felt it to be absolutely certain that the cries they were now hearing were time-traces of what had happened last night. He ran after Philip, calling out. 'Don't go, don't go out there, Phil. There isn't anyone. He's dead already, come back. You're too late, come back.'

But the mirage of sound was still pulling Philip into the waves, the cries for help were siren cries from which he could not be withdrawn by any other voice. He was swimming strongly in the direction of the end of the 'Island' where the rocks turned into the next bay, that of the wrecked ship. He did not appear to hear James shouting, his eyes were set entirely on the open sea away from the land.

When James reached the water's edge he turned. It was instinctive, an act of self-preservation. He flung himself aside and down as the glowing, hissing circular object appeared at the opening into the sand dunes and, with colossal rapidity, began to cross the sand in his direction, following the shallow stream. Even as he threw himself down he was aware that whatever it was was not interested in him, but in Philip still swimming into the next bay.

He heard the wind it created and felt the cold heat of it, white-hot, when it passed into the sea and rose up, slipping, rolling at great speed on the surface of the water. There was an intolerable roar in his ears as if a savage animal was hearing its prey, about to leap upon it and devour it. From his position on the sand, he looked up and saw it springing across the calm water, hopping like a flat stone thrown in a game of ducks and drakes, and knew the meaning of the burns on the back of the drowned man.

He was entirely alone on the beach. He flung off his clothes and dashed into the sea, swimming with all his strength in the direction of Philip and the 'Island'. He was unaware that he was yelling, 'Look out, Philip, look out' as he swam. He heard Philip's cries when he was halfway to him and went on and on until he reached him, the sea like a bath of syrup about him, the screaming gulls overhead a doom. He was only just in time.

Even here, in the sea, he could smell burnt flesh and see Philip's back lacerated by the fire weals. He pulled him over and began swimming with him between his legs towards the shore. They were entirely alone in a sea tinged with Philip's blood and the savage cries of the sea birds and the last half circle of the sun miles away, like a Cyclops, menacing them.

He pulled Philip to the edge of the sand and, with the strength of exhaustion, heaved him over on his stomach and examined his back. The burns were deep and livid and running with sea water. He'd have to go for help, he couldn't move him any farther and he wasn't, then, sure whether he was alive or dead, whether he had been burnt to death or drowned before he could get to him. Before he could decide, and still mesmerised by the circular burns on his friend's back – so exactly the same as those on the drowned man earlier in the day – Philip began to come round.

'God, James, you were right,' he seemed to be saying, his hands clutching the sand in agony. 'There's no one out there. Not tonight.'

'Lie still and don't talk.'

'God, my back, my back.'

'I know, I know. I'll have to go for help. I can't move you alone. Lie still, you'll be all right.'

Philip did not answer. His head had fallen into the sand, a little saliva was coming from his mouth. James laid his shirt gently over the lacerated back, uncertain whether Philip was alive or dead, and running as hard as he could, he set off towards the cottage.

He was lucky. The life-guards on late duty in Treyarnon Bay came to his help. A doctor who lived nearby, in the first house beyond the dunes, was at home and, in a surprisingly short time Philip was in an ambulance on his way to the City Hospital, Truro.

They went down to see him the next day. He appeared to recognise them though he was still under sedation and could not speak. He was lying on his stomach, his face half turned to them. Mary put her hand on his forehead. He seemed to respond to her action with a half smile.

'Wonder he's alive,' the doctor told James, 'those burns on his back! As it is it will take time and a lot of skingrafts. But he'll come through all right. At least we've been able to do something for the pain. And he's constitutionally strong. How did it happen? I mean I'm used to drownings on the north coast, but these burns? And in the sea, too?'

'I don't really know.' It was useless to try and explain here in the hospital where everything was normal, work-a-day, where bells were ringing and nurses hurrying to and fro. The doctor was going on. 'Those weal-like burns on his back, and tracks. As if he had been run over. I suppose . . . ?'

'No. It was in the sea. I pulled him out. It wasn't a car.'

'Quite. More like a waggon wheel. Red hot before it's shrunken on to the rim, heavy and red hot.' The doctor got up and walked to the door of the small room. 'Odd thing is a man was drowned just in that bay, a day before, though he wasn't washed up till a few hours later, in fact, on the morning your friend was attacked. I know this because the body was brought down here for examination, the police weren't satisfied. He had similar burn markings on his back. Never seen the like before.'

'I know,' James said, 'I saw the body just after it was found in the same bay. I think my friend tried to save him.'

The doctor raised his eyebrows. Shock did odd things to people and it was clear to him that James was still under considerable strain. But this was talking nonsense.

'Twenty-four hours too late,' James added and left the room.

XIII

The Sacrifice

Denys Val Baker

Mark's Carn stood in a lonely world of its own – a vast landscape of Cornish Moors, cleaned almost to the granite bone by the Atlantic winds that whistle over the purple-heather cliffs. From the top, the world below – a huddle of village cottages, a church, some distant farmhouses, cliffs, sea, the smoke of a tramp steamer – all seemed doll-like, unreal. And between this lower world and the Carn stretched all the infinite mystery of the moors, vast in space, shrouded in eternal mists. Only the Carn was real, standing high on the moors, chimney stack reaching to the sky, cottage growing out of the wet ground as if it had been there since the first dawn. Here, complete, was a secret place in which anything might happen.

That's what I always thought, from that very first time when Mark and his wife Shelley took me climbing up the steep moorland path. Shelley as a girls' name always used to seem highly affected to me; but not after I met Mark's wife. Somehow it was just the right name for her – small, boyish, puck-faced, with her dark hair cut short. She walked with swift, lithe movements that might almost have been a boy's – yet she was always conscious of her almost feline femininity. Yes, Shelley was her name; it could have been no other.

I didn't know that first day that I was going to fall in love with Shelley. Or did I? And she – did she know? I wonder. The questions hover around like shadows, belonging indeed to that secret world of the Carn. For somehow, once you had climbed over the moors and stood high up, with all that doll-like world spread at your feet, you were inclined to be more emotional, more intense, supersensitive to atmosphere and feeling.

And so, in a way, perhaps there was an immediate contact between Shelley and me – only now, long after, I can't remember it. There's so much in life of that ephemeral nature, which we forget too quickly, and that is so vital in shaping our destiny. I often wonder if Shelley realised just how important our meeting was.

It was a fine, glistening June afternoon when we first went up. I'd met Mark and Shelley in St Ives, an artists' colony on the north coast of Cornwall. It's a gay, colourful place, the houses built around a tiny harbour, with blue and white fishing boats bobbing about like corks. In the little pubs by the wharf, painters and their friends gather in the evenings and argue about Picasso and Matisse and Henry Moore. It's all cheerful and stimulating, and a good way to spend an evening, if you happen to feel in the mood.

But sometimes you don't, and it was on one of these occasions that Mark and Shelley invited me out to the Carn. I was glad to get out of St Ives, sitting cramped in the back of Mark's open car, winding up the long, long hills. I was glad to feel the fresh, seaweedy air on my face, blasting away the cobwebs. I was glad to be heading upward, towards those craggy hills, reaching towards the sky.

Most of all, I suppose, I was glad to be sitting just behind Shelley, so that I could study her profile, the strong lines of her face, the way her nose tilted slightly, the gleam of white teeth between rose-red lips. She was beauty, sheer beauty, the beauty of those very hills and granite cliffs – clear, exquisite, ageless. I did not at that stage reflect about the other side of the coin – that granite is hard, the rocks cruel, the hills remote and uncaring.

We left the car just off the coast road, and walked across two fields and up the steep path that led to the Carn. When we reached the top, there was the cottage – a long, rambling, intimate sort of building that for all its remoteness suggested warmth and comfort. Inside it was all that it promised. The walls had been whitewashed and decorated with modern paintings, and along the shelves stood delicately glazed pieces of local Cornish pottery. Two or three couches, covered in richly coloured hessian, and a thick white rug in the centre gave the main room an air almost of luxury – into which, I noted at once, Shelley fitted perfectly.

I expect I was shown round the rest of the cottage – the two small bedrooms, the kitchen with its old-fashioned Cornish range, the long, low veranda room which Mark used for storing his archaeological finds – but I don't really remember. What I remember most clearly now is the three of us sitting around the big granite fireplace, drinking first tea and then bottled beer, and talking all the time. And I remember Shelley curled up on the white rug, rather as a cat, suddenly stretching herself in that same feline way, so that under her sweater surged all the hidden beauty of her living body. And I also remember how I wanted her so desperately, so irrationally, that I had to turn my head away and stare blindly into the unlit fire.

That was how it began. I became friendly with Mark and Shelley; with Mark because it was polite, with Shelley because at least it enabled me to be near to her, often. I pretended an interest I really did not share in archaeological explorations, and accompanied Mark on several little expeditions among the Penwith Hills. As a trained archaeologist, he was much in demand, and there was a certain interest in accompanying him, for he explained so much that would otherwise have been mystery. I think that side of the thing attracted Shelley, too, for a while. And we had some pleasant times, the three of us, camping out beside some trench-scarred patch of land, out of which piece by piece, we were uncovering the everyday utensils of a bygone age.

Then Shelley stopped coming, and with that, my own interest waned. I knew by now, of course, that I had fallen madly in love with her, but as yet I did not quite know what she felt. I could guess at her awareness, from an occasional exchanged glance, a sudden interrupted reverie. But – I could not be sure.

When Mark went off on his next expedition, which would keep him busy for nearly a week at the other end of Cornwall, I made up my mind to find out.

Waiting until it was nearly dusk, I caught a bus from St Ives to the nearest crossroads, and then walked a mile or so over the fields and up to the Carn. There was a light burning in the dusk, which helped to guide me; though I was so familiar by now with the track that I felt I could find the way blindfold (and indeed there was a curious, faint aroma associated with the Carn, as if, even amid so much fresh air and clean winds, there remained the musty tint of old granite and ancient mortar. And perhaps, who knew, what memories of past occupants? For up at the Carn, one actually felt the belief that anything was possible).

Just as I reached the porch of the cottage, the door swung open. Shelley stood framed in the doorway, the light behind lending a tinge of fire to her ghostly shape.

'Hullo.'

'Hullo. . . .'

Somehow it was all said, in those two simple words, in the passive way she stood aside, in the positive way I strode in. For a time we stood passing conventional remarks, almost as if others, or at least a third person – Mark – might be present. All the while, I remember, Shelley walked restlessly about the room, and again I was reminded of the rootless, apparently purposeless way in which a cat will pad about – until suddenly it freezes, silently, and pounces.

'Can you imagine what it is like to live here?' said Shelley abruptly, swinging round. She stood in the centre of the room, dark mystery against the blazing-white rug. She had somehow become like the hills, the Carn, remote and complete: a world of her own. It was impossible to associate her with Mark, with anyone; she so obviously belonged to no one.

'At first I didn't mind, the solitude, the loneliness. It was new, and in a way, exciting. Then I began to notice things – about the place, I mean. There was a feeling – I can't think of any other word. A primitive sort of feeling – do you know what I mean? Something to do with age, the past, what's buried in the stone Mark says. . . .'

Shelley paused suddenly and looked at me with round, wide eyes. Large, luminous, green cat's eyes.

I never knew what Mark said, nor did I care. I think perhaps she had begun the sentence without intending to finish it, knowing that the spark would light the bonfire.

I took her in my arms. She was all flesh, soft warm flesh that melted towards me. Her face bent towards me, smiling, the eyes bright, the teeth parted. I felt in her a surge of passion against my own desire. As we kissed, I imagined that I encompassed in my embrace all of her, the whole mystery, forgetting that no woman was ever so captured, and least of all this woman.

And yet . . . How much do we delude ourselves? Even now, when I remember, it is the light I look for, rather than the dark. When I think of Shelley, it is of the girl I knew in those precious few days – a taut, vital girl, wearing blue jeans and an old fisherman's jersey, with a garland of sea pinks wound into her hair. She was, to me, beauty incarnate. As we wandered about the lonely hills, the sun beating down, the air humming with heat, I marvelled and rejoiced at her presence. To feel her hand in mine, was to feel warmth and passion, ecstasy. Swept up, consumed by such emotions, it was impossible to think of anything else: Mark, for instance.

Does that seem inhuman? Somehow, that world of Shelley's and mine was inhuman. You could almost feel it in the atmosphere all round. Something aloof, something pitiless. The Carn was desolation, a place of lost souls – to exist there you had to snatch, hold hard to happiness.

'Are you happy?'

It was a question I asked ceaselessly, and it was never answered.

'Why analyse? What is happiness?'

And Shelley would look at me with her deep, sea-green eyes. I used to tease her about them.

'They are mermaid's eyes. You have come up from the sea.'

'Perhaps I have.'

Meditative, she had a cool, quiet beauty. It was difficult to believe that fire and passion lay below. Looking at her, I could seldom resist touching her to prove to myself that she still lived and breathed – and the touch was itself like fire.

Then, of course, I saw only one Shelley. I did not know there were others, each one unique, complete, and indestructible. Perhaps that was the trouble: one could not accept the fact, one could not resist trying to destroy all those other, shadowy figures. Until at last. . . .

During those few days, Shelley and I were lovers. There were no pretences, no half-measures. For a time, the rest of the world did not exist. We made love, we laughed, we wandered, we sat by the fire in the evenings. It was idyllic; I can never forget it. I cannot believe, even now, that it had no meaning for Shelley. Why, I can still remember her slow smile, the way she rested her head on my shoulder, or some other unexpected touch of affection, as she passed me in the cottage. But then, that is how all lovers remember, isn't it? A sweet memory.

On the fifth day Shelley sat up in bed, shook herself, then ran her hands through her hair, as if to brush away cobwebs.

'Darling, you'll have to hurry and clear out. Mark's due back this morning.'

Even put baldly like that, the sentence does not convey the full impact as I felt it, that morning. It was spoken so naturally, with such lack of doubt, that it was almost impossible for me to speak in answer. But – what – why? How could any phrase of mine seem anything but humiliating?

I got up without a word, dressed, and went downstairs. When a few minutes later Shelley came down. I was wandering restlessly about, trying to compose myself. It seemed to me that she could not possibly comprehend how much she had hurt me.

'Shelley,' I began desperately, 'what are we going to do? I mean. . . .'

She went and curled up on one of the settees.

'Give me a cigarette, darling, will you?'

I handed her one. She lit it and puffed up a cloud of smoke. As if mesmerised, I watched the little cloud rising up until, almost imperceptively, it vanished.

'Darling, don't be a bore.'

'But, Shelley. I mean. . . .'

I floundered. It was hopeless. At length I spread my hands out in a gesture of despair.

'Don't these past few days mean anything?'

Shelley took a slow puff at her cigarette.

'Of course, they do, silly. It's been lovely. But the fact is even lovely things come to an end. And I'm expecting Mark back at eleven o'clock. Don't you think, under the circumstances, it would be tactful for you not to be here?'

I gave way then to humiliation.

'But – when will I see you again?'

She shrugged. Sitting felinely on the couch, Shelley shrugged.

'I don't know, darling. But we'll fix something. . . .'

I think it was then that I first began to hate her.

The next few weeks were horrible. Despite myself, Shelley had become an obsession. I could not keep away from her, even though – indeed, immediately – a part of me had recognised the folly and hopelessness of it all.

It was not only a lingering desire to be near her. There was also a morbid fascination. I wanted to be able to be there when Mark was there, and to think secretly – ah, little do you know.

And more than that – well, perhaps, you might say, I had some queer intuitive foreknowledge of what was to come.

And what was that? How can I best describe the process of events? It was like the stitches in some old tapestry, inserted thread by thread, pattern by pattern. Altogether, the events spread over a year, perhaps a little more. I remained friendly with Mark and Shelley, a constant visitor. Every now and then Mark went away. And each time he went away . . .

Well, in St Ives there was a wide assortment of attractive men – painters, sculptors, writers, sometimes a fisherman. Perhaps it sounds incredible, but I witnessed all this, because I made it my business to follow to the bitter end my betrayal. During that year, Shelley had several lovers, of whom I was merely the first. She was, in fact, a natural nymphomaniac, completely self-possessed and totally unconcerned with anyone's feeling save her own. Thus equipped, she was able, adroitly, to manage a number of affairs, each one of which, I do not doubt, appeared to her chosen companion as something unique and wonderful.

And Mark? Was he really so unperceptive, so stupid, that he never noticed? Did he ever wonder how his attractive wife spent her time during his absence? Did he, in fact, suspect? About that I did not know. I wondered, I tried to guess, but I could not be sure. My very curiosity prompted a new interest on my part in Mark, and I tended to spend a good deal of time in his company. His attitude, apparently, was as friendly as ever. A big, rather shy man, with a reflective and guarded manner, he was a difficult person to pin down. Indeed, I often felt, exasperated, that if I were to ask him point blank: Do you realise your wife has deceived you not once but many times? – he would have looked at me cautiously and said slowly, 'Well, I'll have to think about that.'

Rereading that paragraph, I am conscious of my failure to give any sort of clear picture of Mark. And yet, in a way, he was the rock around which the pieces revolved. Despite all that happened, Mark was always Mark, pursuing his occupation, living intermittently at the Carn; and Shelley was always his wife. Looking back, I can see there a clue to the whole thing. In a way it was Mark's very solidity, perhaps his stubborn acceptance, that provoked Shelley into fresh outbreaks – and yet, tenuously, held her captive. If Mark had been different; if I had been different; if any one of her lovers had been a stronger, or even weaker character – if Shelley herself had not been Shelley! But then . . .

Sometimes I accompanied Mark on short explorations in the Penwith Hills. There was Chyauster Settlement, an old Celtic site, where you could follow the outlines of ancient encampments. And farther along the coast there was a deep pit at Gwithian in which unfamiliar pieces of pottery and other old utensils had been uncovered. Watching the reverent way in which Mark handled these, the real excitement in his usually unemotional face, I gained some clue to his inner character. I learned slowly that a part of him – perhaps all, who knows? – lived in this Celtic past, this world of primitive, yet cunning people who lived by different gods, different values.

One day Mark took me up Trencrom Hill, a great bare plateau, spattered with huge boulders.

'This is where the ancient Druids used to practise their rites. Terrible rites . . . yet in a way beautiful.'

I watched Mark curiously. His face had an almost tender expression. I laughed uneasily.

'I can almost imagine you as one of the priests.'

'Can you?'

He looked around slowly. It was a bleak, lonely place, haunted by unimaginable ghosts. It was, in fact, very like the Carn.

'Two thousand years ago this place was alive. The priests came up that path, then they formed around the big stone. Fires were lit. Men carried in the sacrifice. There was the smell of myrrh and incense.' He paused. 'And blood.'

I looked around. I felt a shiver of fear.

'What was the sacrifice?'

Mark stared at the flat stone, now covered with moss and weeds. It was not difficult to imagine the scene – the flames, the writhing figure.

'A woman,' he said shortly.

I found it difficult to forget that day, that visit. Every time I visited the Carn after that, I remembered Trencrom. And looking round I thought: this is the same, this belongs to that world. In my mind's eye I saw the priests coming up the hillside in their long berobed procession. Priests! Priests of darkness, rather. And yet, the very hint of evil and devilment held its own fascination.

I began to study the subject. I got one or two books out of the library. One writer described, among other pagan rites, the Black Mass. It was a vivid, excellent description, horrifying, yet fascinating. I was not surprised, reading on, to find that some of the customs had lingered in Cornwall. Cornwall, this brooding land of ancient ghosts, flaked with ghoulish memories, was the home of all that was mysterious and inexplicable.

Up at the Carn, I would talk for hours to Mark. My interest was towards the dramatic, the sensational. I became far more emotional and excited than Mark, who retained something of the scientist's attitude. So I suppose it was my influence, really, that aroused Shelley's interest. I think, too, she was bored, bored with her succession of secret lovers, with her pursuit of pleasure. Secret that is, one assumed, from Mark. Almost everyone else seemed to know. And yet, in a curious way, there was the feeling that the situation, intangible, almost unreal, could continue indefinitely, perhaps for ever.

'These Druids and their performances sound fun,' said Shelley one day, curled up on the sofa, smoking.

'Fun?' said Mark. 'I'd hardly call it that.'

‘Perhaps,’ I ventured, ‘if one uses a little imagination. . . .’

‘Mark hasn’t any.’ Shelley’s green eyes seemed to narrow, as she contemplated some future scene. ‘I say. . . .’ Into her voice crept the lilt of excitement, and her lips pouted – at once she was vivid and alive, as she was when she captured men’s eyes, hearts, bodies, and souls. ‘What about having a party here at the Carn – a sort of pagan party?’

Well, it was her own suggestion. That at least I can vouch for. I wonder though, sometimes, whether words are put into our mouth by – other forces? Or even, other minds?

‘We could dress up.’ Shelley was bright with enthusiasm. ‘The St Ives crowd would love it. Think what Rudi would look like as an old priest – and Elly. And Vernon and Max, and Perrys. . . .’

She elaborated, weaving fantasies that caught at her imagination. Gradually, even Mark took to the idea. A sort of Ancient Britons’ party at the Carn. Yes, it wasn’t a bad idea.

It was not a bad idea at all. It had verve, originality, and a sort of morbid attraction. Behind the jovial conception of dressing up, having long beards, wearing costumes, lay a secret curiosity. Celtic rites – black magic – pagan rituals . . . ? The art students of St Ives, the painters and their mistresses, the fringe of that crowd – everyone caught excitedly at the new bubble. By the time the date of the party was fixed, it seemed that half of St Ives would be coming.

And on the night itself, that weird, unreal night, the lights of cars streaming out along the coast road seemed never ending as they climbed up the hill and parked on the grass verge below the Carn. I counted nearly twenty as I stood down there holding a storm lantern to help the guests across the bracken slopes of the moor. Everyone was dressed up, of course, though not always exactly in the correct period. They made a bizarre group, as they wended in single file across the moor, and up to that remote cottage where Mark and Shelley waited, in a room garlanded with honeysuckle and heather, and lit with candles and flares – while outside, on a plateau just above the cottage, stood the sacrificial stone, a flat white slab which Mark and I between us, had rolled down the hillside and polished clean. But of that, for the moment, we said nothing.

Inside, there was hot punch and plenty of other drinks waiting for the visitors. Mark and Shelley made good hosts, passing round continuously and ladling out fresh cupfuls of the hot, invigorating punch. I remember watching them for a moment, standing in the shadow of the door – and for a moment wondering, hesitating. There was something intrinsically honest and good about Mark. How had he been drawn to a woman like Shelley? Was there something in her that he saw, that no one else saw? How could there be? Had *I* not known her too, as intimately as one can know any human being? Wasn't she, indeed, as she seemed: the eternal, feline, faithless, utterly pitiless cat?

Then I got swept away into a chattering group. There was Rudi, the sculptor, a lion of a man with grandiose gestures, majestic, wild ideas; his wife Elly gypsy-like, with long earrings and sharp brown eyes, curiously kind and gentle; Mervyn, a painter, Welsh, a true Celt, with his soft, musical voice; and Tom and Vernon and Angela and Guido and all the other gay, light-hearted visitors. Their punch glasses emptied, were filled, emptied, were filled. Soon the chatter of voices rose up in a crescendo of jovial sound. Before long, someone wound up the old horn gramophone. The floor was cleared, and couples began dancing.

I stood outside. It was dark and still. Somewhere far away an owl hooted. The moon rode uneasily behind shifting clouds. On such a night, many centuries ago, perhaps others had stood here? I hesitated, uncertain, and looked across at the white gleam of the distant stone.

When I returned inside, the party had become wilder. Under the influence of the punch, people were becoming what they were, rather than what they liked others to think of them. Rudi and Elly began doing a wild Apache dance. Soon they would be shouting at each other, perhaps fighting. Vernon and Guido, who hardly spoke to each other normally, now chattered happily in a corner as if free from some terrible bondage. Husbands and wives danced for a time, then inexplicably became mixed up; the amorous patterns become confused.

But somehow that night – perhaps because it was *that* night – Shelley caught the eye, as vividly as if she were flame in the dark. She wore a tight-fitting garment, made from old fishing nets painted with phosphorescent green – so that in the candlelight, swirling into a dark corner, she seemed to glitter and glow. I had never seen her look so sensual and lovely, so desirable, so mesmerising. As never before, I was drawn to her as a moth to the light.

Despite all my resolutions, I found myself dancing with her, holding her close, the feel of her awakening age-old memories. For a moment, too, I had the illusion that she melted towards me, that she sensed my feelings and shared them, that we could recapture those brief lovers' days.

'Shelley . . . Shelley . . .' I whispered in her ear. 'You look lovely tonight. . . .'

She held her head back and smiled; her eyes shone like the sea at night.

But she didn't reply. She just laughed, a silent, solitary laugh, in which I could not share. We whirled round and round, and the room seemed to turn with us, so that I was hardly conscious of the other dancers, or even of the room itself – as if perhaps we were whirling into space itself. I wish we had. Oh, I wish we had!

I was conscious of a curious pause, a momentary silence, and then there was laughter, all round me. Pulling myself together, I found that I was dancing on my own, that Shelley had twisted and whirled away out of my arms into the waiting arms of another dancer. And I was left standing, looking quite foolish, to the amused glances of those watching.

It was like that all the evening – as if Shelley had become possessed by some sly, whipping devil, challenging her to flaunt herself as never before. Drunk she was, no doubt, but as much with bravado as from the punch. For the men she danced with were past lovers, each of them linked to her in some subterranean way, as I had been linked to her – as, I knew, I still was, even though love might be hate. Is not hate love?

And if we felt like that, each of us, what did Mark feel? I looked for him sometimes out of the corners of my eyes. Once I saw him, bent over the punch bowl. With his false beard, he looked indeed like some priest of old. He seemed fascinated, as if he were reading some strange fortune in the rust-coloured surface.

I saw him once again, at a later stage, when the dancing had become wild and furious. He was leaning against the door watching, his eyes a little bright, on his face a faint smile. As Shelley flamed by, I saw his eyes rest upon her, and I wondered how he felt; if he felt as I did, deep down within. But in fact, the look on his face hardly changed; if anything, it lightened with a curious sort of tenderness, as if – as if – well, I could not somehow put it into words. Pity? Understanding? Sympathy? Love . . . ?

Momentarily, I was exasperated. I felt more comradeship with Mervyn, who worshipped Shelley blindly, with Vernon, who I had seen in tears over his rejection – with any of the dozen or so lovers gathered here, all possessed by demons of love and hate, hate and love. At least their emotions were real and vivid, whereas

Mark's – well, I suppose I felt a sort of frustration, because still I did not know, and could not tell.

It was in the early hours of the morning that the party moved to its ordained climax. Somehow word had got round about the weird edifice on the hill outside. Gradually we gathered at the doorway, singing lustily, waving our glasses, and then plunged out and up on to the hillside.

What a beautiful night it was! Still and clear, with a moon riding high above trailing clouds. In such a light, the hill, the Carn, the whole scene took on a strange, medieval, atmosphere. This was no longer our world. It was as if the party had been a transitory preparation for stepping from one generation into another. Now, in the silvery light, and wearing the ancient costumes with the cowls raised to add to the mystery, everyone looked as if he belonged, indeed, to those bygone centuries.

In the weird light, momentarily silenced by the mysterious nature of the scene, we all became quiet, so that the shuffling sound of our feet could be heard, eerily, as we padded over toward the raised, white stone. Nobody quite knew what we were going to do; yet, almost by instinct, we were drawn into a sort of ritual. Without anyone speaking a word, we all gathered in a half-circle around the gleaming-white stone.

Then one of the hooded men stepped forward. I recognised Mark's voice as he explained briefly the nature of the pagan rites which we were now to perform in mock fun, the meaning of each act, the importance of the sacrifice – the symbolism of blood.

Was he drunk like the rest of them? I often wonder. His voice did not sound blurred; indeed, it echoed beautifully on the night air. He spoke with assurance and confidence, like one who knew exactly what he had to do.

When he had finished speaking, and suddenly produced from the folds of his robes the long, gleaming sacrificial knife which I had often picked up in his room, there was a gasp among the onlookers – just such a gasp as one could imagine filling the night air in the times of pagan Celts.

Mark smiled and laid the knife along the edge of the long, flat stone. Then he turned, as if waiting; at the cue, we all turned.

And there was Shelley, pale, glowing, advancing across the grass, her figure even more beautiful, even more ghostly in the faint moonlight.

There was a murmur, then a swelling cry of acclamation. Here was the sacrifice. Perhaps at the sight, something stirred in all our blood and bones, for we all began shouting and crying out, and the mass of cowled figures gathered nearer to the stone. It seemed to me that while we were half-pretending to behave in a pagan way – yet, deep down, we really were experiencing those ancient feelings.

I looked up at the sky. As I had imagined, the great clouds had billowed in, as so often they did with the turn of the tide. Now they bore down thunderously upon the waning moon. In a few moments, the brilliant light would be no more; the darkness would have us for its own.

Mark began chanting some incantation. As he did so, smiling softly, catlike, Shelley climbed up on to the platform. She was very drunk. Her body performed movements, her face smiled, while all the time her deep, hidden being was given up to strange ghosts of a dream world. At least this is how it occurred to me, and how I like to remember.

At a sign from Mark, Shelley stepped up and climbed on to the long slab. With delicate grace, she stretched herself out and lay still and glowing, a shimmering figure of beauty.

It was an unforgettable moment. It was entirely primitive, of the blood and the darkness enhancing the whiteness of the stone, the knowledge that well-nigh perfect flesh was lying in offering – beauty incarnate, yet devil-made – gleaming and glowing, yet radiating Shelley's hidden, perhaps satanic nature – the woman that was harlot, the cat that was cruel, the devil that was rampant in us all.

It was the moment, too, of decision. I looked around at the hooded figures: this one perhaps Rudi, this one Vernon, that one Guido – standing back a little from the stone, Mark. There was something at once strange and yet fitting in that we, her lovers, should be gathered around that white sacrificial stone. I looked across for the last time at Mark, wondering. . . .

And then with a weird sense of timing the great clouds reached the moon, swept over its gleaming face, and plunged the hillside into deep and fearful darkness. There was a momentary, terrible stillness. Then out of the night came a wild cry, the like of which none of us had ever heard before – dying away even as it sounded on the still air.

At once, all was confusion. Hooded forms moved frantically about; there were cries and counter-cries. Fear spread like a fire among us. Somebody struck a match which flickered out at once. Others fumbled their way back to the cottage to bring lights. At last two of them returned, holding aloft a storm lantern.

The scene that met our eyes was the terrrible, final one. On the long white slab Shelley still lay, but now there was a curious stillness about her. Protruding from her breast, still quivering, was the long sacrificial knife. And over her perfect whiteness, with the awful inevitability of a deed done, bright-red blood flowed unquenched on to the white stone and dripped down into the dark earth. The sacrifice had been made.

I have tried, inadequately, to capture the atmosphere of that evening, because in a curious way the atmosphere was everything. The Carn, the strange silence of the hills, the moonlight, the loneliness – these things as much as the drink and the pagan imitations, were responsible for the mood. What that mood was I can only hazard. That it did not belong to our normal, sophisticated world, I am sure. We were all of us caught up by the primitive unknown; our very bodies, as Shelley herself revealed in her behaviour, were possessed by some spirits of old. In such an atmosphere, so stripped of convention and falseness, is it not likely that primeval urges, primitive emotions, would have their way?

It seems a long time ago now, though it is but a few years really. You may remember the case – a difficult one, indeed, for any jury to decide. With so many 'interested parties' present, it was difficult, and in fact proved impossible, to say whose hand murdered Shelley. There were no fingerprints on the knife. No one could say for certain that they had seen the deed done. Some suspicion naturally was turned towards Mark, for in such cases the husband is always suspect. Yet his very real grief, his complete breakdown at the time – these things did not suggest guilt. And though he was brought to trial, no one was very surprised when he was acquitted.

I least of all. For it had become evident to me, even before the night of the party, that Mark loved Shelley with an infinite, unalterable love. I shall never forget his look of tenderness that night, in which there was something so pure that it almost compensated for Shelley's behaviour. At that moment, I must confess, Shelley's fate hovered in the balance, if only because of the very strength of her husband's love.

But then – I hated her. And sometimes, don't you think, hate is even stronger than love? It can make a man do anything, especially on the spur of the moment – even murder.

XIV

The Ghost at the Old Ford

C. C. Vyvyan

The river has ugly moods and cruel ones. It is not only a fairway for ships, a setting for pleasure-parties, a refuge for wading birds and a place of meditation for the solitary. It can be threatening, dangerous, even fatal, as it proved to be for a certain old mender of roads when he took a chance on one dark night of winter. The tide will wait on no man and William-John Ivey should have remembered his school history book and the tale of King Canute.

The Old Landlord would often speak of the ancient ford, a place where, according to local legend, a man could cross the river on horseback at low water, some eighty or a hundred years ago. Once, at the very spot which he had described to me, I waded out at dead low tide as far as the middle of the narrow channel and there I stood on the hard bottom in about a foot of water, facing the mud bank on the other shore and afraid to climb it. The ford is never used today, although the old men love to talk about it still, relating tales of those who rode home that way, some of them sober and others market-merry, crossing on horseback from one muddy shore to the other. Whether it ever really did exist as a recognised passage I cannot tell. The whole thing may just as well have been an old man's fancy, some tale for telling 'between the lights'.

As for William-John Ivey and Mrs Lamley, did they ever really meet in that strange fashion or was her own part in that encounter due to an attack of indigestion? Indeed I cannot say. How the Cornishman does long, when he lives in the tropics, for one good day of the soft west-country rain. We, in our twentieth century climate of incandescent publicity, are sometimes truly thankful for the survival of a little mystery. I can only relate the story as I heard it.

Why it should have been a 'foreigner' and not one of ourselves who was summoned by the ghost of that old man to search for his body by the ancient ford, no one ever could explain. It is hardly likely that his thoughts should have turned to Mrs Lamley in those last moments when he was struggling with mud and water. Yet things do happen like that sometimes, things past all believing, and when they happen so there is nothing more to be said.

Did we not travel six hundred miles through the Arctic solitudes and see only a single caribou, standing on the muskeg at dawn between our two camp beds, while we peered at him for a fleeting moment through our mosquito-bars? And then, after we had boarded the tourist steamer at the Fort, did we not hear that caribou had been seen in their thousands by those sedentary tourists who rested on the deck of the S.S. *Yukon?* Did not Saul go seeking the asses of his father Kish and return home with a kingdom? And did not Little Claus begin the story with his single horse while Big Claus had four, and did he not end it with a whole herd of cattle after throwing Big Claus in a sack to the bottom of the river? It is a strange world, my masters.

So here, in all its strangeness, is the ghost story of the old ford, of Mrs Lamley reigning in the ancient home of the Menhinnicks and of William-John Ivey, stone-breaker in his youth, trimmer of hedges in his middle-age and, at the time of the tragedy that befell him, the spryest septuagenarian in Churchtown.

The strangest thing in the story is, of course, the fact that Mrs Lamley was a 'foreigner'. Yet even that fact is not the beginning of the story, we must go farther back in order to explain the extreme novelty of Mrs Lamley in her surroundings and in the eyes of her neighbours, a novelty which was, in such conditions, almost criminal. We must go back to the history of the Menhinnick family who had owned and inhabited the Manor for two hundred and fifty years. They were the family in whose honour this ditty had long ago been written:

Sometimes they sings, sometimes they prays,
Sometimes they worship God;
But on the night in question
They stole a head of cod.

Throughout the ages the Menhinnick family had produced not only men of piety but also men of wit and men of wisdom, and nearly all those ancestral figures were men of valour in their own circle, if not of actual renown in national affairs, while some at any rate, as it would appear from the ancient rhyme, were common or garden rogues. Among all these, however, never a single one had come back from the other world to disturb the peace of his descendants, nor was there ever a ghostly presence within the Manor until the reign of Mrs Lamley.

When the last of the Menhinnicks lay dying they had discussed the situation in the Seven Bells.

'Squire's a-sinkin,' reported Joe, the gardener. 'He's took weth information of the kittens an ulsters.'

'Yes, shure nuff,' chimed in Ernie Borgwitha, the smith, 'Doctor he come up my place this mornin to give the wife a bottle of physic like, an 'e sez to me 'e sez, "Squire's fine and waik an 'e may slip through our hands any minnut". That's what Doctor sez.'

'The old Manor wean't be itself weth no Menhinnick living theare,' added Chuggy Pill. 'I mind me granfaather tellin me theare was Menhinnicks livin up Menhinnick ever since the days of Solomon, and *he* was a wise man ef ever theare was one.'

Chuggy, being the only bachelor in the bar parlour, looked around him with a fighting air, as if he were waiting for some one to challenge this speech and then, after a long silence, he said:

'Mind you, I doan't knaw as I hold weth Solomon havin all they conkerbines. Simmen to me one wife's is more'n enough for any plain man.'

'Tes a whisht job, that's av it,' said the landlord, who seldom spoke except to pour oil on troubled waters, which manoeuvre always took the form of echoing the majority opinion in any discussion. He spread both thumbs sideways in a deprecating gesture of finality and then poured himself out another pint. 'Theare ded always *belong* to be Menhinnicks livin up Menhinnick,' he added in an aggrieved voice, as if he resented the action of Providence in planning to remove such an essential landmark from the local world.

Within the week Squire was dead and buried and within the year that ancient Manor was put up to auction. Mrs Lamley bought it and no one had ever heard of Mrs Lamley, who was supposed to have come from Yorkshire, and on the day when she arrived to take possession there was the most severe thunderstorm that had taken place in the district within the memory of living man.

'Foreboding oal weather I do call it,' Joe had said in the morning, 'like-as-if somethin terrible was going to come.'

And his saying was always remembered.

However, nothing terrible did happen, only Mrs Lamley settled in without delay and began to work the Home Farm herself, like any bailiff, despite the fact that she was up in years and weighed close on nine-score. Joe and the others eyed her proceedings darkly.

'She've got a passel o new-fangled notions that no one ever heerd tell on avore,' he announced one evening. And the others all nodded their heads in assent and added in a chorus: 'She doan't belong to we.'

Ernie Borgwitha added his quota: 'She wean't come to no good, mark my words, boys.' And all the boys of fifty and sixty and seventy years nodded their heads in solemn assent and Chuggy Pill declared that 'Menhinnick doan't belong to have foreigners messin' around,' and the landlord, seeing no cause for intervention in such general harmony, poured himself another pint. And Mrs Lamley continued to put into practice her belief in mass production and labour-saving machines.

After fifteen years she was still a 'foreigner' to all her neighbours, for all unknown to herself those 'new-fangled' notions, which were really nothing more than the basic ideas of her everyday life, had been like a veil or screen between herself and the people and their country. She remained unaware of the real Cornwall. She knew nothing of the magic that hid in the very boulders rooted on the moorland and the hills, she had never explored those hidden valleys where blackthorn, silvered over with lichen, grows awry in fantastic forms, she had learned nothing of the secrets guarded by headlands that have looked down on scenes of wreckage and lost mariners. Even the ancient Manor would always hide its memories from her.

From the first moment of her arrival she trod heavily about her new little world in Cornwall, setting down her feet in foursquare fashion and putting full weight on each, nor did she ever allow herself to suspect that there were deeper things in Cornish minds and Cornish memories than she could fathom. She never won understanding of the thoughts of those about her and whenever one of her men would speak of 'what we belong to do' or 'what we don't belong to do,' or would quote some cryptic saying of the 'old ancient ones', a saying born of their perennial, racial wisdom, she would brush their words aside quickly as if they had been a cobweb in her path.

Then at last there came a summons, a message, a whisper, call it what you will, from the unknown, a something that Mrs Lamley, for all her nine-score weight and her material preoccupations, could not entirely ignore.

She went to bed one night at her accustomed hour after a full day that had been occupied, like all her other days, with things she could touch and see. In spite of all her drive and determination in matters concerning crops and tractors, pedigree herds, improvement of stock and such-like things, Mrs Lamley was, in her own home, crassly self-indulgent. Her rooms were overheated, her table was overladen with out-of-season foods, her indoor staff had been trained to minister in silence to her comfort as if they were automatons; between the enjoyment of hard work and the indulgence in every luxury that money and thought could supply she, passed through her days and weeks and years with never any pause for reverie.

Even in her childhood, so she would often assure her friends and acquaintances, she never had indulged in day-dreams nor wasted time in building castles in Spain and now, in middle age, it was too late for her to enter the world of imagination. She had probably never even heard of Robert Browning and it never would have occurred to her, even under the experience of a ghostly encounter, to 'greet the unseen with a cheer'. To everything that she met in her pathway she would give due attention, but hitherto only the tangible things had appeared in that self-appointed and carefully regulated course.

On a certain evening she had dined on turtle soup and oysters having been brought up the river from Porth Navas by special messenger; roast chicken had followed and then peach trifle, after which, having sipped her coffee and cherry brandy, she had read a detective story for half an hour. Then she went upstairs to bed, taking with her for perusal in the early morning the current number of *Farmer and Stock-breeder*. She got into her four-poster and settled down in the feather tye and then put out the light but she could not get to sleep. This was a most unusual occurrence. She always professed a certain contempt for people who complained of sleeping badly. She tossed and turned and shifted the pillows and when at last she lay still and began to feel a drowsy calm stealing over her, she became aware of an old man sitting on the foot of her bed.

He had a long white beard, his hat was pulled down a little over his eyes and all his clothes were dripping. His face was strange to her. Although her blinds were down and her shutters closed she could see him as plainly as if there were daylight in the room.

She guessed at first that it was one of those queer village people playing a trick on her and she began to tell the unwelcome visitor, in very plain terms, what she thought of him. She had always looked upon the Cornish folk as strange and unaccountable, nor had she made any secret of this opinion. The old man never moved.

Then she sat up in bed and made a pass at him with one hand to push him off.

Whenever she told the tale she would repeat that gesture with her enormous arm and as a matter of fact it was a gesture better fitted to fell an ox than to test the substance of a ghost. She made this movement just as if she were boxing some one's ears and then, so she always declared, both hand and arm to her surprise went right through the old man as if he were smoke.

She then turned on her light but she could not see the intruder, so she got up and searched every corner of the room. She could find nothing unusual anywhere so she returned to bed and put out the light and immediately he appeared again, sitting on the foot of her bed, his hat still pulled down over his eyes and water dripping on to his beard. She turned on the light again, and again she made a thorough search of the room and after repeating this a third time, and then reading for an hour or so, she put out her light and tried to sleep. But all night long her rest was very broken and every time that she opened her eyes in the darkness she saw the old man sitting on her bed as clearly as if the sun were shining into her shuttered room.

At this point it is fitting that Joe Trebolsue should continue the story, since he took the most active part in the rest of the proceedings.

The cottage of the Trebolsues, with its thatched roof and white-washed walls, was a solitary building some half a mile below Churchtown, standing beside a stream that flowed into a small creek of the river, in a deserted hollow of the land. This cottage was the nearest human dwelling to that point where the creek joined the main channel and that channel was now partly silted up with mud washed down from the high country where once upon a time there had been tin mines at work, where now granite quarrying was the occupation of the people. At low tide the channel here became very narrow and it was at this point that, according to the legend, horsemen used to cross the river. One or two people declared that it was still fordable at that particular spot but no one living had tried it.

'Twas atween the lights ef you take my meaning,' Joe would always begin, 'twadden dark an twadden yet light when I was waked up by a whisht lil oal sound outside the door, like the tappin of a yaffle an the screechin of a whitneck all to once. So I took me life-preserver, what me faather always took when poachin of a night an his faather took avore him. Grandfaather always used to say it was better for company than any musket, an he cud a laid out David an Goliath weth one blow ef he'd a mind to. Howsomever there's a mort o power in a leaden knob an the whale-bone is suent like when goin through the air. No, I caan't say as how I ever used it meself on any person but many's the time of a dark night when I wud pass me hand under the pillow to feel it an I'd say to the wife: "H'em theare all right. Doan't ee be afeard me dearr." Women is always nervous creatures at night.

'Well, I took up me life-preserver as I was sayin an put on me clothes an went down over stairs and theare was a lil boy knockin on the door an cryin. "Granfer's down in the water," he sez. "He cudden get his legs out."

'Twas pore Kezia's boy from across the river and simmen like the old man was late comin home from town, market-merry I spawse, an he thot he wud cross the ford where the old-ancient ones belonged to ride over when he got half ways across hisself the mud caught him an he went under. The boy he got frighted an he come up over the fields to look for we.'

There was always a pause here, as there should be in a good narrative when one approaches the crisis, a pause for appreciatively chewing the cud of facts delivered, for refilling glasses and for anticipating of what is to come. Then Joe continued:

'A-course I went up an told the wife what had happened an said to her to bide in the bed an not be afeared o nithin while I was gone, an then I went to the Manor an knocked up the maidens and sent in word to the Mistress what had happened and then she sends out her orders. "Tell Joe," she sez, "to get the boat to once an all the men an drag the river an I'll be down theare beside ee in a few minnuts."

'O course I knawed better'n that. The Mistress never was one for early risin nor yet for doin wethout her mait. Ef the laast trump was to sound in her crowst-time she'd finish her bite I reckon before she answered up. Anyways we went down to the ford an we dragged the river forth and back, me an Chuggie an Ernie an haalf a dozen more. The tide was maakin an you cudden see no channel, for the water was lickin up they mud flats till it came in close under the oak trees on one side an the other.

'We dedden catch up nawthen but crabs an oyster-shells an sea-weed. An then aafter a brae while we heerd the car hootin an theare it was a-tearin down the lane an the Missus she come down over the rocks to we an stood on the edge of the water in er great rubber boots an started givin orders. She's a rare hand for givin orders an sharp's the word for all when she do spaik, we do all knaw that.

'An just at that very moment Chuggy he sez to me: "Joe," he sez, "we've catched un, heave un in boy?" We all heaved together an up come Granfer Ivey. His legs was doubled under him but he was setting up like-as-ef he was livin, weth his hat on his head an the water drippin from it on to his white beard. An he an the Mistress were glaazin pon one nother like, just as ef they was long-lost brothers but they dedden spaik nary a word, neether one of them.'

I believe that Joe's story was told and retold scores of times in the Seven Bells, whenever there was a stranger there to listen or when the regular clients were in the mood for another rendering of the well-known tale. Many a time have I heard it from his own lips while I sat on his garden wall and he stood beside his cabbages, leaning on his spade. Yet I never heard Joe himself make any reference to that apparition in Mrs Lamley's bedroom, although the story of the ghost soon got around and was circulated freely in the district, sometimes just as I have told it and sometimes with embellishments added by the narrator. And I never heard Mrs Lamley's version from her own lips until one winter evening when I was dining at Menhinnick together with several neighbours who were occupied in farming or in market gardening.

We were all feeling overfed and sleepy as we sat round the fire after dinner. We were drinking crême-de-menthe and our hostess kept passing round a large box of marrons glacés. Presently she lit a cigar and, in order no doubt to relieve the silence and enliven the company, she told the ghost story, very much as I have told it as regards the part of it that concerned her own two visions of the drowned man.

Throughout the telling of her story I was tingling with queer, creepy feelings. I could almost see that old man in the room with us, could almost hear the sound of water dripping from his clothes as I peered beneath the hat, trying to see those shaded eyes; and then I forgot the narrator and I was listening with Joe to that knocking on the door and to the crying of that little boy in the middle of the night. Our hostess related it all in the same matter-of fact tone that she had used during dinner for discussing the weight of sows and the rival merits of two local vets.

When she had finished the story we all remained sitting round in silence. It is not easy for us Cornish folk to comment on such things in the presence of an outsider and we sat about her, a dumb half-circle of guests, applying ourselves with renewed vigour to her liqueurs and sweets. Yet it was clear that she expected applause or questions or perhaps a quid pro quo in the form of our own ghost stories. She had done her best to entertain us; now it was our turn.

'Tell me something amusing,' she said, as she lay back among her cushions and puffed out a coil of smoke.

Then I understood how superb was Mrs Lamley's equipment for the life that she led, concerned only with pigs and turnips, broccoli and tractors and the money they could bring her and the comforts that money could buy. She was encased in a kind of plate armour that protected her from any echo, whisper or reflection from the spirit world. The supernatural might come knocking at her door but it would be in vain. The death of that old man and his strangely-timed appearance in her room had meant nothing more to her than the breaking of a night's good rest and was now become a mere tale for the entertaining of dull and silent people like ourselves.

Yet one thing I shall never understand.

Why, among all the living souls in and around Menhinnick, should this unimaginative woman have been the chosen one when the drowned man's ghost came up from that engulfing mud to pay on earth his farewell visit?

XV

Shepherd, Show me

Rosalind Wade

As I approached the house my curiosity increased. In this uncultivated landscape, punctuated only by derelict mineshafts and an occasional slag-heap, it seemed impossible that any habitation could be concealed. My impression was of the Atlantic Ocean boiling up all around me like a vast cauldron, on the surface of which a couple of distant tramp steamers were no more noticeable than match-heads.

I stopped the car, hoping that no unwieldy farm cart would wish to pass, and studied my directions. Once the car was still, the full force of the gale sounded like giant hand-slappings. Even a gull, irresolutely straying inland, barely maintained its poise.

The instructions were meticulously clear. . . . 'Continue after leaving St Huthy for two miles. At the first bend you will see a farmhouse with the shutters painted bright yellow. I should warn you, it's a one in four descent after that, but it leads you straight to Lancevearn . . .'

Very soon I identified that farmhouse – and why anyone should have chosen such a bilious colour for the woodwork remained a mystery. I skirted it with caution and changed gear, speculating as to what manner of man had written that letter. '. . . I do indeed hope you will forgive me for being so presumptuous as to trouble you, a complete stranger . . .' it continued, 'My only excuse is that a very old friend of yours, Miss Queenie Newton, has told me of the wide experience you have in so many spheres, including that unknown quantity, the power of mind over matter. I myself know virtually nothing about 'spiritual' treatment and so I am quite unable to cope with my present predicament which, briefly, is that my wife is completely dominated by a couple of faith-healers. And so, seeing that you are spending a few days in the St Huthy neighbourhood. . . .'

I began then to form a mental picture of him as a fussy, precise person, practical enough when describing a route but a crank and, even more deplorable, husband of another crank. This could be a case of *folies à deux*, and it was more than ever puzzling to know what I was expected to do about it.

Almost without warning I came upon a pair of elaborate stone gate posts set in the high granite wall which enclosed the grounds of Lancevearn. On one side the boundary sliced through a strip of moorland; on the other, a narrow path led directly to the sea. Within, a riot of escallonia. A young gardener was hacking away apathetically at the overgrown plantation. The house appeared to be of medium size and rather squat in appearance; the wonder was that stone and timber had even been transported to this inaccessible spot.

An agreeable-looking maid opened the front door to me. She was very dark, although her eyes were china blue, suggestive of a lingering element of the Spaniards who, in remote times, had invaded these shores and intermarried with the indigenous Celts. She led the way across a large square hall to the drawing room. The furniture was strangely heterogeneous and I paused to inspect one of the most striking pieces. At that moment I heard my name spoken and turned to greet my host. With difficulty I concealed my astonishment. For here was no elderly eccentric but an undeniably handsome young man.

'You *are* Mr Stephen Hallam?' I inquired unncecessarily.

He nodded. 'Let me say straight away how terribly grateful I am to you for coming to the aid of a complete stranger. I was feeling quite desperate when I wrote to you, but Queenie assured me you wouldn't mind. I mean, you have so much experience. . . .'

I raised my hand to ward off the unwelcome and undeserved compliment. 'Please, Mr Hallam, may I make this absolutely clear? I am not an authority on faith-healing; nor, indeed, on anything else. It's true I'm interested in a great many subjects, but purely as an observer and, if you like, a commentator.'

'You're far too modest. Why, Queenie was telling me. . . .'

Not for the first time I shook my fist, figuratively speaking, at Queenie. Her interpretation of the obligations of our lifelong friendship was to belittle such modest talents as I possess to my face while recommending them fulsomely in other quarters.

'But how did you happen to discuss me with Queenie in the first place?' I asked. 'I haven't seen much of her since she became Matron at St Benyn's school, although we keep in touch in a vague kind of way.' Frankly, I could not see my garrulous, muddle-minded little friend in this man's orbit.

'We often have tea together in her sanctum; at the school, that is.'

'You're a schoolmaster, then?' I exclaimed.

'Does it astonish you so much? I should have mentioned in my letter that I'm on the staff of St Benyn's.'

'Forgive me,' I begged him, 'I didn't mean. . . .'

'I don't look like a teacher?'

'Well, no. . . .'

'Then what do I look like.'

The question at first sounded a mere provocation until I realised that he was attaching a quite disproportionate importance to my reply. I inspected him covertly. His eyes were amber-coloured; his hair combed back to conceal an unobtrusive wave. And his voice, vibrant though unaffected was rich with many cadences.

'An actor,' I replied impulsively.

'Well, that's exactly what I am – or was!'

The explanation proved simple. He had originally trained at a teacher's college and then gone on the stage, following a totally unexpected invitation from a West End manager who had seen him playing in an amateur production. But despite this promising start he ended up in a provincial repertory company and it was there that he met his wife, Mira. Alas, the strain of the life told on Mira and she suffered a complete breakdown after the loss of an eagerly awaited first child. And so it seemed wise to get right away from the theatre and fortunately he was able to return to his early profession in an ideal post at St Benyn's.

I listened attentively to this story, filling in the gaps, wondering whether the affinity between acting and teaching was sufficient to support his *amour propre*. And then I found myself voicing the inevitable query. What precisely was I expected to do about it?

'You've every right to ask that after listening to my tale of woe so patiently. Mira was much better by the time we came here but she still wasn't off the sick-list. She injured her leg, you see, when she collapsed.'

'She's not actually crippled, or lame?'

'No, no. Nothing like that. Her leg just needs massage or "light" treatment. You know the kind of thing.'

'And she isn't getting it?'

'I'm afraid not. A few days after we came here – in January that was – I registered with the local doctor, asking him to call on Mira as soon as possible. For some reason he didn't come at once. I was rather annoyed about it, at the time. Anyway, when he did appear at Lancervearn it was too late. By that time the faith-healers had moved in on us and Mira was entirely satisfied with them. In fact, she got furiously angry when I questioned their qualifications. Since then the doctor has looked in several times and been sent away by Mira – rather rudely, I'm afraid. Unfortunately, I was out each time. I should think it must have been about mid-March that he telephoned me at school and put it pretty clearly that there was nothing further he could do.'

'Well,' I suggested, 'is it possible that she really has recovered from the breakdown and wants to establish the fact?'

'I'd like to think that. It did occur to me at first. But no, I believe she really needs quite a bit of help. She still suffers from insomnia. I see a light under her door all night. And there's the leg. I'm sure she's in pain. Anyway, it's bad enough to keep her in bed. She hasn't been downstairs for weeks now.'

'That's terribly frustrating for both of you.'

I found myself considering two kinds of faith-healer; one, a visiting lay preacher conducting a service in the parish church with people queueing up to receive his blessing without noticeable results; and the other, a frowsty spiritualist of the kind a woman of my acquaintance consulted in a fit of emotional despair. Into which category did the present practitioners fall?

His answer was surprising. 'I can't say I've never seen them. You see, weekends and holidays when I'd be home, they've never shown up. They don't wish to meet me, obviously.'

'Then why don't you write or telephone them, forbidding them to call here except by appointment with you personally?'

'That would be the obvious thing, of course, if I knew their names and where they come from. But Mira absolutely refuses to tell me. Naturally, I've asked her again and again.'

As though a curtain had been abruptly drawn back I witnessed the extent of his inner turmoil and deprivation. 'You could easily find out' I answered gently. 'There can't be so many faith-healers in the St Huthy district! But, in any case, is it so important? I expect she will come through, with or without a doctor.'

'Perhaps. But you see, it isn't only a matter of her health. In some strange way, these people have turned her against me. She hates me now. When she speaks to me, which isn't often, she's like a hostile stranger. The summer term starts tomorrow and they'll be back, for sure. That's really why I wrote to you, to ask you to talk to her for me, before it's too late.'

I refused unconditionally. As a stimulus to my creative imagination the complexities of the human predicament might have their uses; yet I shield away from actual participation in them. But he persisted. Just *because* I was a stranger I might break the impasse. . . . And in the end I capitulated, reflecting that I undertook very little of practical service to fellow humans less fortunate than myself.

He fetched a decanter and glasses and together we sat out in the conservatory. His hand trembled as he poured the wine. Tentatively, I sought to distract his attention. What chance had led him to settle in such an unusual place as Lancevearn?

'Oh, simply seeing an advertisement.'

He had rented the house furnished, for one year, at a surprisingly modest figure. Eventually, the place would be auctioned as part of a much larger estate. Lancevearn was built some seventy-five years earlier by a Cornishman who had spent most of his life in the United States and made a fortune there. Nearly all the furniture had been collected in the United States and shipped to England. Each piece was listed with the price paid and where purchased in a large leather-bound volume reposing on the hall table. We laughed a little at this evidence of Victorian precision.

But soon he was glancing at his watch. 'I have to go into St Huthy to fill up with petrol,' he explained. 'And I may need to have the engine looked at. After you've seen Mira, do you think you could wait for me until I get back? Our maid, Rhoda, would get you anything you wanted. And then, if these people should show up you could cope with them, for me; or, better still, persuade them to wait until I get back.' He assured me that he had already told Mira that a great friend of Queenie's would be calling and she had raised no objection. Presently I heard the engine of his car purring away up the track. For a full minute I waited on in the conservatory, gazing out at the incomparable view.

The surface of the hall floor shone like polished ebony. The carving of the balustrade struck me as unique. But it was the magnificently sited landing window which finally captured my attention. Set within a large recess, the alcove afforded the illusion of being built right out over the sea, with Godrevy, a gleaming platinum strip, just visible on the western horizon. There was some furniture, conveying the effect of a small extra room, a rocking-chair and a most unusual escritoire or 'lady's bureau'.

Of the six doors opening on to the landing all but one were closed. 'Is that my visitor?' a faint voice inquired and I braced myself for the ordeal, for the thought of the invalid, immured from the morning freshness, was repellent rather than pitiful.

I do not quite know what I expected her to look like, although names do conjure people and 'Mira' is the 'variable' star. At any rate, the person who greeted me from the vantage of an enormous four-poster bed was one of the most beautiful women I had ever seen and I thought what a striking pair the Hallams must have made at that Repertory theatre. But that she was genuinely ill I now had no doubt. There were about her mouth the traces of deep suffering. And as she shifted her position she winced involuntarily with pain.

'Come and sit down,' she invited, quickly mastering it. 'Stephen told me you were going to call this morning. You're a great friend of Queenie's, aren't you?'

'We were at school together,' I explained. 'I'm sorry you're ill. How very disappointing for you when you've just moved in to this glorious place.'

She acknowledged my sympathy with a polite nod. 'Well, we've been here nearly four months now, you know. It might be disappointing if I didn't know for certain that I can be completely cured. In fact, I *am* cured, although that's rather a negative way of putting it because, actually, there never was anything the matter with me. It's just a matter of time until my own faith is strong enough to banish all these – illusions – of "evil". I have to fight all these wicked whisperings which try to tell me I'm an invalid, but also I have to stand up against – er – people who try to make me believe my body and my mind are still sick.'

She outlined her problem in a common-sense manner which would be hard to combat. She wore a lace-topped nightgown and through it her breasts showed firm and opaque. It was not difficult to imagine the emotional frustration which her husband suffered.

'All that might be so, in a general way,' I agreed cautiously. 'But does it apply to every kind of ailment? Haven't you hurt your leg? I think I noticed when I came in that it was paining you. A thing like that can do with some orthodox medical treatment, surely?' I was uncomfortably aware that I was catechising her, and until this moment she had not appeared to resent it. But my last comment stung her to anger.

'You mean, by a doctor? I wouldn't have one inside the place. Don't you know that they are mere "purveyors of evil". "Confectioners of disease", someone once called them and that describes them perfectly!' I saw then that her husband had not exaggerated. She spoke with such concentrated venom that the immediate effect was of an actress rehearsing an unpleasant part.

'Aren't you a bit hard on the profession?' I countered lightly.

'I feel sure your husband would be greatly relieved if you would agree to, say, a routine check-up?'

'Then I must resist him.'

I was shocked and shaken: 'But you do have some advice don't you, Mrs Hallam?' I cut in quickly, determined to keep control of the situation. 'What kind of people are they, these "faith-healers" of yours?'

'Oh. I see he *has* been complaining about them to you. I thought as much.' Her lips tightened into a thin vindictive line. 'Actually, they are two charming, very devout people, who certainly have my interests at heart!'

'I'm sure they have. Do they call regularly? Are they both women, by the way?'

'They come when they can. No, it's a man and a woman. *She* is quite elderly and rather delightfully old-fashioned. *He* is much younger, but not at all "modern" in the way he talks and dresses. I *think* they're married but I've never been quite sure. Anyway, they have a perfect mutual understanding,' she concluded rather wistfully.

'I can see they mean a great deal to you.' I stood up and held out my hand 'I do hope you'll soon be up and about again.'

'Oh, but I *do* get up, nearly every afternoon. I sit in the window recess.' She spoke quite pleasantly as though unwilling to part on bad terms. Perhaps because of Queenie?

I responded in the same spirit: 'On the landing, you mean? It's lovely there at the moment.'

'Well, I may not trouble today.'

I paused at the alcove, thinking that the reclining chair and the low bureau might have been specially constructed for an invalid. Idly, I rested my hand on the leather-topped desk and as I did so I experienced the strangest sensation. It was as though an over-mastering personality took complete control of me. Darkness obscured my vision, while insistent voices reverberated in my head like a distorted radio. Involuntarily I took a step backward and stood very still, waiting for the attack to pass. Gradually the scene lightened and silence reigned. Though still trembling, I began to feel normal again. By the time I reached the hall the odd, frightening indisposition might have happened only in my imagination.

On the table lay the leather-bound inventory Stephen had mentioned. I turned to the relevant entries. 'One lady's correspondence bureau, one reclining chair, Boston, Mass. (1911).' Also, from the same source, an umbrella-stand in the hall. I was quite amazed at the price paid for these three items. At that moment the telephone bell rang and the maid, Rhoda, came hurrying from the kitchen quarters to answer it.

The caller was Mr Hallam. The garage at St Huthy needed to keep the car for a couple of hours. Thus, he must not detain me if I wished to leave. 'In that case,' I said to Rhoda, 'I'll be getting along.' Through the open dining room door I could see the table laid for one. 'I suppose Mrs Hallam won't be coming down for lunch?' I inquired.

'She has never done so since I've been working here,' Rhoda answered. 'When Mr Hallam is at school I take her up a tray and see she has everything she requires before I go home at two o'clock.'

'That's very helpful. I do hope she'll soon be better. I understand she is being treated by faith-healers,' I remarked with assumed detachment. 'Do they strike you as reliable people?'

Now her china-blue eyes were directed at me with merciless disapproval. If I had anticipated the co-operation of a garrulous Mrs Mopp I was doomed to disappointment. 'I really couldn't say,' she replied coldly, 'I've not been here when they called.'

Outside, the sun's rays were quite scorching. I negotiated the track carefully, castigating myself for having handled a delicate situation so clumsily. By the time I reached the cross-roads I was still smarting from the rebuffs I had received. And who was responsible? Why, Queenie, with her inveterate passion for putting in her oar. On impulse, I decided to tell her so without waiting for our pre-arranged meeting three days hence.

Skirting St Huthy, I was soon bowling along a coast road ribboned by the azure sea; the skyline notched by dolmens and barrows. Within this narrow strip of territory was contained the very essence of early Cornish civilisation – the witches' wishing stone and the foundations of the oldest Christian church in the Duchy. St Benyn's school, once a vicarage, was situated just beyond the ruins.

Queenie seemed surprised and not too pleased to see me, although she invited me into her sanctum, which was stacked with bed linen and trunks. She switched on the electric kettle and set out a tea-tray while listening to my complaints. 'I thought you'd be only too pleased to help Stephen, the poor lamb,' she protested indignantly. 'Tied down here as he is all day while these wretched people sit closeted with Mira, poisoning her mind against him. Oh, it's too cruel. And his teaching suffers. I've heard some of the staff say so.'

I began to wonder whether she was in love with him, and repeated the basic question, 'But why pick on *me*?'

Her answer really astounded me: 'As you were brought up a Christian Scientist, I thought you'd know about faith-healing, and that kind of thing.'

'But, Queenie, that was *years* ago.'

It was perfectly true that my parents had been close adherents of that faith; but they died when I was ten years old and I was brought up by a humanist. For this reason, I had virtually no contact with any organised religion during the formative years; since when I had given the matter very little thought. Briefly, I reminded Queenie of my guardian's views and of the fact that in general terms I had accepted them. 'So if that's all you had to go on,' I concluded, more amiably, 'please explain to your friend that I don't really want to get involved with his problem.'

'If you say so, boss.' She pushed a brimming cup towards me with scant grace. I could see how seriously annoyed she was that her impulsive suggestion had so badly misfired. I confirmed that I would be expecting her at my hotel to lunch on the Sunday. She acknowledged the invitation with a curt nod and left me to see myself out.

The hotel at which I had elected to pass the week of my enforced solitude was picturesquely situated in a charming woodland glade. Yet my spirit was no longer attuned to the pleasantness. I hurried through dinner and as soon as possible returned to the lounge for coffee. The waiter mentioned that a visitor had arrived to see me. Inwardly I groaned. Queenie!

But the caller was Stephen. 'Mr Hallam,' I began as he came forward to greet me. I'm so sorry. . . . '

'No, please don't apologise. How could I expect you to spend a whole day of your holiday hanging around Lancevearn? . . . ' He explained that the work on his car had taken longer than expected. It was past five o'clock before he reached the house, only to discover that 'the worst' had happened. Mira admitted that the faith-healers had been with her for most of the afternoon. 'I protested and accused her of caring more about them than for me. It was most unwise. She flew into a terrible rage and then, suddenly, she went quite calm and cold. She told me that she had decided to leave me and go to live with them if I interfered or criticised them any more. And I could see she meant it.'

'But how could she leave Lancevearn? She isn't well enough?'

'That's what I said. "Taunting" her, was what she called it.'

'You must see them,' I said. 'It's gone too far.'

'Then *you* will have to help me to find them,'

This time I raised no objection for suddenly I felt curiously uneasy and apprehensive about the situation. We went into the bar and carried our drinks over to a corner settee, trying to assess what little information we had to go on.

'There's just one thing I've suddenly remembered,' he exclaimed after a long pause. 'Quite soon after we came here we had a very heavy fall of snow and I nearly skidded getting my car round the farm-house. Mira seemed surprised when I told her because she said the faith-healers hadn't mentioned having any trouble. She was quite willing to talk to me about them in those days. It suggests they were familiar with the Lancevearn track or they'd have stayed away in such bad weather.'

I agreed. 'Oh, they must be local people. No doubt about that.'

I could only promise to do my best. Soon after midnight a gale blew in from the Atlantic rendering sleep intermittent. My dreams, too, were disturbed. In one of them I was with my parents, walking along a river-path, until suddenly they were drawn from me into a swirling torrent. I awoke, jaded and heavy-eyed, to an enveloping mist through which I could barely identify the golden landscape of the previous afternoon.

After an early breakfast, I set off in my car, driving straight into a bank of fog so that soon I was completely lost. Presently, a grey stone building loomed ahead of me. This was a typical Wesleyan chapel. Placards affixed to the gate exhorted the sinner to repent while time was on his side. 'Hell-fire awaits the wicked. Ye shall be saved when ye see Christ.' At that moment the minister rode up on a motor-bicycle and inquired if there was anything he could do.

He was a genial man with an open rugged countenance. I mentioned my interest in the Wesley brothers, and he invited me to step inside. A woman was practising the harmonium; the atmosphere struck agreeably warm and musty. When we had spoken of the eighteenth-century sectarian divisions in Cornwall I decided to make a tentative inquiry about the faith-healers. And gave him, briefly, such details as I possessed.

'Faith-healers?' He seemed astonished; even resentful. 'No, I've never heard of any practising in these parts. Our mission is to heal the spirit rather than the flesh, by the unquestioning acceptance and acknowledgement of God's will. We would have nothing to do with such people in our ministry.'

I realised that I had drawn a complete blank. The minister had lived in the St Huthy district all his life, yet he could not identify these people, nor any remotely like them.

And that was the uniform reaction I received throughout a long sodden morning, during which I called at churches and chapels, even at the Citizens' Advice Bureau. The nearest I came to a clue was the casual mention in a village post-office of a bone-setter at Tintagel, but it appeared that his remarkable 'cures' were due simply to manipulation and he claimed no more for them. By early afternoon, when the drizzle had become a steady downpour, I admitted defeat. The time by then was three o'clock. I considered whether I should telephone Stephen at St Benyn's from a call-box or wait to ring him from the hotel during the evening, and decided on the latter course.

And then, as disconsolately I drew level with the Lancevearn cross-roads, a new thought struck me. Was not this the very hour at which the faith-healers usually called? While I exhausted myself running hither and thither on this inclement morning, wasting my own time and everybody else's, the prize lay all the while within my grasp. I had only to break in upon them, insist that they remained until Stephen returned, and my unwelcome involvement would be at an end.

The approach to the house was a quagmire. Rain fell with a chattering sound on the leaves of the escallonia. The place looked utterly deserted. An enamelled bin stood in the porch with an order for bread scribbled on a piece of cardboard. Fortunately, the front door was open and I stepped thankfully into the hall, depositing my mackintosh and umbrella on the hat-stand. As I did so I became aware of loud voices; at first a mere jangle of conflicting sound, but presently identifiable as a man's vigorous recital of a prayer, followed by a woman singing a hymn in quavering, falsetto tones.

> 'Shepherd, show me how to go,
> O'er the hillside steep. . . . '

Hastily I withdrew, taking my mackintosh and umbrella with me; ignoring the rain and slanting wind, for I had decided to revise my tactics. It would be far more effective to waylay the faith-healers just as they were leaving, thus obviating any risk of Mira warning them against me. There was a gazebo on the far side of the drive, with windows facing the sea. Into this I retreated to watch the wind playing weird games with the oncoming tide. Far more time than I realised must have slipped away. Had I, while resting comfortably in a wicker-chair piled high with cushions, actually fallen asleep? I never knew; only that, when belatedly I glanced at my watch, the hands pointed to four o'clock.

The rain had almost ceased. As I hesitated for a moment in the porch I was conscious of the gentle ticking of the hall clock and the distant throbbing of a refrigerator. Apart from that, silence enveloped the house like a blanket. I could not bear the possibility that I had missed the moment of departure. I looked into the various rooms, not liking myself for doing so. But there was nothing to see – two guest apartments, a small library, Stephen's bedroom and a second staircase leading to the domestic quarters. Mira's sewing and a book lay on the escritoire in the window recess but she herself was asleep in her bed. From the doorway I stood for a full minute watching the rhythmic rise and fall of her breast.

Somehow they had eluded me. Bitterly I upbraided myself: but then, as I paused before a small window looking on to a kind of enclosed inner yard, the question slid into my mind as insidiously as an asp. When did they leave Lancevearn – and how? For it seemed impossible that a vehicle could have driven out through the main gates while I was in the summer house without attracting my attention.

At that moment I heard a car outside and hurried downstairs to the porch. I could hardly conceal my disappointment when I realised that the sound came from the baker's van. The roundsman was the gardener whom I had seen working among the escallonias on the previous morning.

'Have you just passed a car in the lane?' I inquired breathlessly.

He shook his head. 'Who'd be out on such a day? I wouldn't myself, but people must have their bread.' He explained that he had a puncture just as he passed the St Huthy cross-roads and spent half an hour mending it.

I made a rapid calculation. If the faith-healers had driven up the track while I was in the gazebo they must have passed him.

'Is it possible,' I asked, 'that anyone could leave Lancevearn by some other route? Or even without a car? There's a foot-path to St Huthy, isn't there?'

He deposited a couple of loaves in the bread bin and glanced at me pityingly. 'On a day like this? It's every bit of five mile to St Huthy round by the cliff.'

'As much as that? Well, it certainly doesn't seem very likely. But I mustn't keep you,' I added, for he seemed to be waiting, though unwillingly.

'Good day to you, then,' he said, 'I'll be getting along. I've still most of the round to do,' and away he went up the track in a cloud of petrol fumes. I noted that I could see and hear the van until it reached the farmhouse.

When he had gone I concentrated my gaze on what could be seen of the foot-path from where I stood. The boundary of the Lancevearn grounds on this side of the estate was little more than a collection of leaning posts. I pushed aside a strand of trailing wire and stepped over it on to the moor. Bushes and thistles pressed around me as I followed the path until it terminated abruptly at a sheer cliff face. Far, far below, I could see white ribbons of foam as the incoming sea licked at the sides of the ravine. On the opposite side of the inlet, at a distance hard to estimate, the path re-appeared, meandering towards the sky-line, against which a deserted mine-shaft provided a distinctive landmark. With the wisps of grey mist clinging to the vegetation and the leaden sky above it was the most desolate place imaginable, untrodden for months, even years by the look of it.

Clearly, the two faith-healers could not possibly have left Lancevearn by this route. The ageing woman, even with the assistance of a much younger man, would never have been able to negotiate it in the time. Somewhere, they would still have been visible from my vantage point above the ravine.

So where were they then, and what in heaven's name was the explanation of their disappearance? For a moment I waited, still scanning the forbidding landscape; and then, almost without realising it, I answered my own question. They had never been on the cliff-path: nor in the house for that matter, *because they did not really exist.*

I could not possibly have explained by what means I arrived at this extraordinary conclusion. Yet once stated, it was unanswerable. A cold terror seized me then, so that I shivered violently while my body temperature seemed to drop to a degree far below normal.

I ran from the place in a kind of panic frenzy, averting my eyes from the house lest I should glimpse the phantom forms awaiting me there in the porch. I started up the car and covered the distance between Lancevearn and St Huthy with more speed than caution.

From the porter's desk I telephoned St Benyn's, leaving a message for Stephen that I had been unable to locate the two people of whom we had spoken, and that as I would be out the entire evening it would be useless for him to call or ring me at the hotel. In fact, I went straight to bed, fortified by two hot-water bottles and an electric fire. Yet still I shivered convulsively, as though suffering from malaria or ague. Release came only when, half drugged by aspirin, I fell into deep sleep.

As on the previous night, my dreams related to childhood. I was standing on a dark stairway leading from the Christian Science Sunday School which I attended while my parents were at the morning service. I feared they had forgotten me, but when my sense of abandonment and loss became unendurable, a porter, with the face of the Lancevearn gardener, appeared to comfort me: 'Silly kid;' he chided me, 'your mum and dad won't be long. Listen, they've just started on the last hymn.'

And so they had. The reverberating swell of several hundred eager voices rose to engulf me like a cool, lapping wave.

'Shepherd, show me how to go,
O'er the hillside steep,
How to gather, how to sow,
How to feed thy sheep.'

And I was warmed by a rosy comfort which alas, was short-lived. For that incident, or something very like it, really happened a few days before the accident in which my parents lost their lives.

The trouble with dreams, as Jonathan Swift once remarked, is that they tend to leave us very much as we were before dreaming! I awoke abruptly some hours after midnight, still shivering. Nevertheless, the words of that hymn remained quite clearly in my mind, although I had not consciously thought of them in all these years. I recited all the stanzas unhesitatingly. By the time the sun rose, on a very chilly dawn, I was beginning to understand.

I dressed before anyone was up, roaming about the hotel garden in the soft bright light of early morning, while I attempted to analyse and assess the situation. That I myself was acutely sensitive to supernatural manifestations I already knew as a result of a very disturbing experience. This concerned a brooch purchased from a small antique-dealer in my home town. Whenever I wore it I was subject to moods of such acute depression and fear of the future that I thought it worth while to investigate the history of that brooch. I learned that it had belonged to a young woman who had committed suicide. This was my first intimation than an inanimate object could be permanently invested with the personality of the individual who had once possessed it – also that certain people, myself in this casé, might unwittingly tune in, as though on a kind of one-way radio telephone, to span the limbo which separates the living from the dead.

My doctor, who insisted that he did not for one moment

accept the possibility, none the less urged me to get rid of the brooch as quickly as possible and this I did, by throwing it into a pond.

I could not reasonably expect such tidy, conclusive proof in the present situation. All the same, I decided to seek some confirmation of my theory, if that were possible in this out-of-the-way locality.

Immediately after breakfast I drove into the nearest of the coastal towns and there by sheer good fortune discovered in the public library a copy of a book on faith-healers which I remembered reading some thirty years earlier. In it I found reasonable corroboration of my own grotesque conclusions.

I knew then that I must remain no longer in the St Huthy neighbourhood. For I dared not risk brushing even the garments of the supernatural. I gave notice at the hotel, packed, and wrote a letter to Queenie saying that I had been unexpectedly called away and so was obliged to cancel the invitation to lunch. And early in the afternoon I drove off, feeling infinitely relieved, with the intention of reaching my own home sometime on the following day.

But as I passed the Lancevearn cross-roads a dark cloud of guilt descended on me. I alone suspected the true identity of the Lancevearn 'visitors': yet I had taken no steps to warn Mira either about her own occult sensitivity or of the 'other-world' influences to which she was being subjected. More important still, should I not have told her husband? For whatever principles the two faith-healers might have upheld when living and breathing in the material world, their motives seemed to have become frighteningly distorted while breaking the barrier between this universe and the Beyond.

I could imagine Stephen's astonishment only too easily.

'But of *course* the faith-healers are real people. Certainly, they have a peculiar hold on Mira and I mean to put an end to it. That's why I begged you to help me to find them.'

So rather than face a conversation along these lines I was putting distance between Lancevearn and myself. And yet . . . If I made no attempt to communicate my reading of the situation, surely I would always despise myself? So, torn by one of the strangest conflicts I have ever experienced, I turned the car and drove back to the Lancevearn turning. The sun was stronger now; cotton-wool clouds floated high above my head. Away towards the sea, a kestrel hovered: and I heard lark song on the still air. It would have been difficult to imagine a more tranquil scene, and deeply I regretted leaving it after so short a stay.

I reached the house just after four o'clock. Once again, the place seemed utterly deserted. The front door was slightly ajar, as before. This time a plastic container with an order for the butcher propped up against it stood just inside. Although not unexpected, the silence was uncanny, for there was something final and menacing about it. And yet on the surface, all seemed normal: the dining table set for supper, and through the open conservatory window great gusts of clean, billowing sea-air made nonsense of my apprehensions.

I braced myself to ascend the stairs. Gently, I knocked on Mira's door, but there was no answer. 'Please may I come in, Mrs Hallam?' I called out, 'I have something very important to say to you.' But had I? Suddenly, I was no longer sure.

At last I looked into the room, not quite sure what I expected to see. Mira was not there. The bedclothes had been carefully folded back into position and several small toilet items removed from the dressing-table. There were no clothes or books lying about and the thought struck me that Stephen must have prevailed upon her to leave Lancevearn for a while and recuperate elsewhere. He would have had no obligation to tell me of any such arrangement after my telephone call to the school and if this was really the case I need have no further feeling of responsibility.

I did not linger in this room, scene of so much suffering and acrimony, for suddenly I felt spent and exhausted after the anticlimax of finding her gone. I almost fainted as I crossed the landing and sank down on the rocking chair, resting my head against the escritoire, until the blood flowed slowly back to my brain. At that moment I saw them, in the diffuse grey light which made a startling contrast to the brightness outside, yet distinct in every detail. A slight, elderly woman, plainly though expensively clad in a dark enveloping garment made of some kind of brocade with, at her throat, a diamond brooch in the shape of a cross. She moved with extreme difficulty; yet maintained an air of authority and purpose. The man who supported her wore an old-fashioned jacket and knee-breeches. His manner was solicitous and quietly deferential.

I have often wondered how eventually I found courage to follow them down the stairs, although I felt certain they would be gone before I reached the hall. And I was right; not even a wraith of mist remained; although the conviction was hard to put to the test.

In the weeks that followed I sometimes speculated as to where

Mira had been that afternoon and whether she was by now fully recovered. Yet soon, with the press of family and other interests, I forgot her. But before that happened I had found time to look up various biographies and reference books in an attempt to clarify my impression of the two figures who had appeared before me on the staircase at Lancevearn. From prints and reproductions I recognised without any hesitation the Founder of my parents' faith, Mary Baker Eddy; by her sparse, carefully waved white hair, the material of her dress and the diamond brooch. There was no picture available of her companion; but sufficient published information for me to identify him as one of the two principle 'disciples' who supported the closing years of her long, tempestuous life. In a photograph of one of the rooms at her last home, Chestnut Hill, Massachusetts, I noted pieces of furniture identical to those on the landing at Lancevearn, and the wonder was that they had ever come into the market, rather than the high price paid for them, which at first surprised me.

Gradually, I came to accept the extraordinary experience as a fact. I had no wish to arrive at a final judgement. Whether ultimately a force for good or the reverse, I realised that the projection had been trapped between cross-currents of time and resurrection at the most autocratic and doctrinaire period of a controversial career. I asked only to forget the Lancevearn episode as quickly as possible.

But this alas I was not permitted to do. My contact with Queenie had reverted to a state of suspended animation. I feared she must have been very annoyed at my abrupt departure and it might be that I would never hear from her again. But early in December a Christmas greeting arrived. Much information about her activities was compressed into a small space in almost illegible handwriting. I was relieved that she bore me no ill will: although as I read the postscript on the back of her card, a kind of electric shock seemed to pass through me.

'I don't suppose,' she had written, 'that you ever heard about the tragedy the day you left St Huthy. Mira Hallam was found drowned in the Lancevearn cove. Later on, her suitcase was washed up farther along the coast and the coroner said she must have been trying to leave home while "the balance of her mind was disturbed". It was a terrible shock for Stephen. You see, he blamed himself. The only thing you can say is that in some ways it was a "happy release". . . . '

The room in which I sat seemed to darken. I crumpled the Christmas card in my hand, dropping it into the heart of the fire. . . .

XVI

The Lost Ones

Mary Williams

It was late afternoon when I saw the village, and the yellowing Autumn dusk was closing quietly round the humped line of moorland hills, so that the great Cromlech became submerged – crouched into the shadows like some ancient beast taking its rest. There was no sound save the thin high crying of a gull from nearby, and the rustle of dead leaves as I walked down the lane. I had wandered farther than I had intended that day, taking a cross-country route, and I was no longer sure of my exact locality. But that did not matter to me; complete freedom is one of the virtues of a walking holiday on one's own, and no doubt there would be an inn or some cottage where I could put up for the night. If not, I would surely be able to find transport of some kind to take me to the nearest hotel. Or – wouldn't I?

I realised suddenly, how tired I was; and with the knowledge came a swift unexplainable depression. This was odd because one expects to be tired after a day's tramp over the Cornish moors. But I could not shake off the sensation. The nearer I drew to the village the stronger it became.

The very silence grew sinister, charged with an evil that no words can adequately describe. There was nothing obvious to account for it; before me was a typical Cornish hamlet perched mid-way between the hills and coast, consisting of a dozen or so cottages and a farm or two grouped round the church. The lane zig-zagged towards it, through a rising mist pungent with the damp smell of bracken and blackberries, mingled with the salty tang of rime. I made an effort to dispel my sense of foreboding, but it was no good; the feeling persisted. From the adjoining fields large boulders emerged, which to my heightened imagination had the appearance of animal shapes in the fading light. I could picture them coming to life with an elemental movement of their own – fancied, as I watched, that strange fungi pressed their foul spotted heads through the earth and grew before my eyes. I could almost smell and taste their earthy odour, feel it closing about my throat with furry insistence, so that involuntarily my hand went to my neck.

Then I pulled my nerves together, telling myself not to be a fool, and walked on. My legs which had been shaking, became steadier. I was ashamed of what had been, after all, no more or less than a neurotic fancy, and in a further effort to regain complete normality, I sharpened my pace, whistling as I walked.

A little ahead of me I saw a figure moving across the road.

'Hey,' I called, 'Hey – good evening – excuse me – .'

The man turned and stared at me; he was oldish, a farmer probably, thick-set, with a fresh complexion and greying moustache. A completely ordinary looking man, and yet – the way he paused, turned, and looked at me for some moments without speaking, was – furtive somehow, unpleasant.

'Well?' the voice was expressionless, without interest.

'Do you mind telling me what village this is?' I asked him, 'I've been walking and lost my bearings.'

'Gwink,' he answered. That was all, just – 'Gwink'. Then he turned and cut in front of me to a gate leading into a field. A minute later I could see his squat form shambling past some gorse bushes into the fading rim of earth and sky. Soon his figure was obliterated by the mist, and I went on my way, between straggling stone walls, and grotesque wind-blown trees with twisted branches clawing through the air. Apprehension rose in me again; I hurried, fighting an absurd desire to rush away – anywhere – leaving the dread village of Gwink far behind.

Then commonsense re-asserted itself; it was ridiculous to be afraid of a village, and it *was* only a village, I told myself emphatically; I was over tired, on edge, nothing more. Perhaps it had not been such a good idea after all – to spend my holiday alone. With a friend I should not have had such fancies, indeed would have enjoyed the whole thing.

Just then the lane dipped down abruptly, and I found myself at a cross-roads, facing some cottages on one side, and the church on the other, with a lane twisting on towards the headland. Odd lights glimmered through the twilight; the scene was picturesque, but the silence was oppressive, uncanny. I could see no sign of an inn, but a woman came along the lane carrying a bucket. When she saw me she would have passed me by, but I stopped her and asked, 'Can you help me I wonder? I'm looking for somewhere to spend the night – or a car, perhaps – I've been walking. Is there an inn here?'

Into her eyes came the same veiled hostility I had seen on the face of the farmer. And simultaneously I felt a pricking creeping feeling at the back of my skull. Terror, in cold waves chilled my blood. I knew that I had come to a bad place where bad people lived. The very air of Gwink was evil.

'The inn beant used any more,' she said curtly. 'Not by visitors.'

'But – but why not?' I shouted, 'in God's name why not?' What's wrong with this place?'

Her eyes narrowed. In the uncertain light her features were pale, pig-like.

'If it be lodgings you do want, best go to the parson's,' she said in a curiously flat voice. 'Mebbe he'll help 'ee, 'tes likely he will.'

The vicar! of course, I thought with relief. Where there was a church there must be someone in charge, a man of God who would help me as she had suggested. It became in that moment, of vital importance to me that I should find him.

'Which is the Vicarage?' I asked, trying to keep the agitation out of my voice.

She cocked her thumb over her shoulder, to the right. It was a large thumb, and her hand was large, pale like a moon-face.

'Up there.'

I left her, and made my way past the square tower of the church and a primitive ancient stone cross on the other side of the road. The tomb-stones glimmered from the tangled grave-yard as I passed, and two children went by me, with eyes averted. Yet when I turned they were crouched against the wall staring at me, and I knew with sickening conviction that they were half-wits.

There was only one house up the lane, a typical country vicarage, large and square surrounded by a few straggling trees. A gleam of light streamed through the curtains from one window, and though the sight should have been welcoming, I was possessed suddenly by a contrary reluctance to go inside. I paused at the door, irresolute, an odd deadness in my limbs, with the chained nightmare feeling upon me of being unable to move. Then, almost automatically, my hand reached for the heavy knocker. A hollow clanging sound disturbed the silence, and a bird rose squawking from the undergrowth.

Presently I heard the pad of footsteps from the house. The door opened and I was confronted by a small stout figure in clerical attire. The face was genial, under a wide intellectual forehead surmounted by a thatch of white hair. His eyes were remarkable; in the first second or two, despite the uncertain light, I was aware of their power, of an intensity of purpose which left momentarily tongue-tied, and – afraid. Yes, quite suddenly my terror had returned, only this time there was no escape; I was caught.

Then he spoke.

'Good evening, what can I do for you?'

Instantly my nerves and body relaxed. His voice was so ordinary, frail and light, the kind of voice one instinctively connects with a reverend gentleman getting on in years.

I explained my quandary and he invited me inside.

'But of course,' he said, as he showed me in. 'We can put you up for the night. Of course – of course. My wife will be delighted. We both will. Visitors, as you may guess, are so few to this remote spot. You must certainly stay with us sir.'

I mumbled my thanks, and he took me into a room, presumably a study or library, in which a log fire spluttered fitfully from the grate. The glow was acceptable. I discovered that my hands were cold, and that my teeth were on the verge of chattering. I lay my rucksack down and he indicated a chair by the fireplace.

'There,' he said, 'do please make yourself comfortable, Mr – Mr – ?'

'Renton,' I told him, 'Geoffrey Renton.'

'Ah yes; Renton.' He smiled, and the smile discomforted me, for it belonged only to the bland rather thick lips, leaving the eyes calculating, without warmth. I shivered, with my hands outstretched to the glow of the fire. He poked at the logs remarking casually, 'The mist, you know – it penetrates. That's the worst of these out-of-the-way places. But we get used to it. And of course, we have a very active social life in the village.'

'Do you?' I said.

'Our nights,' he continued, 'are very busy indeed. Oh yes, quiet as it is, Gwink has its activities.' He paused. 'Well Mr Renton, I have business to attend to, so I will tell my wife of your arrival and she will be with you in a few minutes. I will see you later.'

'Thank you,' I answered.

He left me alone, and for the first time I had a good look at my surroundings. The room was large and high ceilinged, having one wall lined with books. The furniture, consisting of a heavy table, large tallboys and leather chairs, was drab and unprepossessing. But the pictures! – as I stared at them I was shocked. They were so completely foul; sensual elemental paintings, obscene in colour and feeling.

One in particular revolted me, a large work depicting a growth of curious fungi shapes all with the spotted heads in dull reds, greens, and blues, which I had visualised on my walk down the lane to the village. Those had been figments of my imagination only. Yet here they were, vividly portrayed in disgusting detail. As I stared their sinister vitality encroached upon my senses, emitting again,I fancied, their evil smell.

I jumped to my feet, with the sweat damp on my face and hands. It seemed to me that the room was clouding with damp waves of mist which crept under the door and through the cracks of the windows. I was still staring when the door opened and I heard a feminine voice.

'Good evening Mr Renton. You are interested in the paintings?'

I turned sharply to see a woman standing there. She was fair and slim, wearing a green dress with a fitted bodice and full skirt falling almost to the floor. I was surprised. She was so unlike anyone I could have conceivably pictured in that musty room. In my astonishment I forgot the paintings until she came forward saying,

'I am so pleased to meet you and so glad to find you have noticed my husband's pictures. Startling, aren't they?'

She was smiling; and her smile was lovely. With her face to the light I saw that she was beautiful in a strangely disturbing way, childlike almost, yet seductive, with a full sweet mouth curling upwards at the corners and highly modelled cheek bones that gave a tilt to her green eyes under the slanting brows. Noting my astonishment she laughed gaily, and the sound was infectious. My tension lessened as she prattled on – 'I am sorry I surprised you coming in so suddenly. And you were so deep in thought.'

'I am the one to apologise,' I said, 'behaving like a gauche schoolboy. You must forgive me, Mrs – .'

'Daryan,' she told me. 'Fenella Daryan.' She paused, then continued more seriously 'I'm glad you're going to stay with us; we both are. Simon, my husband, will be grateful to have your opinion of his paintings. He does quite a bit of it you know.'

I temporarily evaded discussion of the pictures by diverting the conversation hurriedly into more ordinary channels. Whether she was deceived or not I did not know, but after chatting for some minutes by the fire she jumped up remarking, 'Well, I must go and see to your room. Or –' she paused, throwing me a look half pleading, half doubting – 'would you like to have a look at the garden first, before it is quite dark; it stretches to the headland you know –'

Although this was the last thing I wished to do I could not resist her, and answered weakly that I should like to see the garden very much.

Despite the chilly air she wore no coat, but went as she was, in her green dress, showing the toes of absurdly small scarlet shoes. I followed her along a path skirting the side of the house. She walked lightly, gathering her dress in both hands. Soon we were almost running along the track; I was surprised at her speed as she darted over stones through the rough furze and bracken. Once she turned and gave me her hand. The tips of her fingers were cold as ice.

'This is the rockery,' she said presently, 'all kinds of sea-flowers grow here. Soon we shall come to the headland.'

Glancing down I saw, in the twilight, a riotous confusion of strange star-shapes and globular plants gleaming luridly through the tangled undergrowth.

I remember treading on something soft which squirted liquid over my foot, and I was repelled. I would have gone back, but at that moment Fenella smiled at me. 'We're nearly there,' she said. Her voice, the strangeness of her face pale and flower-like in the mist, fascinated and held me. Ancient ungovernable emotions rose in me struggling for fulfilment. The blood pounded in my ears. My limbs shook with the desire to crush her body to mine, to feel the sweep of her soft hair against my eyes and lips, and her cool mouth under my own. It was a lustful dark thing I felt out there, and I have thanked God many times since for my escape.

We came to the headland from where the cliffs dropped precipitously to the sea. The tips of their crags emerged through the mist, but veils of vapour shrouded the waves, twisting and writhing into snake shapes about the rocks. Through the haze, a disc-like moon was creeping into the sky.

'Well,' she said softly in my ear, 'how do you like this?'

A clinging tendril of hair brushed my cheek. I turned my head. Fenella was smiling at me; and as she smiled her dress fell to the ground, and she stood naked before me, green lights striking the whiteness of her flesh. Her face was raised, with her lips curled cruelly, seductively.

I knew then that no evil in Gwink was darker than the evil of Fenella Daryan. My heart raced, bringing a trembling to my whole body. I was clammy with a cold fear.

'All this could be yours,' she whispered, 'for ever.' She came closer, and I placed my hand to my face, shielding my eyes. Then I heard her saying – 'Look at me, you fool! Look at me.'

I faced her again, and seeing my expression a change came over her. The youth and beauty crumbled into a contorted witch-like mask with twisted features and lusting mouth. Her hands were raised, claw-like, green-white hands, creeping closer – closer – reaching for my throat.

I stepped aside quickly, calling upon God for deliverance, instinctively crossing myself. She screamed; and the shriek was that of an animal in torment. Shrill and agonised it pierced the silence, ending in a long drawn out howl.

I turned and ran, scrambling over stones and through bracken, falling and picking myself up again, not pausing to look round or take my bearings, but running blindly, as one runs in a nightmare – anywhere, anyhow, from the horror in pursuit.

How long it took me to reach the highway I do not know. But I must have fallen unconscious, for when I came to myself I was lying by the roadside, with the first glimmer of dawn lighting the sky, and a cold wind creeping down from the hills above.

Several years have passed since my sinister adventure, but last summer I visited Cornwall again, with a friend. We stayed at a fishing cottage in Port Ia, and one evening as we chatted with my landlady, I asked her casually, if she had ever heard of a place called Gwink.

'Gwink;' she echoed, 'well now! there *was* a village of that name, but that was many years ago – a hundred, quite. There was a landslide they do say, and everything fell, even the church. I dessay 'twas a good thing. Gwink was an evil place – evil because the parson was evil too. My grandmother would have it that he married one of the 'strange 'ones – a green woman of the ancient race – and that black mass was held regular in Gwink church. I don't know, mind you, but that's what I've heard said.'

Next day my friend and I went in search of the spot, which we found towards evening, lying bleak and lonely under a leaden sky. What the woman had said was quite true; all that remained of the former village were tumbled walls round the desolate shell of a fallen church. From between the stones, stunted trees waved their witch-like branches in the wind, and when I looked down I saw the crowded malevolent heads of fungi pressed close against their roots.